HART & SEOUL

Hart & Seoul

A NOVEL

KRISTEN BURNHAM

www.mascotbooks.com

Hart & Seoul

This is a work of fiction. Names, characters, businesses, places, events, and incidents are either the products of the author's imagination or used in a fictitious manner. Any resemblance to actual persons, living or dead, or actual events is purely coincidental.

For more information, please contact:
Mascot Books
620 Herndon Parkway, Suite 320
Herndon, VA 20170
info@mascotbooks.com

Library of Congress Control Number: 2018914662

CPSIA Code: PRFRE0319A
ISBN: 978-1-64307-314-9

Printed in Canada

For You.

One

There have been rumors that K-pop boy band Thunder has broken up, but the managers at Seoul Music want to assure fans that this is not the case. Updates will be coming soon.
Press release of Seoul Music,
posted by KThunderfangirl.com

There were not enough sparkles in the picture.

I glared at the offending image in question. No matter how hard I tried, the blasted thing didn't do him justice. Perfect jawline? Check. Sexily tussled hair? Check. Fuzzy sweater and bedazzling wrist cuffs? It would be a challenge to get the right shade of Oscar-the-Grouch green for the sweater when I filled it in with pens, but check.

But there's just no way to capture his sparkliness.

Usually, when I worked on my weekly cartoon panel, the hardest part was coming up with the best twist, combining the right amount of realism and comedy. The next challenge was turning a drawing into something that anyone could relate to. I created a new cartoon each week, with each panel capturing some event that happened to me. It had started as a homework assignment in third grade, and I loved it so much that I just kept going. As a result, I had a hand-drawn portfolio of my life's events. Most people carry around mental records of striking but fleeting memories that randomly surface. I, on the other hand, had a bunch of sketchbooks on my bookshelf to flip through whenever I wanted to remind myself of the day I met Bree in kindergarten, when she shared her bag of Doritos with me because I didn't have a snack. Or the moment I first received positive feedback from a member on DeviantArt. And that day a year ago when I'd read the worst text ever. Row upon row of cartoon panels that outlined the good and bad in my life.

But today might be the day that creativity fails me.

Grabbing my eraser, I furiously scrubbed at the page. I don't know why it mattered so much to me to add that one last detail, but the urge was beginning to get to me.

Seriously, why should it matter at all?

Our encounter had lasted all of three minutes, and he'd made his disdain abundantly clear. And I hadn't been able to forget it. The guy was a royal jerk.

Dang it! Why can't I get the sparkles right?

The day had started off normally. I was walking around the neighborhood, trying to get over the serious case of jet lag that I couldn't shake, no matter how many naps I took. It had been several days since my dad and I had returned from our two month trip to Australia (there are benefits to having a military consultant as a parent) and while Dad was fine and able to return to work without a care, I was left to spend the last few days of my summer vacation walking around like a zombie. In a desperate attempt to stay awake, I'd dragged myself outside, camera in hand, in case I saw anything that triggered a panel idea. You never know what inspiration could be waiting for you around a corner. Or come tearing around the corner, as the case may be.

One minute I was alone, desperately blinking to try to stay awake, and the next minute I was in the middle of a scene from *The Fast and the*

Furious, the star being our neighbor, Ms. Park. I stood on the sidewalk staring as she swerved towards her house, the tires squealing on the asphalt like nails on a chalkboard. Now, I could count on one hand the number of things I knew about Ms. Park, and being a deranged race-car driver was not one of them. She was an older woman who'd moved next to us some years ago, and usually kept to herself. She seemed to be really nice, always smiling as she greeted me. But she definitely wasn't smiling now as she jerked her blue car into her driveway. I flinched and shut my eyes, waiting for her to crash into her garage door.

But there was no crash. Opening one eye, I saw what had to be the worst case of road rage to hit our sleepy community. She was screaming at her steering wheel, flailing her arms around like a manic conductor. Rush hour must have been *bad*, I thought. Either that, or I was witnessing a mental breakdown of epic proportions.

Suddenly, she hopped out of her car, slammed the door, and marched to the side of the vehicle facing me, where she proceeded to have a staring contest with her reflection in the tinted windows. I was debating whether to say anything or just sneak into the house when she yelled something completely indecipherable and wrenched the back door open.

Whatever she said, it must have been along the lines of, "Move your butt out of the car!" because two legs encased in tight leather pants appeared. So, maybe it was not a mental breakdown after all. Although, given how she was glaring at whoever was in the car, she might have still been on the verge of one. Frazzled didn't even begin to describe her. I could tell the owner of said legs was tall, even though the rest of him was still hidden from view. A deep voice shouted something from the recesses of the car, muffled (but definitely angry), and Ms. Park hollered something back in an even louder voice. And that was finally enough to make the wearer of the tight leather pants unfurl from the car and stand, towering over her.

The guy could be summed up in three words: tall, hot, and sparkly. Seriously, the guy glittered like a comet, from the gel in his hair to his shiny shoes. Even his face twinkled! Staring at him, I was overtaken with the desire to draw him. My fingers twitched like a wannabe gunslinger prepping for a showdown as my mind automatically ran through my inventory of supplies in search of the right ones to capture his image. And right then, my eyes met his, their almond shape emphasized by perfectly smudged eyeliner. Now he was tall, hot, sparkly…and angry.

"What are you looking at?" he snarled across the yard in a deep, slightly accented voice, glaring at me as if I were the cause of all things evil.

My eyes widened in surprise. "Who, me?" I actually turned around, half expecting someone else to be behind me and the focus of his disdain. Because it couldn't be me.

"Is there anyone else here?" he sneered.

Well, alrighty then—I guess it was me. I could only gape at him, my sluggish brain trying to process why he was clearly furious with me. But he couldn't be mad at me. We'd just met. No, not even met. Wait, what had happened?

He rolled those perfectly lined eyes as if *I* were the weird one. "*Oegugin.*" By the way he spat out the word, it was not a compliment— that much my brain registered. If only I could come up with a snappy response. But my brain just refused to cooperate, and I remained mute as I eyed him warily.

Muttering under his breath, he grabbed an impressive number of suitcases from the car and stomped towards the house, throwing glares over his shoulder at me. The dramatic effect was ruined because he had to wait for Ms. Park to come and unlock the front door of the house for him. He scowled at me, daring me to laugh, as he waited impatiently for her to open it. But laughter was the farthest thing from my mind, because my brain had just gotten over the shock and was fast approaching righteous indignation. The minute the door was open, he lunged through it. Meanwhile Ms. Park beamed at me as if I'd done something amazing before gently closing the door, all signs of her earlier anger gone.

Ummm…what?

I squinted at the drive way, at Ms. Park's front door, and back at the parked car, as if I could somehow connect the dots of the living comet's anger. But nope, there was no logic behind it. I'd just been walking, minding my own business, and just happened to make eye contact with a guy who looked like he was auditioning for *America's Next Top Model*. And he thought it was okay to take his bad mood out on me?

A glint of something in the grass caught my eye. He'd dropped a wrist cuff, like a stray sparkle that he'd shed in his wake.

I should leave it. Just mind my own business and avoid Sparkle Boy.

But the sky was becoming overcast with heavy, dark gray clouds that signaled a fast-approaching downpour, and my conscience won out. The guy had just arrived, after all. So, like the good neighbor I was, I picked up the cuff and deposited it on the front porch, intent on leaving it and making my getaway. But the door suddenly burst open, and Sparkle Boy stood with legs braced and arms crossed.

"I told you to leave me alone! No pictures!"

"I'm not here to take your picture," I snapped back, all the righteous neighborly feelings replaced by irritation. "Why on earth would I want to take your picture?"

"You don't want to take my picture? Why not?" he barked, sounding insulted at the idea.

"Wait, what? You're mad at me if I do take a picture and mad if I don't? You know what, never mind. I was only returning this." I shook the cuff at him. "You dropped it."

He jerked back as if I'd slapped him as one hand flew to his bare wrist. Snatching the cuff from me, he immediately snapped it into place, glaring at me all the while. I just glared back. This was ridiculous. He was ridiculous. And me still standing there on his porch was ridiculous.

He was making no move to thank me. Why would the jerk start being polite now? Rolling my eyes, I spun on my heels, throwing a sarcastic "You're welcome" over my shoulder.

He muttered something under his breath, and I twisted around. "What was that?" I hissed, ready to fight his insults.

"Zankyou."

"What?"

"I SAID THANK YOU!" he bellowed loud enough for the whole neighborhood to hear before slamming the door in my face.

I almost screeched back "SCREW YOU!" but stopped myself. The Harts didn't yell in public. Even if they had just encountered the most infuriating boy who ever walked the planet. Or at least this neighborhood. Sparkle Boy? More like Sparkle Jerk.

Teeth clenched, I marched into the house, stomped upstairs, and plunked myself down on my window seat, fuming.

As if I'd want to take his picture. Ha! He wishes. The fact that I wanted to draw him didn't count, because...well, just because.

Seriously, his ego was something else. No wonder Ms. Park had nearly lost it—the guy was like mood kryptonite.

It took a good ten minutes for me to calm down enough that I could hold a pencil steady, but when I did, I eagerly vented my frustration in the best way I knew how: a new panel, sketching a cartoon version of the most bizarre event I thought I'd ever have. Nobody on DeviantArt would believe it, which made it all the better. The more I drew, the better

I felt, each movement of the pencil helping to literally draw the anger out of me as it soothed my jangled nerves. I even started chuckling as I imagined what my face must have looked like when I first saw him.

But try as I might, I couldn't make him sparkle.

Although maybe I shouldn't be worrying so much about the sparkle. Devil horns were more accurate. I added them to the sketch, taking way more pleasure than I probably should, before pulling out my alcohol ink pens to color in each panel. A lot of cartoonists use India blue ink to go over the outlines, and then scan the images into a computer and use software to add colors. But one, I didn't have money for that kind of software, and two, I liked using a different medium. It was not that I was the only one who used alcohol ink, but it was still uncommon enough that I felt my work stood out because of it. I'd developed quite the collection of pens over the years, although I know for a fact that I definitely did not have a sparkly one.

Through the window, a flash of brilliant red hair caught my eye: Bree. Grinning, I put my supplies aside and went downstairs to greet her on the porch. Sparkle Boy would just have to wait. Opening the door, I said, "About time you got here."

She rolled her eyes as she wheeled her bike up to lean it against the porch. "Yeah, yeah, I know. What can I say? Work's been crazy. And messy. The air conditioning broke *again*." Another eye roll.

"I thought that you were going to quit," I said.

If there's anything Bree hated more than scooping ice cream, I certainly didn't know what it was. Not that I blamed her; she was stuck in a tiny kiosk, day in and day out, serving sundaes and battling with the old AC unit while people complained about their ice cream melting.

She fumbled a bit with the bike, almost dropping it. "Stupid thing! Sorry, yeah, I was going to, but I wanted to hold out a little longer. Need all the savings that I can get, you know? Now, come here and let me see how much more awesome you've become."

Laughing, I gave her a bear hug. We'd kept in touch online, but with the time difference, plus both our busy schedules, it'd been a long two months. I'd missed my zany bestie.

"Obviously way more awesome. I can now say g'day properly," I told her.

Bree hugged me back, then abruptly shoved me away. "Don't do that again, okay? I mean, traveling is all very well and good, but things just aren't the same without you."

"Need me to keep you on the straight and narrow?"

Her bright green eyes darkened briefly. But she tossed her bright hair and laughed gaily, so I must have imagined it.

"Something like that," she said. "So, let's grab a snack and you tell me everything, starting with how to say g'day like a native."

We raided the pantry and hunkered down on the family room couch, where Bree listened with wide eyes as I described Sydney—she was as horrified as I had been when I'd discovered that there weren't a lot of Starbucks, and cooed over the picture of a quokka that I'd taken. "That is the most adorable animal in the history of animals. And you got a selfie with it!"

"My friend Ema took me to the island where they live, said it was much better than seeing one in the zoo. And she was right."

"Ema?" Bree asked. "Who is Ema?"

"I met her family at the church Dad and I went to."

Ema had taken one look at me and pronounced that I had not lived until I'd done her version of an Australian foodie tour. With anyone else it might have come out as an insult, but Ema had made it sound like it was the highest of honors, and I didn't think twice about saying yes. One outing turned into another, and soon we were getting along like we'd known each other for years. Scrolling through my phone, I pulled up a pic that had been taken in front of the Sydney Opera House. "Here she is," I said.

Bree leaned forward and whistled. "Wow. She could be a model. Look at that hair!"

That had been a particularly blustery day, and Ema's thick curls were blowing behind her like she was on a runway. With her tanned skin, tall and lean dancer's build, and warm smile, Ema was very beautiful, something that she was aware of but never rubbed into other girls' faces. To her, it was just a fact—something that she'd had nothing to do with, and that was that. I can't remember how many times I looked at her long legs with envy. I was on the short side, with pale skin marked only by freckles on my nose and cheeks, green eyes, and wavy blonde hair that frizzed with the slightest hint of humidity.

"We were talking about her coming to visit next summer, and of course video chatting over the year. I'd love for you two to meet."

"Sure." Bree did not sound enthused, and I immediately felt guilty.

"I'm sorry, I've been going on and on about myself. Catch me up on you."

That was the opening she'd been waiting for, and right away Bree launched into a tirade about how boring her life had been, from working extra hours at the ice cream stand to going through five different types of shampoo to rid her hair of the smell of ice cream. "I kid you not, the manager spent an entire half hour explaining the new flavor to us. A half hour! And it's not even a good flavor! Whoever thought of combining Nutella with root beer needs their head examined."

"That's disgusting. And people actually bought it?"

"Mer, the line went around the building twice. I take full credit for that, of course. We've had a huge increase in sales since the manager let me take over the Instagram account." Bree had always been very active on social media, and was planning on specializing in social media marketing in college. "But other than that, it's been pretty boring around here. Just a bunch of parents not watching their kids. One nearly got hit by a car because his mom was too busy yelling at me about how I should change my gloves more often. I'm like, 'Lady, focus on your child's safety before you get after me on food safety.'"

"Wow. Hypocritical much?"

"And all this in between summer assignments! Summer homework is just cruel. When I'm not working, I'm reading. And when I'm not reading, I'm working!" She gave me a knowing look. "You're already done, aren't you?"

I grinned. "You know me so well."

She rolled her eyes. "Let me guess, you did it all on the plane."

"It *was* a really long flight, and I had to do it twice. So…" I leaned forward and asked in a conspiratorial whisper, "…have you met anyone?"

She went absolutely still. "What do you mean?"

"You know exactly what I mean. What happened with that one guy you said kept coming for ice cream?"

The blood drained from her face, leaving it colorless and almost waxen. "I told you about that?"

"Why wouldn't you? It was right before we left Australia; you said this really cute guy was coming almost every day."

"Oh, yeah. Uh, it didn't work out."

Well, that was definitely not the reaction that I'd been expecting. "Bree, is everything okay?"

Her eyes snapped to mine before shifting away. "Okay? Of course everything's okay. Why wouldn't it be?" She tried to laugh, but it was strained and a tad shrill.

"I don't know, you just seem to be a bit tense."

"I'm fine."

"You sure?"

"I'm fine." Her chin set with determination, a look I was all too familiar with. If she didn't want to talk about it, nothing would convince her otherwise.

In an effort to break the strange tension that had suddenly sprung up between us, I changed the topic. "Luke said he'd be coming by tonight—"

"Luke's coming here?"

That time her voice was definitely shrill. And somewhat panicked. I eyed her warily. "Yeah…why do you sound surprised?"

"Right. Yeah. Sorry." Bree stared at her lap, brows furrowed in concentration as she picked at her shorts.

"Um, Bree, are you sure everything's okay?"

"Huh? Yeah." She jumped to her feet. "Sorry, I need to go. I forgot that my mom wanted me to, uh, fold laundry."

"Fold laundry."

She gathered up her bag, avoiding my incredulous stare. "Yeah. I'm really behind."

"I haven't seen you in two months, and you have to go home and fold laundry?"

"Awful, isn't it? But I'll make it up to you, I promise."

And just like that, she was out the door, not even bothering to close it behind her before she launched herself at her bike and careened away. I stood in the doorway, watching her pedal down the street.

She never once looked back, and disappeared around the corner right as a shiny red pickup turned onto the street, its handsome driver waving at me with a big grin on his face. "Merri!"

"Luke!" I came down the porch steps and was waiting for him before he'd put the truck in park. He climbed out, towering over me, and immediately wrapped his strong arms around me, his lips eagerly searching for mine. I threw my arms around him and kissed him back. Two months was a *long* time to go without seeing your boyfriend.

He reluctantly pulled away. "Merilee Grace Hart, don't ever leave for that long again."

"That's exactly what Bree said."

His head whipped around. "Bree's here?"

"You just missed her, actually."

His shoulders relaxed and he pulled me closer. "Too bad." His lips trailed over my jaw. "Guess you and I have some time to ourselves."

Warmth tingled through me as he focused his attention in that spot right by my ear, the one he knew was extra sensitive. "Just you and me and…"

"Luke." My dad appeared from nowhere.

Luke had me at arm's length before I could blink. "Hi, Mr. Hart. Didn't see you there, sir."

Dad raised an eyebrow. "Obviously."

I bit back a smile and cleared my throat. "Luke's going to hang out for a while. Okay, Dad?"

"Sure."

When it came to Luke, Dad tended to keep to single word statements. I don't know if it was just a dad thing, but he had never liked Luke. Said he was too smarmy, whatever that meant. But he tolerated him now, so I considered that progress. Eventually he might actually say two words at a time to him.

Luke trailed in after us, waiting until Dad had gone upstairs before relaxing. "Some things don't change, I guess."

"Oh, you know my dad. He's just protective."

"Tell me about it. At least your mom—" He stopped himself and shook his head. "Sorry. Don't know why I said that."

It took everything in me to act as though nothing was wrong. "No, it's okay. Sometimes I forget too." Empty words; how could I forget that she was gone?

"Have you, uh, have you heard from her?"

I shook my head, hoping he'd get the message. The last thing I wanted to do was talk about my mom. "How have you been?"

Taking the hint, he began talking about the special writing course he'd taken over the summer, using up what little free time he had in between life guard shifts. "I'm telling you, Merri, the pool parents are crazy. None of them watch their kids."

"It must be an epidemic; Bree's having the same trouble at the ice cream stand."

"I bet. Do you know that they have this weird flavor—Nutella and root beer? Out of all the ones I've tried, that was the most disgusting."

"That's what she was saying." But she hadn't mentioned that Luke had come by, although of course he could have done it when she wasn't working.

"What else did she say?" he casually asked, reaching out to play with one random curl that had escaped my ponytail.

"Hmm?" I had to remind myself what the question was. "Oh, just that there was a guy that came around all the time, but things didn't work out."

"Too bad." He was inching closer, eyes locked on my mouth, making it obvious where his attention really was. He'd just eased his lips onto mine…

"Dinner," Dad said loudly as he marched past us to the kitchen.

Luke exhaled sharply. "I give up." His phone buzzed, and as he read the message his features tightened. "And I have to go."

I had to fight to keep the hurt from my voice as I asked, "Do you have to? I haven't seen you in so long, maybe we could go for a walk after dinner? I'm still jetlagged, so I'm not really up for going out, but—"

"Sorry, it's an emergency." His tone was abrupt and almost cold, although as soon as he saw the surprise on my face, he forcibly relaxed. "Sorry. Just something's come up that I have to deal with. But I'll take a rain check, okay?"

"Sure." I don't think my smile would have fooled anyone, but Luke just gave me one last kiss. "Thanks for understanding. I'll text you when things settle down."

Text? Not call? But he was rushing out to his truck, and I had just enough time to give him one last wave before he took off.

First Bree, now Luke. What was going on?

Two

The fans were not disappointed at last night's performance. Thunder literally shook the roof as they descended from the ceiling, to the delight of the 3,000 people waiting below. At the audience's insistence, the group members performed their latest hit, Catch Me, four times. Rumors of a new song have been keeping bloggers busy. Will Thunder be releasing a new single?

ARTICLE FROM K-POP NEWS

My life officially sucked.

My dad had decided that dinner was the perfect time to start lecturing me on how I needed to focus on something other than my art, an old argument that always left us both frustrated and determined that the other was wrong. And to make things worse, the next day I'd woken up with a scratchy throat and headache. And I was *still* jet lagged.

I never should have left Australia.

I slumped at the kitchen counter and rubbed my gritty eyes as I did my best to ignore my phone. My silent phone that wasn't lighting up with any notifications. Nothing from my best friend of thirteen years or my boyfriend of two years. Nada.

Luke and I had met when I joined the school newspaper club in sophomore year, initially as a proofreader, until he convinced me I should become their "graphic artist" (meaning hand drawing on a hard copy and scanning it into the computer), insisting that the weekly paper needed more visuals to grab people's attention. It wasn't long after that when he asked me out, although it took him about three weeks to convince me that he was serious. Tall, handsome, intelligent, he stood out from the uber-popular jocks that made up half our senior class, and he seemed genuinely interested in art, something that I must admit I was starving for. We'd been together ever since—even though he graduated to the journalism group while I was stuck being the yearbook's "artistic manager," something that I most definitely was not going to share with my dad.

In those two years, Luke built up a reputation as a good writer. Well, "good" considering what he had to work with. There weren't really any newsworthy stories besides footballs being deflated during games (not by our team, of course), what really went on in swim practice (swimming, go figure), and how to win that elusive title of Uno champion.

Yeah, it was that kind of school. Tucked away in a corner of Northern Virginia—which, as residents know, is completely different from the rest of Virginia and always referred to as *Northern* Virginia—Chesapeake High was one of three local high schools. A few years ago, there wasn't really anything here except farmland and trees; now it was a growing suburban area that people were flocking to. But it was still small enough so that everyone kind-of knew each other, and it had the advantage of being close enough to D.C. to visit for a day without having to deal with big city problems. Luke enjoyed nothing more than scouring the local newspapers for said problems and trying to find something comparable in our school. I, on the other hand, was relieved that getting new textbooks and being the first to write in them was considered exciting. But despite our differences, Luke and I worked as a couple.

Or I thought we had. Granted, it had only been a day but, dang it, I was annoyed! We hadn't seen each other for two months and now he doesn't want to see me?

The doorbell was a much needed interruption to my brooding. I almost didn't answer it, since I was in my ultimate comfy clothes—sweat pants and a super-soft hoodie. But it pealed again, and curiosity won out. I got an itch in my nose just as I opened the door but managed at the last second to turn my head to the side, which was fortunate, since I don't think Sparkle Boy would have appreciated me sneezing in his face. He wasn't, however, looking nearly as sparkly. His hair flopped over his forehead, no hair gel holding it in place, and the only makeup he wore was guyliner. And of course he looked good in it.

He bobbed his head. "Hello."

His voice was deep and rich with an interesting mix of Korean and Australian accent. It almost distracted me from the slight smirk, as if he were enjoying some private joke. And the punch line of that joke was most likely me. Was my hair sticking up? Because it felt like it was sticking up. His dark eyes flickered over my head, and his lip twitched. *Yep, definitely sticking up.* I lifted my chin in a vain attempt to keep the top of my head out of his view, which was pointless since he towered over me.

"Bay I hep you?" *Ugh, stupid congestion.* I blew my nose, not caring that I sounded like a goose.

He gave a sharp nod. "My aunt would like to borrow sugar."

He may be handsome, but he definitely wasn't creative. "Good one. Why are you really here?"

He frowned. "Sugar. My aunt needs some sugar."

Oh, he is serious. "Sorry, I thought that you were joking."

"Why would I joke about sugar?"

17

"Because people say that when…never mind. Come on in, I'll get you sugar. Brown or white?"

"What?"

I bit back a sigh. "I'll just get you both."

He followed me into the kitchen and stood by the doorway.

"How much sugar do you need?" I asked as I pulled out canisters and a measuring cup.

"Uhhhh." He was transfixed by the kitchen, eyes wide and curious. Maybe kitchens were different in Korea?

I carefully began to spoon the white sugar into a bag. The silence stretched between us, but I couldn't think of anything to say.

I hated awkward silences. Always had. As a result, I tended to ramble, both mentally and verbally, a horrifyingly embarrassing habit that I knew annoyed Luke at times. Even with someone as rude as Sparkle Jerk, I just couldn't help myself, and would say anything to break the awkwardness. But what do I say?

"You look bad," he blurted.

I was so relieved that he'd started the conversation that it took a moment for me to comprehend that he'd just insulted me. "Excuse me?"

He looked me over again before staring at my now flushed face. "You look bad. Do you need to go to hospital?"

"Hospital?" I squawked.

"You should see a doctor," he continued earnestly. "They will help you look better."

"Look better?" I repeated dumbly. I needed a doctor because I looked awful?

"*Deh.* You do not look your best. Your face is very," he waved his hand as he searched for the right word. "Very white. And tired. Very, very tired. Do you always look this bad?"

That's it, this conversation is over. "Better to look bad than to be a complete jerk." I slammed the canister lid closed. Forget hating silences, I should have been grateful for it.

Sparkle Boy raised his eyebrows, shocked that insulting me had made me mad, but instead of apologizing like a normal person, he just grabbed the bags and bobbed his head at me. And then he just walked out, while I remained in the kitchen, fuming.

I didn't look my best? Did I always look this bad? I needed a *doctor* to help me look better?

Unbelievable. Unfreaking believable. I'd have to be sure to add a tail in addition to the horns to his sketch.

"Horns and a tail? Oh girl, that is a beaut." Ema broke out into peals of laughter. "He can't be that bad."

"He said, and I quote, 'You look bad. Do you need to go to hospital?'" I gave the now complete cartoon panel a shake for emphasis, holding it up to my laptop's camera so she could get a closer look. "That's the very definition of bad."

"Well, you got me there. Although you got to admit that the bloke's definitely spunk."

I'd gotten used to Ema's accent, complete with the Australian habit of making statements sound like questions. But throw in a slang word and I was completely lost. "Spunk?"

"Hot, my dear Yankee. The bloke is hot." She waggled her eyebrows with glee. "And kind of familiar?"

"Riiiiiight."

"Oh, you're just knackered from jet lag. Maybe he'll grow on you."

"Of course you'd say that. He must have spent time in Australia, because he has an accent like yours."

"Either that, or he got an English tutor from here. Lots of Aussies go over to Korea to teach. So, he's spunk in looks *and* accent."

"Riiiiiight." Or not.

It was morning on her end, and the sunlight picked up the blue and purple lowlights in her hair while making her tanned skin glow. She looked like Zendaya, and I know for a fact that she wasn't wearing any makeup. "How's Luke?" she asked, oblivious to my slight envy of her supermodel looks.

"That's a good question. I could answer that if he wasn't avoiding me." Five days. Five days since I'd heard from him. I'd tried texting, but nothing. And of all coincidences, Bree had gone AWOL too. "Part of me thinks that they are avoiding me, but I must be being paranoid." I paused. "Do *you* think I'm being paranoid?"

"Well, I don't know them, but it does seem weird. Maybe Bree was having a funky week, you know? Just give her some space."

"And Luke?"

She squinted as she tried to come up with an answer. "Yeah, he's being a drongo. But maybe he just needs some time too?"

"Yeah. Maybe." Or maybe I wasn't being paranoid.

The front door opened, and my father's heavy footsteps echoed on the hardwood floor. "Merilee?" He came up behind me and put a hand on my shoulder in greeting. "Oh. Hi, Ema. How are you?"

"G'day, Mr. Hart!" Ema gave him a cheery wave. "My dad misses you already. He told my mom that barbequing won't be the same without you."

He grinned, the gesture easing his normally stern expression. "Tell your parents I say hi, and that he needs to come over here for some American grilling. Merilee, I'm going to get dinner ready." He waved to Ema one last time before going into the kitchen.

"Okay, I'll be there in a minute." I groaned inwardly. He had that look he always got whenever he wanted to talk to me, usually about something I didn't like. Might as well get it over with.

"I have to go, Em. But we'll talk next week? Same time?"

"Right. See you then," she gave a wave, and then the screen went dark. I shuffled into the kitchen and sat down at the table, just in time for the reheated pancakes.

Dad smiled at me as he sat down. "Did you have a nice talk with Ema?"

"Yeah." Talking with Ema, good. Subject matter, not so much.

He lifted one gray eyebrow. "You okay?"

"Yeah. Just, stuff. Anyways, is there something you want to tell me?"

"Actually, there is."

He drenched his pancakes in syrup, waiting until they were thoroughly soaked before taking a bite. He gave a sigh of satisfaction, and I smiled. We may not look alike, but one thing my father and I both shared was a sweet tooth, one that we indulged in every Friday night with pancakes and maple syrup. Real maple syrup, mind you, not the fake stuff.

Dad took three more huge bites before continuing. "Ms. Park and I were talking outside just now. She's invited us to go out to dinner with her and her nephew."

I choked on my mouthful. "Ms. Park asked you *what*?"

He sawed on his stack, unaware of my horror. "We're going out tomorrow night. Apparently he's just arrived, and she's hoping that you can get to know him. Maybe show him around."

"Uhhhh."

Finally, picking up that I was not okeydokey with this plan, he lifted his head and speared me with a quizzical look. "Is everything all right?"

"Fine, fine," I lied and reached for some water. "Um, so you said yes?"

"Yes. Is that okay?" he was looking at me funny, that familiar cautious glint in his eyes, like he was trying to discern a hidden meaning in my words.

I'd been getting that look a lot recently. And I hated that there was this tension between us. Tension that I'd put there. So I dutifully shook my head and said, "No, it's fine," before shoveling a huge forkful into my mouth. Anything to avoid any more conflict. Or at least conflict with my dad. No doubt there'd be conflict with Sparkle Boy.

At least I was over my cold, or goodness knows what he would say. Maybe offer to drive me to the hospital? On the bright side, the evening would be interesting, if nothing else. And there would probably be another comic on DeviantArt by tomorrow morning. Art imitating life and all that fun. As Ema would say, the dinner would be "bonzer."

Three

Lee Hyung-kim was noticeably absent from Thunder's interview on the talk show last night. Managers declined to respond. Fans noticed his absence from Thunder's last interview, and now another one. What's going on with Thunder?
K-POP 24/7

By the next day I still hadn't heard from Luke. Or Bree. The only highlight of the day was reading comments on DeviantArt, which housed most of my cartoon panel portfolio. And I loved the feedback (and occasional roasts) I received from other members. The fact that I could be part of a community of fellow artists, a group that gave me the acceptance I so desperately craved, was a gift I cherished.

As expected, they raved about my panel featuring Sparkle Boy, the consensus being that it was just too hilarious to be true. Hah! If they only knew. They also wanted more panels, something that had never happened before, at least not with any previous panels I'd posted. Maybe it was a good thing I'd see Sparkle Boy again. By six o'clock, I was ready—hair freshly washed and pulled back in a high ponytail, skinny jeans and flannel shirt paired with my favorite boots and boot cuffs, just the slightest hint of makeup carefully applied. My charm bangles jingled with each step I took. My favorite was the silver bangle Bree had given me for my birthday two years ago, a tiny otter charm designed to link up with the matching one she wore. The bangle was part of a best friends set, inspired by how otters held onto each other to keep from floating apart.

I held up the charm, fingering the dangling otter. Was Bree starting to float away? Was there anything I could do about it? And what about Luke? What the heck would make him suddenly go cold like that? I took a moment to study my reflection. My wavy blonde hair had already begun to escape the hair tie and dry into curly wisps around my face. Freckles that no amount of powder could cover up looked like cinnamon had been sprinkled across the bridge of my nose and upper cheeks. Curves that had appeared overnight on my thirteenth birthday (at least, that's what it'd felt like) and now conditioned by my daily runs filled out my shirt and pants.

If I were Bree, I'd snap a picture and send it to Luke. She was forever taking selfies and putting them on Instagram, even had a decent number of followers. I preferred to keep my online presence focused on my art—safe and anonymous. But maybe I should message Luke? I shook my head and grabbed my jacket. I was *not* going to worry. I'd reached out to him, to both of them, and now it was up to them. Luke needed space to figure out whatever he had going on, and I was going to give it to him. I refused to chase after him.

Dad was waiting by the front door. He stood tall and absolutely still, years of being a naval officer ingrained in him. His white hair, highlighted with steely gray, shone under the hallway light, and his brown eyes, which used to radiate humor and authority, now had a permanent sadness. I swallowed a sudden lump in my throat. Would that look ever disappear?

He smiled and held out my jacket. "Ready?"

I thrust my arms in the sleeves and grabbed my wristlet. "Ready as I'll ever be. Let's get this over with."

"What?"

"Nothing! Come on, I think they're waiting."

Sure enough, Ms. Park and her nephew were already outside next door, Ms. Park beaming ear to ear. Several years older than my dad, she was slender, with black hair cut in a simple bob that always looked amazing, and always dressed with a casual elegance that intimidated me. Tonight she had on some kind of jumpsuit that on anyone else would have looked awful, but she pulled it off with ease.

And her nephew...he was not sparkly. Not so much as a stray twinkle. Ridiculously, I was disappointed. I had a vision of him being the human equivalent of a disco ball, but nothing. Although, now that I was no longer sneezing and battling watery eyes, I could really see just how good looking he was.

Thick hair so black it had an almost purple sheen to it was styled carelessly around his face, the ends just brushing his shirt collar. His face was perfect. Literally perfect. Tanned skin without a hint of a beard, a straight nose, high cheek bones, and a chiseled jaw line. Almond-shaped eyes, so much like his aunt's, were a rich brown... and currently trained on me with an unblinking intensity, following my every move as I approached him and his aunt. Great. First angry, now brooding.

"You should see a doctor. They will help you look better."

I forced my mouth into a polite smile. Sure, he was good looking, but that didn't change the fact that he was the rudest guy I'd ever met. Still, I found myself standing a little straighter, suddenly glad that I was wearing something besides sweats and a hoodie. Who needed a doctor now, Sparkle Boy?

Ms. Park, bless her, was all smiles as she bowed and greeted us. "This my nephew, 'Eeunim." He gave us a bow and waited silently, almost like he was bracing himself.

I kept the forced smile on my face as I held out my hand. "I'm Merilee. But you can call me Merri—everyone does."

He stared at my hand and finally took it carefully in his. His hand was warm, slightly calloused at the finger tips, and it completely swallowed mine. "Like Christmas?"

I held back a sigh. He was not off to a good start here, although Ema would be tickled pink. "No, like happy and joyful."

"So, like Christmas," he persisted, and I honestly couldn't tell if he was serious or teasing. If it was the latter, he had a fantastic poker face.

Yep, this would have to be forever immortalized in a comic later.

Ms. Park elbowed him and muttered something in Korean. Sparkle Boy—what had she said his name was? Ee something? No, must have been Lee—snapped to attention and gave me another quick bow. "It is a pleasure to meet you," he repeated as if on autopilot.

Yeesh, he sounded like he was trying out for a role on Masterpiece Theatre. And it's not as though this was our first encounter; he'd borrowed sugar, for crying out loud. But whatever.

Ms. Park smiled in victory as he bowed to my dad. "We ride together?" she asked.

"I can drive," Dad offered, gesturing to our car. Our small car. Our small car that could barely fit four people, where Sparkle Boy and I would have to squish into the back seat together. And judging from the look of horror on his face, he was not happy at the idea either. But Dad ignored the pleading stare I aimed at him and herded us to the car like it was the greatest idea ever. Ms. Park joined him in the front, while Lee and I had no choice but to clamber into the back. Sparkle Boy was as self-conscious as I was; he had himself flattened against the window so fast that I would have been insulted if I wasn't doing the same. Actually, I still was a little insulted. Luckily, we weren't far from the restaurant so it wouldn't be that long of a ride. But was *Christmas* happy? No, no she was not.

I glared at Dad, who was talking to Ms. Park and oblivious to his spatially impaired daughter right behind him. Being cramped up against the window involved using muscles I didn't have to use for running, and it was embarrassing how stiff I was by the time we got to the restaurant and I had to climb out of the car. Lee seemed to have no problem, his every movement fluid as he sprang from the back seat, the stinker. He stared up at the glowing sign of the restaurant, nose crinkled and arms crossed, as if even the idea of burgers and endless fries was something to be wary of.

That look remained as we checked in with the hostess and were led to a table. Surprise, surprise, I was seated across from Lee. Dad and Ms. Park immediately launched into a conversation about taxes or something equally exciting, leaving me to eyeball Lee as he alternated between glaring at the menu and watching me with narrowed eyes, like he expected me to whip out a camera. I almost wish that I had one; it'd be hilarious to see what he'd do. Maybe he'd need to "go to hospital." Hah! But there's no way that I could sit through a silent dinner—my worst nightmare—so I cleared my throat and jumped in to what would no doubt be a conversation I'd later regret. "So, is this your first time visiting the U.S.?"

His eyes narrowed even more, as if he couldn't figure out whether to answer or ignore me until I went away. "Yes."

Okay. At least he has said something. He'd sounded angry, but he'd talked. "Is it very different from Korea?"

"Yes."

"Are you going to be visiting for a while?"

"Maybe."

And that was clearly the end of the conversation. The question was, do I continue to torture both of us by asking more questions when he obviously hated being there and detested talking to me? His brown eyes, sharp and glinting with that unexplained anger, zeroed in on me as he watched my internal struggle. *Staring at the menu it is, then,* I decided.

The truce lasted until we got our drinks. Lee's eyes went round when the glass of water was put in front of him, staring at it like it had a shark hidden in its depths. In Australia, they'd put pitchers of water on the table along with small glasses so that people could serve themselves. I personally had missed big glasses filled with ice—lukewarm water is not my favorite—but maybe things were done the same in Korea? I couldn't resist asking, "Is something wrong?"

"This glass is so big. Why is it so big?"

Yup. Definitely a Korean thing too.

"They're always like that. See? Mine's the same size."

"You drink that much water?" He made it sound like the worst of insults, which immediately made me bristle in defensiveness...over water. Could I get any more ridiculous? I'm pretty sure the Aussies hadn't looked down on big drinking glasses so much as being practical.

"Is there something wrong with drinking that much water?"

"It is bad for your health."

My mouth opened and shut like a gasping fish. "Bad for your health," I repeated, thinking I must have misheard him.

"It is unnecessary. Korean food doesn't make you need that much." For a moment his face glowed with pride, then quickly twisted with disgust. "Not like here. Everything here is the same."

"What do you mean?"

"The food all sounds the same. Everything looks the same. There are no *bulgogi* or shrimp burgers, there is no *gochujang* sauce." He sighed angrily even as I marveled how being miserable apparently made him so chatty. "And no *kimchi* anywhere."

I blinked. "Did you say shrimp burgers? What's a shrimp burger?"

He looked mournfully at the menu. "Not here, apparently. Do they have any sweet relish or mayonnaise?"

"I assume so." I scanned the menu but came up empty. "Is that different from regular relish or mayo? I guess you'll have to ask the waiter."

Lee glanced at the side of the table, sighed as if the weight of the world rested on his shoulders, raised his hand, and then proceeded to shout at the top of his lungs, for all the restaurant to hear, "EXCUSE ME!"

Everyone at our table and within a five-table radius jumped about a foot in their seats. For a moment we all just stared at him, some (myself included) with a hand plastered against our chest as if to keep our hearts intact. His aunt was the first to recover. "'Eeunim," she hissed even as she nodded and smiled at everyone in an unspoken apology. "What are you doing?"

"Calling for our waiter," he replied like it was the most natural thing in the world to bellow like an ape in a public building. "There is no button."

"Not like that! We not do that here. We wait for waiter to come back."

He scowled, but then just as quickly smoothed his expression into bland compliance. "*Deh.*" I assume that meant yes, because he wordlessly retreated behind the menu, holding it up so high that I could only see the tip of his purple-black hair and the tanned fingers clutching the paper in a white-knuckled grip. He probably would have happily stayed there for the rest of the meal, except the waiter, who hurried over as soon as he could to avoid another bellowed summons, came for our orders. Lee perked up when he found steak on the menu and ordered the biggest size possible, while I went with an old favorite of chicken tenders and sweet potato fries. I handed my menu to the waiter; Lee, on the other hand, had other ideas—he clenched it like it was a lifeline. Probably to use it as a shield from me. The poor waiter had to actually rip it from his hands, and raced off before Lee could take it back.

Without his prop to keep his attention, Lee did a one-eighty mood change and set his sights on me like the convenient target that I was. "Merry Christmas, your hair is yellow."

It was said so bluntly, just like the other day, that I was momentarily stunned. "Excuse me?"

"Your hair is yellow," he repeated loudly as if I were hard of hearing.

"It's Merri. Not Merry Christmas. Just Merri. And yeah. It's called blonde. And yours is black," I retorted. Black and, at times, sparkly.

He squinted and leaned over the table. "You have freckles on your nose."

"Yep."

"Have you tried to get rid of them?"

"*Excuse me?*"

He leaned forward with a glint in his eyes. "This upsets you? *Wae?* It is a fact."

"Like how I looked bad earlier this week?" *Dang it. I didn't mean to say that.*

"But you did. You were sick?"

I gave a begrudging nod as I braced for the next inevitably ridiculous statement. He'd probably blame it on me drinking too much water.

He leaned back in satisfaction. "I knew it. Koreans always tell the truth." His lips twitched as he was enjoying a private joke.

I cocked my brow. "Really? *All* Koreans tell the truth *all* the time?"

He shifted. "I meant, if something is true, we will say it."

"But there can be nicer ways of saying the truth. Or just not say it at all. It's not as though I asked for your opinion. The way you say it makes it sound like it's a bad thing." Oh my gosh, I sounded obnoxious even to me. Now *I* wanted a menu to hide behind.

But he didn't seem annoyed. "Not bad. Just different. But I understand your point. *Joesonghapnida.*" He bowed his head slightly.

"Chosoo-what?"

"*Joesonghapnida.* It means 'I am sorry.' I did not mean to offend you."

I wasn't so sure about that, but there was no point in arguing about it. "It's okay. And technically you're right. About the hair and freckles, I mean." I offered him a grudging smile.

His gaze intensified for a minute.

This was an unexpected twist. Was it warm in here or just me? I reached for my *oversized* glass of water and took a gulp, then another. Luke never looked at me like that, like there was something about me that had caught his attention and he couldn't help but stare…I had *not* just compared my boyfriend to Sparkle Boy, and found Luke lacking. What was wrong with me?

Caught up in the hypnotic force of his gaze, I took another gulp of water, which left me eying Lee's still-full one as I wondered how he'd react if I asked the waiter to bring me another one. He might offer to drive me "to hospital" for drinking too much water. All the while, those dark-brown eyes watched me, assessing me in a way that made me want to blurt out my life's story. Darn those awkward silences!

The food arriving saved me from the very real danger of actually blurting who knows what to break said silence. But I couldn't swallow my giggle as Lee took in his steak. Eyes wide once again, he cautiously nudged it with his fork as if expecting it to suddenly bite him.

This went on for a full minute before I just couldn't sit by any longer. "You've had steak before, right?"

"*Deh,*" he shot me an annoyed look. "We even have forks in Korea."

Ouch. Well, I deserved that. "Sorry. I'm afraid I don't know much about Korea." Make that anything besides the Korean War.

He nodded, not at all surprised. "Most Americans do not. I expected that."

"Still, I'm sorry. No, wait. Choo…chooosong," my tongue tripped over all the vowels.

"*Joesonghapnida*," he supplied with that slight quirk of his lips. Amazing how so small an expression eased his stern expression. "And this," another poke at the meat, "is a lot bigger than what I am used to." He cut a small piece, ate it, and winced. "And tasteless."

"Really?" I eyed his plate. "Looks fine to me. There's never been an issue before. My dad loves the steak." We both turned to look at the man in question, who was happily sawing away on a piece like Lee's.

Lee shuddered. "We marinate ours with different sauces. It tastes…more."

"More is good. Hey, want to try some of my chicken?"

"No thank you." He speared a piece of lettuce from his side salad and braved a bite. Yuck. Even from here I could see that it was limp and soggy.

I pushed my plate to him. "Have a sweet-potato fry. They came out all right." He hesitated, but hunger won out. He reached for one. Then another. Hmmm, Sparkle Boy had a salty tooth.

Feeling that we'd exhausted the topic of food, I moved on down the conversational checklist. "So, why are you here?" *Wait, too accusing.* "I mean, what are you doing here? What I mean is—"

"I know what you mean."

Oh good, because at this point I don't. What is it about this guy that makes me such an idiot?

"It has been years since my aunt moved from Seoul, and I wanted to visit her."

"Are you taking a break from school?"

He rolled his shoulders back like the question made him uncomfortable. "I've already graduated from school."

That surprised me. He didn't look like he was old enough to have finished high school. "And how long will you be visiting? Will more of your family be joining you?"

It was like watching a blind being yanked down over a window, although he replied evenly, "I am not sure how long I will be here." But he rubbed at one of his wrists, scratching under the leather cuff. And he offered nothing about his family.

Something was up. His answers were robotic, like he had rehearsed them over and over and over again. Almost like he was hiding something.

As if sensing my suspicion, he took charge of the conversation, tilting his head as he studied me. "Is your mother not here?"

I stiffened, but he just gazed back at me in innocence, unaware of the dangerous topic he was skirting around. *Merri, chillax.*

I was getting paranoid. I'd just asked him a bunch of questions, why wouldn't he? And he had to be curious why it was just my dad and I at dinner. "No, my parents are separated. So, what do you like to do in your spare time?" *Smooth transition there, Merri. Not obvious at all.*

If possible, he got even more tight-lipped. "Normal things."

As opposed to abnormal things? That's reassuring.

Ms. Park leaned in beside him. "He runs. Like you, Merri."

"Oh." I guess I shouldn't be surprised that she knew I ran, but she said it with an eagerness that seemed a bit excessive.

"You should go together."

"What?"

"*Bo?*"

"Yes." She ignored our mutual horror. "Lee should exercise."

"Uhhh…" I frantically looked to Dad for help, but he just gave me a blank stare, eyebrows raised in surprise. No help there. Right. Up to me to do damage control. "Actually, I don't think—"

She said something to Lee in Korean, and he muttered something back, something that did not sound like "*deh*," so he clearly was as reluctant as me. Ms. Park laughed. "Of course, Merri not mind. She is a good girl," she beamed at me. "You will, yes?"

"Uhhh, well, yes, I guess."*Oh good job, Merri. Effective.*

"You go tomorrow," Ms. Park said, although it came out as more of an order.

So much for damage control. More like the damage had just controlled me. Lee was blinking madly, and I'm pretty sure my jaw was touching the table. Ms. Park just smiled with all the innocence of an angel.

"Tomorrow," I repeated.

Lee's throat bobbed in a gulp. "*Deh.*"

Deh, indeed.

Four

Thunder has just announced that they are participating in a charity event. Guests will bid on the chance to spend a day with each member of the group. All money will be donated to an orphanage in the Guryong village in Seoul. Tickets for the event have already been sold out. But will LHK be a part of the event? Or will he still be AWOL?

K-POP DREAMZ BLOG

I barely managed to keep a lid on it during the car ride home, which was THE MOST awkward ride of my life. I leaned my head against the window and stared at the traffic, while Lee slumped against the window as if the thought of spending more time with me was more than he could bear as the adults chattered to fill in the resentful silence, broken only by my phone dinging with notifications from DeviantArt. Every single comment was about the panel I'd shared featuring Lee's grand entrance into the neighborhood, and all were positive. Guess I'd definitely have to do another one now; maybe I'd show how he practically broke his neck trying to get out of the car when we pulled into our driveway. Although, to be fair, I was just as eager to escape. Giving Ms. Park a vague smile and wave, I waited until Dad and I were safely inside before exploding. "What the heck was that?"

Dad snorted as he hung his coat in the hallway. "That, sweetheart, was you being out maneuvered."

"Out maneuvered? She practically steamrolled us into that play date." I yanked off my jacket and stomped into the kitchen, flinging it on a chair on my way to the fridge. "He obviously hated the idea as much as I do. Can't she take a hint?"

"Ms. Park told me that she was worried that Lee doesn't know any-one his own age," was all Dad said as he trailed in after me. "It's just one run. Will it hurt you to go this once?"

"No, but it might very well hurt him. He treats me like I'm con-tagious or something. And don't get me started on his opinions of my freckles. The guy is ten different kinds of special, let me tell you."

He laughed. "More like extreme social awkwardness. Just do your normal run and get it over with. And later on I can help you look at schools."

My stomach plummeted at his casual words. With anyone else, that didn't signify anything dramatic. But with us, there was a wealth of history weighing down that statement. I knew, and he knew that I knew, what I wanted. And what I wanted was the exact opposite of what he wanted. But I also knew that Dad was determined to change my mind by ignoring the problem and acting as though everything was fine.

Words bubbled up inside me, old arguments that I dismissed as soon as I thought of them because I knew they were pointless. And I was just too worn out to take on this battle, so I answered back just as casually, "Sure, that'd be great."

He grinned, clearly relieved. "Well, I'll head on up then. Goodnight, Merri."

"Night."

I watched him leave, back straight, no falter in his step. So sure of himself, so confident of what he wanted to do. As if his wife of twenty years hadn't left him last year without a backward glance, leaving him with a broken home and sole custody of a bewildered teenage daughter.

Mom had texted me. *Texted* me. While I was at school. I got on the bus that day with a mom, and by the time I got home she was gone. And not just gone, but gone-gone; she'd somehow managed to pack all of her things and leave. Dad came home to find me in hysterics, frantically calling her friends to try to hunt her down. But of course it didn't do any good, and a year later we still hadn't heard from her. If it hadn't been for the text, Dad would have called the police. But it was pretty clear by the "I'm sorry, plz forgive me" message she'd sent that she was in full control of the situation and knew exactly what she was doing.

The sad thing is that a part of me wasn't even all that surprised. How could I be, when the fights had gotten worse and worse over the years? Mom hated how long Dad would be gone on the ships, hated how we didn't live on base so she could have support from the other naval wives, hated when we did live on base because there wasn't enough to do. When Dad had finally decided to retire from the Navy and work as a consultant, she'd been excited to settle down…but it wasn't long before she was back to complaining.

They never argued in front of me, but nothing prevented their raised voices from surrounding me as I hid out in my room. And the cold silences that followed were even worse—days of Mom slamming everything around, while I stayed quiet and did my best not to make her even more angry. You never knew what mood you were walking into each day, and I'd learned quickly to go with the flow. If Mom was feeling happy and lighthearted, then the day could be spent shopping, going to the spa, baking or binge-watching old movies. If Mom was unhappy? I kept my head down and got a lot of homework done.

Still, I'd never thought that she'd actually leave us. Leave *me*. How could you hate someone yet miss them at the same time? All of her funky colored pots that had once hung over the stove were donated to the nearest thrift store. Her endless supply of magnetic notebooks, where she kept lists for everything, all recycled. The dry erase calendar where she'd kept all of our schedules, thrown out the day after she had left. Now the kitchen was stark and bare, just like the rest of the house; the absence of her things just a reminder of how little she cared about us.

Needing air, I quietly slipped out the front door into the blanket of silence interrupted only by the gentle chirping of the crickets and frogs. The evening breeze had the slightest of bites to it, a welcome contrast against my hot face as I sat on the hanging bench on one side of the porch, tucked away from the front door.

Out of habit, I pulled out my phone and opened that last text from her and read it for the millionth time. The abrupt words cut just as deeply as they had the first time I read them, even after a lifetime of living with sharp words thrown at me whenever a bad mood hit.

You are just like your father: no imagination.

Why can't you try to push yourself more?

Sometimes you really disappoint me, Merilee. Don't you want more for yourself?

Tears burned the backs of my eyes, and I leaned back against the seat, anchoring my foot on the porch so that I could swing the seat back and forth, the chains squeaking as I rocked out my frustration. Putting my head back to rest on the hard curve of the swing, I squeezed my eyes shut against the sting of tears as anger and guilt raged in me. Anger over my mom's selfishness and how unfair it all was. And guilt because I was following in her footsteps.

Although the text didn't say it, Dad and I both knew ultimately why Mom had left: to pursue her art. Over the years she'd grown more and more obsessed with it, and at first I was grateful. It was something else for her to turn her attention to, especially when Dad was away. And she'd been so happy when I'd shown talent in it as well; it was one of the few things that she was always encouraging about, and in her better moods, she would sit down with me and help me practice. But over time art became the only thing that she was interested in—there would be days I didn't see her because she was locked up in the spare bedroom (her self-proclaimed art studio), painting at an almost feverish pace. She attended local workshops, traveled to conferences and somehow became convinced that the only thing keeping her artwork from becoming famous were the distractions of her suburban life, aka her family. So, just like that, she'd decided to leave. No wonder my dad was so against me studying art.

I understood how he felt, I really did. I could see how everything was stacked against me: I was essentially a carbon copy of my mom when it came to looks, and we both loved art, which was driving a wedge between my dad and me more and more each day. I used to show him my weekly cartoon panel, and he'd laugh at the scenes and look at me with pride. But those days were long gone. Dad was determined that I wouldn't end up like my mom, insisting that I study something more practical—like technical writing or business—if I planned on him paying for my tuition.

I could apply for art scholarships, but was it worth it to disappoint him that much? He'd already suffered so much, how could I make it worse?

I took a shaky breath and rubbed at my eyes—grateful for the quiet as I struggled to rein in my frustration.

"*AISSH!*"

I just about jumped a foot in the air as Lee erupted outside, a phone pressed to his ear, yelling at the top of his lungs. His voice echoed in the night, but since it was all in Korean, I doubted he cared if anyone overheard. However, one encounter with him tonight was enough for me, especially since we had our orders to run together tomorrow. Shrinking into the shadows, I had no choice but to watch him give the person on the receiving end an earful of his wrath, every word deep with anger and derision.

Back and forth, forth and back, Lee cut a trail through the grass as he paced, randomly kicking at the ground as he made noises that alternated between loud and bewildering, at one point sounding like he was clearing his throat hard enough to scrape it raw. I remained frozen on the bench the entire time, hardly breathing for fear that he'd see me. It was dark, so maybe he wouldn't notice me. Not daring to move, I was forced to watch this whole thing unfold as he got madder and madder until he finally, and rather anticlimactically, hung up.

His chest rose and fell like he had been sprinting for miles; dropping his phone, he gripped his head, his fingers burrowing into his hair and clenching into fists. *"Aiiish!"*

Achoo!

Of course that's the moment I would sneeze. Stupid Virginia allergies. He might not have seen me, except our automatic porch lights came on just then, like a spotlight. Life hated me, apparently.

Lee's head whipped around. "Christmas?" His deep voice was hoarse and rough sounding, although whether from emotion or from the yelling was impossible to tell.

Achoo!

"Hello," I said flatly as soon as I could talk again. Let him take the hint and leave me alone.

But did he? Of course not. Instead of stalking off, like I fully expected him to, he came closer. "How long have you been there?" he demanded, the accusation clear that I'd dared to eavesdrop on him.

I sat up tall in a vain effort to appear unaffected. "I don't need to answer that."

His shoulders remained tense, his voice tight as he muttered to himself, although his breathing slowed as he visibly tried to calm down.

"Why are you here?" he asked, his voice no longer angry, although there was a challenging note to it, one that immediately got my back up. Why was *I* sitting on *my* porch? More like why was *he* still talking to me? "I *live* here," I snapped, not bothering to keep the snarky tone from my voice.

His eyes narrowed briefly, then he leaned forward over the porch railing, intent on me. "Why are you *outside,* upset?"

"What makes you think I'm upset?"

"You've been crying." He pointed to my face, and I slapped a hand to my cheek in horror. Crap. I wiped off the tears impatiently.

"Christmas?"

"My name is not Christmas," I snapped at him. What would he say if I called him Sparkle Boy to his face?

A puff of breeze caused his hair to flop on his forehead in a surprisingly endearing way, and the fact that I'd noticed made me even angrier.

"You have yellow hair."

"Yes, you said that before."

"Like a star."

I had a bad feeling that I knew where he was going with this. "You're saying my hair is like a Christmas tree topper, aren't you?"

He just smirked.

"Tell me this, do you work at being rude, or does it just come naturally to you?"

The smirk widened to a broad grin. "Korean girls do not seem to mind, *Christmas.*"

"Yeah, well this American is immune to your charm."

"So, you think I have charm?"

Did he not realize that "charm" could be used in a negative sense?

I guessed not, since he was still grinning cockily. Lacking the energy to fight with him, too, I just rolled my eyes. "Sure. Let's call it that."

"You called it that, not me."

All right, that's it. Time to turn the tables.

"Looks like your charm wasn't working a minute ago, hot shot. Everything okay?"

That grin of his immediately vanished, wiped away by my question, and he gripped the railing till his knuckles were bone white. "It is fine."

"Really? Because it didn't sound like it." I smiled not so innocently at him. "I mean, I don't speak Korean, but some things don't need translation. Like when your aunt first brought you home. She seemed *mad*. I bet she didn't find you charming."

He scowled. "She had just found out why—" he cut himself off before I could find out just why Ms. Park had been so furious that day. "Never mind. I am not the only one angry. *You* are angry at my aunt," he fired back at me, crossing his arms over his chest. I did *not* notice how the movement pulled at his shirt and emphasized his broad shoulders. "You were obviously upset with her for making you run with me."

I mirrored his movement, as much out of defensiveness as the cool breeze. "I wouldn't put it quite like that."

He arched an eyebrow.

"Okay, fine, you're right. But come on, you weren't exactly happy about it either. Didn't it bother you?"

He shrugged as if he hadn't just been yelling his head off at his phone, the faker. "I am used to it."

Somehow I had a hard time envisioning Ms. Park bossing him around all the time from the other side of the world—unlike my dad who, once he got going, excelled at micromanagement no matter what time zone you were in. But perhaps Lee meant the rest of his family? Maybe I could talk him into canceling tomorrow. He probably resented being bossed around as much as I did. Easy-peasy. Clearing my throat, I oh-so-casually said, "You know, it's okay if you don't want to run tomorrow. I mean, I'm sure you have other things that you need to do."

I held my breath as he considered, eyes raking over me, a quizzical light in them. He appeared to be confused about something, although I couldn't figure out what. What was he waiting for?

He eventually nodded. "I do not."

"Great! I mean, you can tell your aunt and—"

"No, Christmas. I do want to run tomorrow."

I blinked at him in confusion. *What the heck?* "You're kidding, right?"

"Are you afraid?" he asked, eyes bright with challenge.

"Why would I be afraid?" I scoffed. "Nothing I can't handle."

"Good."

What I did next can be blamed on the smug expression on his face. Before he could blink, I'd taken a picture of him with my phone. With the flash on. Hah! I gave him my most obnoxiously sweet smile. "I'll see you tomorrow morning."

But instead of getting mad, like I'd expected (and hoped), he settled back on his heels and nodded again, pleased as punch about something. "I will see you tomorrow. G'night, Christmas." The Aussie accent drawled out the words in a sexy rumble, the thread of amusement putting my teeth on edge.

I stared at him as he strutted back to his house. It might have been my imagination, but I could have sworn I heard him give a wicked chuckle before going inside. With an angry huff, I got up and stomped into the house, remembering at the last minute not to slam the door.

I went to bed filled with purpose that can be summed up in five words: Sparkle Boy was going down.

Please let him still be in bed. Please let him still be in bed.

I stood in the front yard, clad in my best workout gear (I was *not* going to run next to Mr. Model wearing old and sweat stained clothes), all stretched and ready to go.

No sign of life from the Park household.

Maybe, just maybe, the universe felt bad for the trouble it had given me last night and was making up for it today. Sparkle Jerk was probably still in bed—he seemed like the type that would sleep in past noon, and it was already almost one o'clock—which meant I could go for a peaceful run by myself and then spend the rest of the day working on a new panel that involved a certain someone hollering for a waiter.

The door opened, and my hope vanished as Lee stepped out, eyes bright and a spring to his step I didn't trust, especially when he flashed me a grin. Even the way he was dressed was suspicious. He was clothed from head to toe in some serious exercise gear: black jogging pants, a bright blue windbreaker with some pretty wacky black stripes zig-zagging all over the place, running shoes that were scuffed with the marks of an experienced runner, hair pushed back with a thin band in a way that highlighted his handsome features. He meant business.

I was doubly glad I had opted for my best workout clothes. At least I wouldn't look shabby next to him. And on the bright side, given what he was wearing, it was clear he was used to working out, which meant we could get this over quickly. No more Merry Christmas and sexy accents and confusion. "Well, Lee, let's get this over with."

He stiffened. "What did you just call me?"

"Lee. Isn't that your name?" He was frowning, his thick brows pulled down until they almost covered his eyes. What, had I gotten it wrong? His aunt had said Lee *Something*, I was sure of it.

"Yes. No. It is," he sighed impatiently. "Never mind."

He muttered something else I didn't even want to translate and shook his head as he began to stretch his toned frame with practiced ease. Seemed awfully grumpy for someone who had passed on an opportunity to back out. *Well, let him regret it.* I wanted to get this thing over with, do a panel featuring one heroic neighbor going above and beyond to make her grumpy neighbor feel welcome, and move on.

We started out at a brisk walk, neither acknowledging the other beyond making sure that our arms didn't whack each other's. Oh man, this was so awkward. Forget needing a proper warm up because I was burning up with embarrassment from my head to my toes.

I didn't realize that I had started jogging until the smacking of Lee's feet against the pavement as he caught up with me jolted me from my inward cringing. And when he did catch up, he easily matched my pace. I stole a quick peek; even while running he looked like a model, hair falling just so, biceps just taut enough as he swung his arms. He caught me looking and flashed me a knowing grin. He knew how hot he was, darn him. And now he knew that I had noticed.

But would he look so good at a faster pace? *All right, buddy, let's see how you do in a real run.*

I rocketed down the path, a rush of competitive adrenaline pushing me to a pace just shy of a sprint. Lee kept up easily…scratch that, it was clear he was holding back, and he wasn't afraid to make me know it. He shot me a challenging look that clearly said, *Is this the best you can do?*

Game. On.

I poured every ounce of power into my legs, the energy like rocket fuel propelling me even faster. My vision narrowed until all I could see was the next step, the next stride. Legs tore up the track as my strides lengthened to their full range.

This! The exhilaration of muscles stretching and flexing in rhythm to your heartbeat, a breeze of your own making cooling you, the blood pumping through your whole body. This was why I loved running. I hadn't been able to do it so much in Sydney because we'd been staying in the heart of the city, and there was no good path for me to use, and I'd probably regret pushing myself like this later, but for now everything—all worries, stress, even Lee—melted away as I sprinted down the path. I heard a voice call out, but didn't pay it attention. Who cared? I was running and nothing could—

"Aaahhhhhh!"

Pain seared up my leg, sudden and piercing, and my ankle crumpled under me, causing me to skid on the gravel before landing with a final "*Ooooomph*" on the grass.

Exertion and pain stole my breath, and I desperately gasped for air. My ankle, my poor, poor ankle, was throbbing in time with my thundering pulse, sending waves of agony up my leg. I reached out with shaky fingers, but wimped out.

Lee dropped to his knees beside me. "Are you okay?" he huffed, chest heaving from exertion. "You did not hear me? I was telling you to watch out for the pothole."

I glared up at him, latching on to annoyance to distract me from the ever-growing pain of my swelling ankle, which kept giving me breath-stealing spasms of agony.

"I did hear you...thanks. That hole," (*gasp*) "wasn't there" (*gulp*) "before." That thing had so not been there before I'd left for Australia! It was like a crater had sprung up in the span of a summer.

"*Aiish*, look at it. It is already swollen." He made a move as if to touch it, and I cringed away. Even cringing hurt.

"Don't touch! OUCH!"

"I will not hurt it, I just want to feel if it is broken. Can you move it at all?" His long fingers surrounded my ankle, applying a gentle pressure that still sent spasms up my leg.

I shook my head and hissed. "I think it's a sprain."

His grin was sudden and bright. If I hadn't been writhing in agony, I would have admired it. "No kidding, doctor. Do you have your phone?"

"Here." I gingerly pulled out my phone, being careful not to shift my weight too much, only to deflate when I saw the huge crack now running down the screen. Something rattled loose inside, and when I tried to turn it on, the screen remained dark. "Oh. What about you?"

"Left it at the house." He ran his fingers through his hair, making the thick strands pull loose from his band and stick straight up.

"Can you walk on it?"

"I'll try," I said, face burning in humiliation. Of all the stupid things to do!

He took both my hands and braced himself as I hoisted myself up and stood on one leg. Still holding on, now in too much pain to be embarrassed, I touched the ground with my injured foot.

"Yaaaaaa-aaaa. I don't think so." The pain was too intense, and I felt the blood beginning to drain from my face as I fought waves of nausea.

Lee turned his back to me and crouched. "I cannot believe I am doing this," he muttered. "Get on."

"What?"

"I will carry you on my back."

I stared at his broad shoulders. "Are you serious?"

He twisted around. "Or you can wait for me to bring some help. But it might take a while. Do you want to be left alone here?"

And just when I thought things couldn't get any worse.

He was right. Waiting around for help while my ankle continued to balloon up did not seem like the best of ideas, although it sure as heck would leave me with more dignity than would be left by what I was about to do. But since my ankle had surpassed the grapefruit stage and was now heading towards cantaloupe proportions, there was no choice but to climb on.

I hopped up onto his back with a very indelicate grunt of pain, and laced my arms around his neck. Feeling very much like a piece of wet laundry pinned to a line, I held on for all I was worth as he smoothly stood up like there wasn't a full-grown girl dangling from his neck. He hooked my legs around his arms, again with a gentleness that startled me, and to my absolute horror, my skin pimpled in goose bumps, as if it welcomed his touch. But if Lee noticed, he didn't say anything, thank goodness. He just started retracing our steps at a mercifully slow pace. I'd like to think it was because he didn't want to jostle my ankle, but the weight of a full-grown girl around probably was a more likely reason for the lack of speed. But it didn't matter, because I had just made a discovery: Sparkle Boy had muscles! Biceps, triceps, back muscles all rippled together in a rhythm that made me very aware that they existed. I'm not very tall, but I am curvy, and it couldn't be easy to carry a gal after running the way he had. But Lee didn't show any sign of being strained at all, although when he turned his head to look as a bird swooped past, I caught sight of clenched jaw—the muscle twitching as if he was holding in his anger.

This was awkward. Didn't help that it was all my fault. If I hadn't been determined to outrun him, I probably would have noticed the stupid pothole and avoided taking a tumble that would be played in a slow motion replay later tonight as I tried to fall asleep. I would have been happy to just stew in the silence and count each step closer to the sanctuary of home, and I assumed that Lee felt the same, so I was surprised when he asked, "Does it hurt much?"

A fresh wave of pain me hit as he shifted his grip on me. I clenched my teeth and grunted out, "Yeah."

"Ah." He seemed to be considering something. "So, did you hear me? Or were you ignoring me?"

Well, gee, someone doesn't hold back their punches. It was kind of disconcertingly refreshing, though. Awkward, but refreshing.

I waited until the pain had eased to a dull throb before answering. "I was not ignoring you." (Okay, maybe a little. But was I going to admit that? Nope!) "When I run, I tend to block things out. Actually, I do that any time I'm focusing on something." Hours have gone by as I draw, and the only way I know is by how stiff I am at the end of it. "What about you? You seem to be…" (I wanted to say intense, somewhat moody) "…a focused guy."

He nodded. "*Deh.*"

"Okay, what does that mean? I'm assuming yes?"

"*Deh.*"

"You like yanking my chain, don't you?"

"What chain?" He kept his eyes fixed on the path ahead, but I could tell from his serious tone that he was legitimately confused.

"It's just an expression. It means that you like to tease me." And come to think of it, it was a really random saying. Even though his English was excellent, it was easy to forget that it was not his native language.

Lee stiffened. "I am not teasing you."

I snorted. "Yeah, right."

"I am not," he insisted. "Why would I tease you?"

There was that brutal honesty again. "Sorry. I thought you were being sarcastic."

"No," he said, turning his head slightly. Suddenly, his lips were alarmingly close, and I got to see just how attractive they were. Not too thin and not too full. Attractive lips that were now parted just a bit.

I jerked my face away, pulling back from his shoulder. My cheeks felt radioactively red at this point. What was I thinking? I couldn't stand this guy, and I already had a boyfriend. *And what, now I am flirting with a pretty face? Okay, not so much pretty as…ARGH! Stop it!*

I caught sight of Bree's house. There was a path that cut from beside her house right to my street that would make this journey end that much sooner. But maybe I'd get lucky, and she'd be outside. She'd have a perfectly normal explanation as to why I hadn't seen her, and it would all be fine. "There's a shortcut here that you can take."

Lee followed the direction I pointed to and made his way through the woods at the edge of Bree's house. I tightened my grip as I raised myself up to see if she was outside, and that's when I saw it. A red pickup truck in the driveway.

Oh.

My.

Gosh.

It was Luke's truck. And it was Luke's familiar blond head bent over Bree's as they made out like they were auditioning for a soap opera. Luke and Bree were kissing. Each other. Luke and Bree…

I must have made a noise, because Lee jerked to a stop. "What is it? What is wrong? Did I hurt your ankle?"

Ankle? Who cared about a freaking ankle when MY BOYFRIEND WAS KISSING MY BEST FRIEND?

"Christmas?"

They were *still* going at it!

"Merri?"

This could not be happening to me. No way that my best friend and boyfriend were—

"Merilee!"

"What!" I snapped.

"Are you okay?"

"Okay? OKAY? That's my…and she's my…they're…"

He was somehow able to fill in the blanks. *"Aiiish."*

The two broke apart for some long-overdue air, and that's when Bree spotted me staring in horror, clinging to my neighbor's nephew like a demented monkey. Her whole face constricted in dismay, and I could see her mouth a curse word that would have had her mother reaching for a bar of soap if we were younger.

Luke whipped his head around and met my horrified stare. His jaw dropped and he went bright crimson in five seconds. His brows came down in bewilderment as he saw me holding onto Lee even as his face tightened with guilt, his jaw clenching tight. Anger was not far behind as he took in the fact that I was being carried by another guy, his face taking on a purplish tone. He made a move to get out of the truck, but Bree grabbed onto his arm.

"Lee, take me home. Please." My voice was small and weak, all feeling numbed as shock settled in.

Lee grunted and strode away, managing to go at almost a jog without hurting my ankle. He didn't offer any words of reassurance because they would have been fake. And Koreans, according to my completely unbiased source, did not lie.

American teenagers, on the other hand, apparently did nothing but lie.

Five

"Music is living; you experience life when you listen. Your dreams, sorrows, victories—all can be found in a song."

RHEE JIN-SO, MEMBER OF THUNDER

"Merri? Honey, do you want something to eat?"

"Nope."

"Are you sure? You've been up here for a while."

"Yep."

Dad's sigh was so deep it's a wonder it didn't open the door. "Well, I'm here if you want to talk about it."

"Okay."

"Okay. I'll, uh, I'll just be downstairs."

"Okay. And Dad?"

"Yes?" he immediately said, sounding so hopeful that I felt guilty.

"Thank you for understanding."

"You're welcome, sweetheart. I'll just be downstairs if you need me," he repeated, clearly not knowing what else to say. His heavy footsteps almost drowned out his mutterings about how he'd known Luke was an idiot, and I was once again left alone.

I curled up on my window seat and tightened my grip on my

comforter as if to shield myself from the world as I glared at the trees that marked where Bree's house was.

Cheating. The two of them. Together.

I still couldn't believe it, even though the signs had all been there. Now I understood why Bree had been avoiding me, why Luke had suddenly dropped off the face of the earth (although why did he even bother to see me when I first got home?). They didn't even try to deny it, not after me seeing them kiss right out in the open like Romeo and Juliet.

It had been three days since they had been spotted, and they'd run the gamut of stupidity. At first, both tripped over themselves with excuses and apologies. *It was a mistake. Never should have happened that way. So sorry to have hurt you.* If Luke expected that to make me feel better, he was beyond idiotic.

Then, it was on to, *Well, it's not as though there weren't problems, or else this never would have happened.* Again, not one of Luke's better moves.

And, my particular favorite, courtesy of Bree: *You should have seen this coming.* Yes, silly me, how could I have *not* anticipated that she'd hook up with my boyfriend the minute my back was turned? He was probably the ice cream cone mystery man that she'd boasted about…the idea that they'd been flirting with each other while I'd been blissfully unaware sickened me.

Luke had actually had the nerve to accuse me of basically doing the same thing, saying that obviously I would move on fast with the guy I was "hugging." That was the only time I responded to his message. I fired back to remind him that I had *never* cheated on him, and if he hadn't had his tongue down Bree's throat he would have seen that my ankle was the size of a basketball and I obviously couldn't walk.

Radio silence from Luke after that.

Not once did either try to talk to me face to face. Oh no, that would have meant that at least one of them had a sense of decency. This was all done through text. Cold, impersonal, safe texts—just like with my mom. Two more people who had decided that the best way to destroy my world was to do it via text. Sparkle Boy didn't seem so bad after all, compared to them, although my cheeks burned at the memory of him carting me home, hyperventilating down his neck until he all but dumped me into my father's arms. (It was a fun trip to urgent care, let me tell you. Dad tried to order everyone around like they were navy staff, although the doctors did not pay him one iota of attention.)

The following few days were, in a word, hell. I had missed the first few days of school because of my ankle. On the one hand it saved me from having to see people. But on the other, it gave me endless minutes to replay every second of that scene in graphic detail. Over and over again.

Luke holding Bree close, fingers tangling into her red hair. Bree running her hands through his curls, tilting her head to bring him closer. The sympathy on Lee's face when he carefully lowered me down on the porch…

Apparently, when I'm upset my memory plays out like a corny romance novel.

On the third day after the ankle debacle, desperate to distract myself before I descended into absolute melodrama, I forced myself to get up and take a shower. This was, I'll admit, much-needed, but it was difficult because I couldn't put weight on my foot and had to stand like a drenched flamingo, one hand pressed into the shower wall. By the time I finished up it was dark outside, and I had just enough energy to fall into bed. But as with the previous nights, I couldn't go right to sleep. Instead, that replay started up again, the pain not far behind, welling up from the knot in the center of my chest. But no tears. I refused to spill any more tears over them.

If only I hadn't left for the summer.

If only they had told me.

If only I had tried harder to talk to Bree, or ask Luke what was going on.

If, if, if.

The maybes of an alternate reality chased off any hope of getting sleep. My phone buzzed with another WhatsApp text from Ema, who had no idea why I had been ignoring her over the past few days. I'd even missed our video chat. But she must have spider senses, because all it said was, *I'm here for you.*

I rubbed the screen. Ironic how someone whom I'd known for only a few months had already shown more loyalty than someone I'd known most of my life, even when I was avoiding her. Time to stop hiding.

- *I've been better.*

- *You want to video call?*

- *No, that's ok. But there's something I need to tell you.*

- *OMG U R SICK!!!*

- *No, I'm fine. Ankle is sprained, but that's not it.*

- *YOU NEED SURGERY!!! Is it your kidney? Do you need a donor?*

That brought a smile to my face. Small, but still a smile. No one could say that Ema was without a healthy imagination. I began typing another response when another message pinged in.

- *YOU'RE MOVING!!! TO AUSTRALIA?!?!*

Dang, she could type fast.

- *NO!!! Luke cheated on me.*

That apparently shocked her so much she couldn't type anything, so I added fuel to the fire. *With Bree.*

- *WHAT?!?!*

A split second later my phone began ringing. Knowing Ema, she'd want to know everything in minute detail, and I now braced myself to relive it. I couldn't hide in my cocoon anymore. I was just lucky that I had a friend like Ema to turn to.

I could do this. No, I *would* do this. And when I was able to walk again, I would show Luke and Bree how mature I was by ignoring the both of them. And maybe kick Luke hard enough to make him squeak when he talked, as if he had been huffing helium, for the rest of his life.

Taking a deep breath, I answered Ema's call.

The blank page of my sketchbook mocked me, the untouched paper a glaring reminder that despite my best efforts to pick myself up from my emotional plummet, I had zero inspiration, just visions of Bree and Luke playing tonsil hockey.

Argh!! I shoved the book away in disgust and flopped back on the mounds of pillows I'd amassed at the head of the bed, being careful not to jostle my propped-up foot. The doctor had wrapped my ankle, given me some fresh bandages if I needed them, along with a pair of crutches and orders to rest for a few more days before going back to school. Something about a strained tendon and needing to not strain it further. Whatever. It was a green pass to continue to avoid the world and come to grips with the fact that I'd spent two years with a jerk and been best friends with a liar.

Dad was out doing manly things with some of his buddies, so it was just me and my self-disgust. How did I suck so badly at picking up some key character flaws? The stillness in the house pressed in on me, until finally I'd had enough. I shoved the covers back and, grabbing the crutches, made my way downstairs. Somewhere in the kitchen there was a box of Fruit Loops with my name on it, and I was in the perfect mood to feed my sorrows with a sugar high followed inevitably by a sugar crash.

I was halfway to the kitchen when the doorbell rang, and I hesitated. Who would be here at seven on a Saturday night?

Lee, apparently. Perfect, airbrushed Lee, clothed in a ribbed yellow sweater that had probably been made in the nineties, ripped black jeans, and yellow slip-on sneakers. A bright pink sack, with something bulky inside, dangled from one of his hands, while the other was brushing back some of his artfully messy hair. He froze as I opened the door, lined eyes widening ever so slightly before he dipped his head. "Good evening. How are you feeling?"

Courteous words, but there was an edge to them, like he was annoyed by something. If he *was* annoyed, why was he here? Well, if he could speak the truth all the time, so could I. "I've been better."

He nodded. "May I come in? I have something for you."

I blinked in confusion. "Uh, sure?" *Uh, why?*

I held the door open for him like the good (and now curious) neighbor that I was. He carefully took off his shoes and put them by the door before heading straight for the kitchen, me hobbling behind him and talking to fill the silence.

"I wanted to thank you. For the other day. You know. For everything." My foot caught on the barstool, and I flopped against the counter with an *oof*. Stupid crutches. "I mean, it was awful," I continued, somewhat breathless, "and I'm sorry you had to see it. I just had no clue, you know? It came out of nowhere, and I had no warning at all. I'm not normally the type to cry or freak out, and you were carrying me and—" *Merri, stop your rambling before he thinks you're an even bigger idiot.* "Anyways, thank you for doing what you did."

He leveled a piercing stare at me. "You still look bad."

It says something that this time I didn't get mad. I knew I looked bad, and quite honestly, I didn't care. He was the one who had decided to come over, he could deal with it. "Life's been bad lately. Why are you here?"

He proudly gestured the various dishes he'd set out. "I have brought you comforted food."

"Comforted" food consisted of various small containers filled with pickled…things. I had no idea what the food was, but the big container held what looked like really flat noodles and chunks of something in a black sauce. He pulled off the lid of the big container. "Do you have a fork?"

I gestured to the drawer behind him, and he grabbed one to mix up the noodle dish, swirling everything around until the noodles were coated in black. "Here," he held the dish out to me. "It will make you feel better."

Really? Because right then I was feeling a little grossed out. It looked like…I won't even say what it looked like. As I gingerly took it from him, my fingers brushed against his. His breath hitched, and he yanked his hands back like I'd burned him. Suddenly the black noodles were the most fascinating thing in the room, because I sure as heck was not about to open *that* can of worms to figure out. "Thanks. What is this?"

He cleared his throat. "It is *jjajangmyeun.* Noodles and black bean paste." The food was halfway to my mouth when he added, "It helps singles feel better."

I froze and stared at him. A noodle slid off the fork and fell to the table. "What?"

He nodded. "Koreans eat it when they are single. It will make you feel better. Korean food is good for your health." He leaned back and crossed his arms across his chest, obviously pleased with himself.

I blinked. And blinked again. "You brought me food because I'm single? Not because I hurt my ankle?" He'd brought food because he freaking felt sorry for me? Because I was now *single*? He knew this better than anyone, since he'd been right there when I became single. And naturally that inspired him to bring me food? What. The. Heck?

Right now, literally RIGHT NOW, would be the perfect time for the universe to make up for all of this and let the earth swallow me up. But not before I chucked a crutch at his big fat head. I slammed the noodles down. "Seriously?"

He reared back in surprise. "You are upset by this?"

"I—and you—this…"

Lee cocked an eyebrow. "You cannot talk. You seem to be that way a lot."

I wanted to scream. "Believe me, it's only when I'm with you." I glared at him, making it clear that it was most definitely not a compliment.

He leaned his forearms against the counter, careless and relaxed. "Just try it." He nodded at the fork still clutched in my hand. "It will help as you forget the *baekchi*. The idiot," he translated. "Both of them are *baekchis*. They hurt you, and I am sorry."

All the righteous indignation fizzled out as my hurt lurched with an emotion too painful to define. *I am sorry.* Just three words. Three words that I didn't know I'd been waiting to hear until he, of all people, spoke them.

The walls I'd been desperately holding up since seeing those two traitors that day faltered, threatening to leave me raw and bare. Not raw to Lee, though, but raw to myself, which was even worse. The pain and rage and insecurity and fear and bewilderment, all of it roiled together in my chest, tightening my throat. I stared at him, not daring to blink, as the dreaded sting at the back of my eyes threatened to spill over.

Lee hesitated, his ears going bright red. Quickly straightening from his relaxed position, he said. "I had better go. Enjoy the *jjajangmyeun*."

He dipped his head, ears still burning, and strode out of the kitchen. The front door clicked behind him, and then I was alone.

Alone to look into the bowl of now cold and slimy black noodles, the official food of singles.

Alone to let my walls come down, if only for a while.

Alone to cry.

And cry I did. Oh boy, oh boy, oh boy, did I ever cry. I cried for Bree, for all the years of laughter and fun and going through growing pains together. For wasting my time with Luke, being blinded by his good looks and flattery.

The sobs shook my whole body, tears falling into the noodles as I just let go. And it felt good. Oh, it felt so good to let the walls down, to stop fighting my emotions and trying to hide from all the self-doubt that had been eating away at me. Good to acknowledge every trace of betrayal as I mourned for what I'd lost and faced the fact that, no matter how much I wished otherwise, things would never be the same again.

It took a long time, but the tears finally slowed to a trickle, and I was able to take a shuddering sigh and actually breathe. The knot in my chest no longer threatened to choke me, and although I had a plugged-up nose and achy head, I felt as though the weight that had been pressing down on me had lightened somewhat—still there, but not quite as heavy.

Lee had been right. The food *had* helped, and I hadn't even had to take a bite. I guess Korean food really was good for your health.

Six

Thunder member Lee Hyung-kim was seen last night with model/singer/actress Park Su-sung. Rumors of the two dating have been hitting all the K blog sites, but neither has confirmed the relationship. Promotional propaganda? Or something more?

ARCHIVED ARTICLE ON K-POP WORLD

I stared at my reflection, taking in the pale cheeks and purple eye bags with a critical stare. Needed more powder. No way I was going to my first day of senior year looking like I needed to *go to hospital*. And yes, a panel featuring that particular statement was almost complete and ready to be uploaded to DeviantArt. At least my followers were getting a kick from all this; I'd never had this many comments on my work before Lee became the main subject. The knowledge that people liked my work, liked it enough to comment on it and even share it with others, was like a balm to my raw emotions. In an effort to distract myself, I'd stayed up late to share links to my page on various social media outlets. Checking my phone, I could see it'd paid off—overnight the number of comments had tripled. I'd been experimenting with the chibi (tiny cartoon characters with large heads) format, and apparently had succeeded, given everyone's response.

The extra foundation powder helped. Now I just looked exhausted. Great. Senior year was not looking good, and the topping on that bitter cake was that I had to use crutches. No glorious and clumsy-free comeback for me. But at least I was armed. If I saw a certain blond, curly-haired, cheating jerk face, I could give him a good whack on the head…or other places. Luke getting pole axed by my crutches—now *that* would be a great panel.

Dad had offered to go into work late so that he could drive me to school, but I'd insisted on riding the bus. What had started out as a great show of independence was now being undermined by being so slow that I had missed the bus. *Oops. Oh well, guess I'll have to wait till tomorrow. Too bad…not.*

"Christmas?" Lee stood near the border between our houses, his face a blend of bafflement and amusement as he watched me hobble back up the driveway.

I jerked to attention, heart suddenly racing. "What are you doing here?"

He sauntered over, hands in the pockets of jeans that were not quite as tight as the pants he'd worn when he'd first made that dramatic entrance into our neighborhood. "Do you need help?"

"I'm fine, thanks."

He bowed his head, which made his dark hair fall against his forehead, drawing attention to his eyes. I peered at them. Guyliner was the perfect combination of smudge and precision. And seriously, how did his skin have no pores?

"Christmas?"

Moving on. "Um, I wanted to thank you. For the food. You…you were right. It did help." (In ways he probably hadn't expected.) "And I really appreciated it." Which was surprisingly true, given how I was ready to clock him when he'd first announced that it was "singles" food. In his own unique way, he'd been trying to make me feel better. That, if nothing else, gave him leeway to call me Christmas. Besides, I was kinda getting used to it.

He studied me, taking me in from the tip of my wrapped foot to the top of my *yellow* head. A blush began to work its way up from my neck, darn it, but I was *not* going to back down. He's already seen me at my worst; I had to reclaim some of my dignity. So, I stood my ground and let him look. After an eternity he nodded, as if confirming something to himself, and said, "You are welcome."

Right then Ms. Park came bustling out. "Merilee! How is ankle?"

"It's fine. I just need to rest." Why was she smiling at me like that?

"You miss the bus?"

"Yeah, but it's okay. One more day at home won't hurt."

She gasped. "No! Cannot miss school! 'Eee Hyung-kim," she turned to him and then gave him an order that needed no translation, much to my absolute horror.

He winced, but dutifully said, "Would you like a drive to school?"

"Oh, no, that's okay," I said quickly. "It's fine, really."

They both gave me identical looks of skepticism. "But, you miss bus," Ms. Park helpfully pointed out. "You need ride."

Lee nodded. "*Deh*. You need my help." He nodded as if to say, "*So there.*"

"You take my car. Hurry, hurry, or you will be late." Ms. Park pulled keys out of her pocket. Hmmm, planned much?

But I just couldn't say no to her face. I mean, I could, but I couldn't. "Yeah, um, okay. Thank you."

Under her watchful gaze, I followed Lee to the car. To my surprise, he not only opened the passenger door for me, but also helped me with my crutches and backpack—probably putting on a show of being the dutiful nephew, but I wasn't going to complain. Well, not about that, anyways. The idea of staying home an extra day wasn't really all that bad.

Lee carefully pulled out of the driveway, eased down the street, and didn't stop until we got to the intersection leading out of the neighborhood. "Where is your school?"

"Just take a left here, and keep going till you see the school on the right."

He eyed the road. "What time does school start?"

"In ten minutes," I answered, looking down at my watch, "but I don't mind being a few minutes late—"

"You will not be late!" Revving the engine with glee, he slammed his foot down and went from zero to breaking the sound barrier in five seconds. All I could do was hold onto the dash, heart in my throat, and pray for deliverance.

I don't know how they drive in Korea, but if it's anything like the way Lee drives then it's a wonder that any of them are still alive. The speed limit was completely ignored, and every car was an obstacle to weave around. I felt like I was on a rollercoaster about to derail. He slammed on the brakes and floored the gas so many times, the seatbelts locked repeatedly, and every time, I instinctively braced for impact. And when he couldn't zoom past someone, he was shouting in a mixture of English and Korean, something about stupid rules and how they made no sense.

"Lee! That's a crosswalk!"

"A what?"

"CROSSWALK. People are crossing! They have right of way in Virginia!"

"*AIISH!*"

"AHHHHHH!!"

Terror. That's what the ten-minute car ride was—absolute mind-numbing terror.

When he pulled up at the school minutes later, all I could do was sit limp as a rag as fear and relief roiled inside me. Had I actually done it? Had I survived Lee Hyung-kim's driving? I would have kissed the ground if I wasn't still frozen in fear.

And he actually had the audacity to ask, "Christmas? Are you okay?"

I clenched my teeth to keep them from chattering. "Am I *okay*? I am never, EVER riding with you again."

"What is wrong?" he asked in genuine surprise.

I glared at him. "As if you didn't know. I don't think I've ever had that many near-death experiences in a row. How you weren't pulled over is beyond me."

He smirked. "Korean drivers are the best."

"I gotta say, Lee, no one can match your patriotism."

On his lips played the beginning of a full-on smile, but right then I caught sight of something that made everything else fade into the background.

Luke and Bree, fingers linked, were walking across the parking lot, both laughing as if they didn't have a care in the world. Bree was wearing his hoodie, looking adorable and tiny.

I'd bought him that hoodie a year ago.

"Are you going to get out?"

"Just give me a minute."

"Why? Do you...ahh." He stopped talking as Thing One and Thing Two walked in front of the car. "Do you want to leave?"

Once again, his kindness caught me by surprise. And, oddly enough, strengthened me. If nothing else, I'd prove to him that I could handle this. "No, I'm fine. Need to get it over with."

Still, part of me cringed as I pulled myself out of the car, and I kept my head down so I wouldn't have to meet anyone's curious looks. Lee once again helped me with my crutches, even steadied me as I pulled on my back pack before getting the crutches situated under my arms. I took a deep breath, pivoted on my heel…and came nose to nose with Bree, who was standing on the curb. Not that she noticed, since she was too busy gaping at Lee.

I cleared my throat. "Bree. Luke." I nodded at them, inwardly rolling my eyes at how he was attempting to hide behind Bree and look nonchalant at the same time. Idiot.

"What happened to you?" Bree demanded as if she hadn't just totally been drooling over the guy standing next to me. So classy.

"Sprained my ankle." I waited a beat, but she didn't make any effort to move out of my way—she was once again taking in Lee, eyes wide and bright with a glint that I didn't like one bit.

Luke didn't either. He inched forward and gave that weird chin nod that guys give each other, his jaw tight and eyes suspicious. "I'm Luke."

"I know." It was hard to read between the lines of Lee's flat response, but I for one was leaning towards the hope that he was not impressed with Luke. Not that it mattered to me what he thought. Nope, it didn't make me want to smile at all.

Luke's eyes darted to me, surprise and hurt glistening in those deep-blue eyes that I used to sigh over. "That's funny," he said, "because I don't know you."

Lee just crossed his arms and leaned back against the car, a cocky grin over his handsome face. "You do not recognize me?"

Luke opened his mouth to reply, no doubt to say something stupid, but Bree elbowed him hard in the ribs before zeroing in on me. "Merri, I really need to talk to you. We," she grabbed Luke's arm and hauled him closer, "we both need to talk to you."

Oh, spare me the soap opera. "But I don't really want to talk to you. I think enough's been said and done." Emphasis on *done*.

"Don't you want us to explain?"

It took every ounce of self-control, but I managed to keep a lid on my anger. "No."

"But how can we move past this if we don't talk about it?"

Who was she, Dr. Phil? "Bree, I don't want to talk about it. Now, will you just leave me alone?"

She leaned her head against Luke, red hair gleaming against the dark blue hoodie that I'd chosen because it matched his eyes, and pain lanced through my chest. Oh my gosh, was she trying to rub it in? "I don't want any bitterness between us, you know? It's awkward, but I want us to deal with it and move on. Maybe we could meet up tonight? The three of us?"

"Gee, as much as I'd *love* that, I have plans with someone who *didn't* lie and betray me. So, yeah, not happening."

If my words bothered her, she showed no sign. "I know you're angry, but come on, Merri. This is important. Can't you reschedule?"

The lid snapped off, and my anger took a hold of my tongue before my brain could catch up. "Lee and I have dinner reservations." Wait, what?

"You do?"

"We do?" Lee sounded as shocked as Bree. That made three of us.

Now it was my turn to elbow Lee in the ribs even as I kicked myself. I couldn't believe I'd just said those words aloud.

I wasn't the only one. "You're, you're going out with *him?*" Luke sputtered.

Lee drew himself up, taking control before I could dig myself even deeper into trouble. "That is right, *baekchi*. We have a date," his voice hesitated slightly over that last word, but his smile was as confident as ever. Turning to me, he said, "I'll see you tonight." He winked—*winked*—at me before shooting Luke a triumphant smile as he got back into the car.

The three of us watched as he screeched away, all of us wearing matching looks of dazed confusion. Had I really just said that I was going on a date? With *Sparkle Boy*? And he'd actually gone along with it?

But there would be time for me to beat myself up over my stupid pride. Right now, I had to escape before Bree decided to try intervention round two. With as much dignity as I could manage while relying on two giant toothpicks for balance, I swiveled and hopped into school, leaving them together on the curb.

Rage burned in my chest like an ulcer of the heart, fueling me during the painfully slow trek to my locker. *Deep breath in, deep breath out. Don't let them see you're hurt.*

I kept my head down and plowed through the morning, managing to grab a seat right by the door in each class. I could feel Bree's attention on me the entire second block, but this time it was me who avoided her. I had nothing to say, and I definitely didn't want to hear anything from her.

Finally, the third block bell rang, which meant that all I had to do was get through lunch and the afternoon classes—a relief because not only was I emotionally exhausted, the crutches had left my armpits raw and my standing leg shaky and tired.

"Hey, Merri."

A girl from my English class sidled up to me as I was leaning against my locker, drained from the hike from the classroom to the hallway. "What happened to your foot?"

"Hi, Cassie. I sprained my ankle running." I waited. Cassie and I knew each other because we were in the same class, but that was it. She had never spoken to me outside of class, so why now?

"Ouch. Sorry. So, um, did you know about, you know, them?"

Aaaaaand there's the reason.

Starting fresh. Losing it is not starting fresh. "By them you mean Luke and Bree and how they were going out behind my back? Yes, I know."

Wait a second. I narrowed my eyes at her. "How long have *you* known?"

Either she was really clueless or just so eager to gossip that she didn't care. "Oh, I've known about it since last month. Saw them at the mall together. But we think they've been together for at least two months."

"Two. Months." I slammed my locker door shut. "They've been together for two months?"

"Uh huh," she agreed. "You're better off without them. I mean, we were all shocked that they would do that."

So there is a "we" now? "Just how many people know?"

She blinked at me as if I'd asked a stupid question, which I had the feeling I had. "The whole school knows."

The *whole* school knew. Of course it did. "Thank you so much for enlightening me, Cassie. It's been real."

Awareness dawned on her, finally. "You really didn't know? I'm so sorry. I'm just glad that you know. No more secrets."

I could feel my lips stretch into a grimace of a smile. "Oh, definitely no more secrets. You heading for the cafeteria?"

"Yeah."

"Great, I'll be right there." And she happily skipped off, most likely to her next unsuspecting victim, leaving me to fume into my locker.

The whole freaking school had known, while I had been oblivious. HOW? School had just started a week ago; had they known all summer?

Pain shot through me as I pressed my lips together, anger and embarrassment coursing through me. The heat radiating off my cheeks was nothing compared to the mounting pressure of the pounding in my chest. I turned towards the cafeteria, jaw clenched. Months. They'd been doing this for two months. And I'd been so stupidly oblivious.

My crutches beat furiously against the cracked linoleum floor. People practically jumped out of the way as they heard me approach. Every step, every vicious swing of the crutches, added to the pressure inside me, each twinge of pain from my armpits feeding my fury. They had known. They had *all* known. And not one person had had the decency to tell me. I brought down the crutches particularly forcefully.

I banged the cafeteria door open with my crutch, meeting all the shocked glances with defiance until I zeroed in on the pair of faces I was looking for. Some freshmen scuttled out of the way as I propelled myself towards the table, staring down the duo until I was right on top of them. I slammed my hand down, the smack echoing through the now silent cafeteria. "Hi there. You wanted to talk about it? Let's talk."

"But—"

"Nope. You don't get to talk, *I* do. Nothing you say can make things better. You both lied, you both cheated, end of story." I was so furious that for once I didn't care what people thought. Hah! No one had told me how liberating this would be. "I'm going to keep this real simple, and you just nod your heads. Did you or did you not hook up behind my back?"

"It wasn't like—"

"DID YOU OR DIDN'T YOU?" Wow, was that my voice bellowing out? Given the stares from the entire cafeteria, yes it was.

Bree's face lit up like a firecracker with embarrassment as she nodded. Luke looked dumbstruck. Or maybe just dumb.

"Great. Next question: have you been doing this for two months?"

"I really think that—"

"Luke, so help me…just answer the question. Two months?"

Once again, it was Bree who responded, almost like she couldn't help herself, although this time she shook her head. "Wait, not two months?"

Another head shake.

"Then how long?"

"Four," she whispered.

Four.

"Four months? You started whatever it is that you two are doing four months ago?" I was actually shaking, literally vibrating with anger.

Luke—stupid, dumb, idiotic Luke—finally chimed in with, "We're as surprised as you are."

"Then you'll never see this coming." My hands snatched up his bowl of brown beans with the speed of a cobra, and before I could talk myself out of it I threw them over his head.

Beans had never been a favorite food of mine, but that changed in that moment. There was something poetically beautiful in the way they dripped off his face, the syrup oozing into his shirt and marking it with stains that I hoped would take forever to get out. I slammed the bowl back onto his tray with a triumphant smack.

"Merri!" Bree's horrified gasp rose above the excited murmurs of students riveted by the dramatic showdown that I, of all people, was giving them. Me! The girl who had never so much as gone to the bathroom without a hall pass.

It felt kind of good.

I eyed Bree's tray, but the only thing on it was a bottle of water, which she snatched up and held protectively against her chest, eyeing me as if she expected me to tackle her, which at that point was a distinct possibility...I wished someone had a bowl of cheesy nachos.

"What is going on here?" a teacher shoved his way through the circle of kids that swarmed around us. He gaped at the three of us, me especially. "Miss Hart?"

Just like that, the anger that had been fueling me left as reality brought in a cold rush of terror. What had I done? Had I really just done that? I tried to smile angelically at the stupefied teacher even as my heart began to pound. I was in trouble. Big trouble. "Hi, Mr. Rosario."

"All three of you, to the office. Now."

Bree and Luke stood up; everyone snickered as the beans slid off Luke's shirt, plopping on the floor behind him as he walked out. Bree hid behind her hair. And me? My entire high school career flashed before my eyes as dread and nausea gripped me. Never, not once in my whole life, had I ever gone to the principal's office. That horror was reserved for students that talked back to teachers or, worse, got into fights. Does throwing beans at your scummy ex-boyfriend count as a fight? Would I get detention? Would this go on my record? Wait, did I even have a record?

Mr. Rosario walked behind the three of us, like we were going to bolt for freedom at the first chance. Actually, that sounded like a great idea, if I could achieve a speed faster than a sloth's. The only sound during our trek through the corridors was the clink of my crutches against the floor and the tapping of feet.

When we finally got to the reception area, Mr. Rosario pointed a finger at the chairs and stalked out of sight. The admin assistant, Ms. Friedmond, continued her typing as if this happened every day. Maybe it did. *Oh, gosh, I have just joined the ranks of rule breakers.*

A stray bean that had been stuck in Luke's hair slid down his face. Bree rushed to get a tissue from the desk, and Luke hunched away from me in misery. I contemplated how I'd achieve the right shade of bean brown when I immortalized all this in a panel later tonight.

All visions of said future panel shriveled up as I caught sight of the walking lecture, aka the principal, who was following Mr. Rosario along the hallway towards us. Tall, slender, with thick, curly hair pulled back into a bun, and green eyes that were a startling contrast to her copper-toned skin, the principal was an intimidating person at the best of times. This was definitely not the best of times.

"Ms. Hart, please come with me." Her voice, soft and with a hint of a southern accent, showed no emotion.

I was so dead.

She was silent as she led me down a hallway that smelled of stale carpet and plastic, and gestured for me to enter her office, a small room with a tiny window and no personal photos anywhere. She waited until I was sitting in the chair in front of her desk before taking a seat, hands folded on the desk. And then, she waited.

I shifted under her direct stare. The look in her cool eyes reminded me of a cat waiting for the slightest movement before pouncing. The silence stretched on and on, with no end in sight, and I finally cracked. "I'm really sorry, Mrs. Parry. It was my fault."

She slowly blinked. "Mr. Rosario tells me that you dumped food on Mr. Evan's head. For no apparent reason, I might add."

I squirmed. "Yes."

"Ms. Hart, part of my job is to know the students of my school. And I can say with confidence that up till now you have never given me cause for concern. I also find it difficult to believe that you acted as you did without cause. Would you like to speak to the school counselor about anything?"

And drag out the embarrassment even more? By all that is good and holy, please no. "That's okay. I'll be fine."

"Hmmm." She leaned back in her office chair as if needing the extra distance to consider me. "Would you like to share why you did it?"

"Um, I, uh, found out some, uh, *stuff* that they had been doing behind my back."

One eyebrow lifted. "Stuff."

I nodded.

"I see. Well, Ms. Hart, in light of what you are saying, and more importantly what you are not saying, I think that this will just be a warning to you." I sucked in a relieved breath, but held it as she continued. "I admire your discretion, but in the future please refrain from expressing yourself by pitching, what was it?"

"Beans," I supplied.

For a split second, her mouth pursed as if fighting a smile, before she reigned it in and composed herself. "Thank you. Please refrain from pitching beans during a disagreement. Understand?"

"Yes, ma'am."

"All right, you may go. Tell Ms. Owens that she is next. Oh, and Ms. Hart?"

"Yes ma'am?" I paused by the door, gripping the crutches as I waited.

The smile broke free. "Between you and me, I would have done the same."

I left that office with a smile on my face and a kick to my step, or rather a hop, and my head held high. I passed on the message to Bree and left Luke sitting in his soggy bean-soaked clothes. I may have been sent to the office for the first time, but finding an unexpected ally was worth it. That, and the sight of that one last bean dripping off Luke's eyebrow.

Seven

Sometimes we lose sight of what is truly important in our pursuit of our dreams. And other times we have perfect clarity of what we need.

PARK MIN-HO, MEMBER OF THUNDER

Dad was waiting for me when I got home from school, a bag of brownies from our favorite bakery on the counter. "How was it?" he asked carefully.

I plopped my bag on the table and collapsed on a stool. "Which part? The car ride from hell, a confrontation with you-know-who, me announcing to them that Lee and I are going on a date, or me dumping beans on you-know-whose head?"

"You did *what*?"

"Don't worry, it was just Luke. I think I showed admirable self-restraint with Bree."

He sighed. "I'm going to need coffee for this."

Three brownies and two cups of coffee later, I was frowning at the crumbs on my napkin and Dad was chuckling into his mug.

"I didn't so much throw as pour—way less violent. Aren't you mad at me?"

"What you did was infinitely more kind that what I'd like to do, and let's just leave it at that." He shook his head and took another sip out of his mug. "I cannot believe that they've been lying to you for so long."

"Tell me about it. Can I be homeschooled? Please?"

He chuckled again. "I'm sure it's not as bad as you think it is. The principal let you off easy, and you know you're not going to do it again. You got the worst part over, right? You saw them and survived. Besides, they'll never know that you aren't actually going out with Lee."

"But you should have seen his face," I winced at the memory.

"Luke's?"

"No, Lee's." I buried my head in my hands, my cheeks warm. "It's like every time I'm with him, the most embarrassing thing happens to me. You know what? I think we should move. Let's go back to Australia."

He just shook his head as he got up to wash his mug. "Merilee, it will be okay. Just take it one day at a time." How many times had we told each other that, clinging to those words in the aftermath of my mom's decision as we struggled to pull our lives together? *Focus on one problem at a time, don't think too far in the future.*

I couldn't think about the whole school year. I would have to see Bree cuddle up to Luke every day and watch while they went to homecoming and prom together, and everything in between. Grabbing one more brownie, I thanked my dad and laboriously made my way up to my room, where I grabbed my laptop and got settled on my bed. A quick check on DeviantArt showed that my latest panel of Lee bringing me "single" food was a hit.

DreamArt, you've done it again!

OMG, yes!! Jjajangmyeun is THE BEST comfort food!

Next one! Next one!

The pain and utter humiliation of earlier faded away as I began sketching out a new panel featuring a certain deranged driver. Taking breaks every now and then, I checked in on the forums and looked at other members' work. Even before my mom left, I'd enjoyed the support and encouragement of the community, but now? It was the only place I could go. I was in the middle of typing out a comment on another member's board when my dad knocked on my door. "Merilee? There's, uh, someone here to see you."

"Who?"

"Lee is downstairs. Says you have a date tonight?"

"*What*?"

Dad raised his eyebrows and shrugged. "You going to talk to him?"

"I…but he…oh, fine."

Confusion, embarrassment and curiosity warred within me as I hopped downstairs. Why in the world was he here? He didn't actually think I had been serious, did he? Because of course I hadn't been. Right?

Lee stood in the foyer, a sheen in his tousled hair, dressed in black jeans that hinted at the muscle beneath instead of shouting it to the world. He looked even taller. Seriously, it was like he had legs up to his armpits. I switched my attention to his shirt, but that was no better. A deep blue, it was snug against his chest, shoulders, and biceps. Those wrist bands were firmly in place. I eyed them suspiciously. He seemed awfully attached to those things. Must be another Korean custom.

And I'd been staring for too long. "Lee? What are you doing here?"

He dipped his head in greeting. "We have dinner plans."

Oh boy. So he *had* thought I was serious. "Lee, I'm sorry for the confusion. It was just so hard seeing them together, and then Bree wanted to talk, so I just blurted that out. But of course I don't expect you to take me to dinner."

"But you told them we were."

I just stood there, speechless, desperately trying to think of something to say, until I caught sight of that ever so slight smirk. "Okay, you got me there. But if you knew that I was, um…"

"Lying," he said, supplying the verb with that faint smile on his face.

"Right, if you knew I was *lying*, why are you here?"

The smile dimmed and he shifted, suddenly restless. "I talked to someone back home and, well, I lied too. And my aunt overheard me and wanted to talk about it. And since we both lied, I thought we might as well make it true. Besides, I need a distraction tonight." He leaned forward and added in a whisper, "My aunt is driving me insane."

Now *that* I understood. Having seen Ms. Park in action twice now, I had no doubt that she was an unstoppable force. Still, did I really want to go out with Sparkle Boy?

Bree leaning against Luke, Luke twining his fingers with her, the two staring at me with pity.

"You know what? I think it's a great idea."

His face lit up in relief, and something else that I wasn't ready to figure out. "Great. How about now?"

He must be desperate, if he was overlooking the fact that I was wearing sweats and an oversized sweater, without a lick of makeup on.

"I'll need a few minutes to get ready," I said. *Like, thirty, minimum.*

"I'll wait."

And he prepared to do just that, crossing his arms and leaning against the wall and looking incredibly sexy. Darn it.

Clearing my throat, I said, "You can wait in the living room, if you want. I might take a while."

"*Deh.*" He bent down, removed his shoes, making sure to line them neatly up by the front door, then strode into the living room and made himself comfortable on the couch.

The minute he was out of sight, I sprang into action. "Dad!" I hissed, gesturing him to come nearer.

"What?" he answered, mimicking my frantic whisper.

"Help me!"

Without batting an eye, he hoisted me over his shoulder and carried me up the stairs and down the hallway to my room, surprising me with his strength. *Not bad, Dad!* He promised to help me back downstairs as soon as I was ready. I chose to ignore how he was laughing as he said it.

My heart raced and my hands shook as I grabbed a pair of jeans, a tank top, and a print sweater. I shimmied into everything—a debacle that required me to remove my ankle wrap and then tug my jeans on while sitting on the edge of my bed. Somehow I did not slip off. I then had to put the wrap back on before I hopped into the bathroom to brush my hair and get some make up on. I eyed the results with satisfaction: no pale cheeks or bags under the eyes tonight. Last thing to do was pick a restaurant, but a quick search on my phone took care of that.

By the time Dad helped me down the stairs, I felt like I had been through ten rounds of bootcamp. I leaned against his chest for a minute, and his chuckle rumbled under my ear. I squinted up at him and demanded, "And just how is this funny?"

"You're going out with Sparkle Boy and you don't think it's funny?"

I gasped. "How do you know I call him that?"

"Merilee, you're not nearly as quiet when talking to Ema as you think you are." His eyes twinkled in mirth. "It's good for you to get out of the house."

I had nothing to say to that, so I lifted my chin and hobbled into the living room. Lee immediately got to his feet, a strange expression on his face. But all he said was, "I will drive. Do you know where we should go?"

"I'll pull up directions in the car. Bye, Dad."

Lee bobbed his head, and away we went, keeping pace to my shuffle. Lee was the epitome of a gallant gentleman, carefully helping me into the car before stowing my crutches. With one last bow to my dad hovering in the doorway, he climbed into the car and eased the car out of our driveway like the car was made of glass.

This lasted for about twenty seconds, the time it takes to get to the main road, where he gunned the engine and once again became the crazed driver I'd grown to know and fear. "You're going to drive slower, right? Remember what I said about the police?"

"We will be fine!" he said, a grin splitting his face. "Just relax. Where are we going?"

"Take a left and...THAT'S A STOP SIGN!"

"AIIISH!"

We careened down the highway, swerving from one lane into another, as I screeched directions and he yelled at drivers. We narrowly avoided at least three collisions. And yet by some miracle we defied all odds and made it to the restaurant in one piece. Well, pieces, if you count my sanity that was hanging on by a thread. I glared at him as he pulled me from my safe, stationary seat. "I thought I said never to drive like a maniac again. That was the very definition of crazy driving."

He grinned as if I'd paid him the highest compliment. "I was feeling homesick."

I took a deep, steadying breath. Not a good idea to lose my temper when he still had to drive me home. "Then I'm glad I chose this restaurant. You'll feel right at home."

He caught sight of the neon restaurant sign and froze. "What is this?

I beamed at him in victory. "This, my friend, is the best Korean barbecue place around. All the reviews that I looked at say it's good."

It must have been my imagination, but it looked like he went white, his pale features highlighted by the neon light. "You picked a Korean *leseutolang*?"

"If that means restaurant with five stars on RateThisRestaurant, then yep. Let's go! I've never had Korean barbecue food before. And hey, maybe they have those shrimp burgers you wanted."

But instead of charging for the door in search of the elusive shrimp burger, Mr. Homesick didn't budge, his throat bobbing as he gave an audible gulp. For a second, I even thought he was going to refuse. He glanced down at my wrapped foot, winced, and squared his shoulders.

"*Deh.*"

"I'll take that as, 'Lead the way.'"

Once again he hesitated, emotions flickering across his face too quickly for me to read. But after a moment he nodded, and opened the door for me.

Why did I have the feeling I'd made a big mistake?

Eight

I need another Thunder mv! Has anyone heard anything on LHK? Share any news you have. Chasers unite!

POST ON KTHUNDERFANGIRL.COM MESSAGE BOARD

The second we stepped into the restaurant, my senses were totally overwhelmed. My eyes widened to take it all in. And there was *a lot* to take in. Posters. Posters everywhere. On the walls, from the top of the ceilings to the floor, some even splattered on the ceiling. Each and every one was an ad for a different Korean product. The majority were pictures of beauty creams held up by smooth-skinned, doll-like models. No wonder Lee had been shocked by my freckles. Who knows, maybe the models had been airbrushed like crazy. Although going off of his own flawless complexion, I doubted it.

The posters were the first line of attack, initially distracting me from the numerous TV screens that were positioned so that no matter where you sat, they'd be in view. Most American places have sports playing, cartoons, maybe, or game shows. Not this place. No, here everyone had a multi-angled view of music videos. Korean music videos.

It was all kind of a blur, with just the impression of people moving around in a dizzying kaleidoscope of colors. The music was just a notch below blaring, so I couldn't tell if it actually matched what was playing on the TVs. The staff were running around, chattering to each other and to customers in Korean as they darted from table to table. And from what I could see, I was the only non-Asian person in the room.

Lee hovered behind me, and I had to nudge him forward with one of my crutches as a young girl about my age approached us. She bowed and greeted Lee in Korean, a bright smile on her face. Lee returned the bow and answered, relaxing a bit.

Wow. Him speaking Korean, really speaking it and not just peppering English conversation with a few words, was unexpectedly attractive, but then what else was new? It seemed no matter what he did, he looked good or, in this case, sounded good. His voice deepened and his face changed, the muscles moving in different ways than when he spoke English.

I shouldn't be watching him so closely.

Not that I was the only one. The girl was practically glowing under his attention. Her smile widened at whatever he had said, and she bowed again before indicating that we should follow her. Once again, Lee hesitated.

Bending down to speak into my ear, he asked, "Are you sure you want to eat here? We can go somewhere else. Maybe a burger place?"

I stared at him, incredulous. "You want to go to a burger place? Americans don't spend all their time eating burgers, you know. Besides, you were complaining about how there's no Korean food anywhere, and now that we're at a Korean place you want to go somewhere else?"

His shoulders drooped, but he nodded before turning to the girl and asking her something. She appeared a bit confused, but bowed and nodded before leading us to a table with a domed grill in its center all the way in the back corner. I slid into one side of the booth and peered through the dark.

"Is it always so dark? Isn't that a light?" I asked, pointing to a fixture in the booth that looked kind of electrical.

"No lights!" Lee snapped. "I mean, there are no lights to turn on. Oh, here is the *banchan*." A waitress placed several small dishes in front of us.

Banchan turned out to be the Korean version of appetizers: salad, rice, some kind of marinated cabbage that Lee told me was *kimchi* (so *that's* what he'd been going on about at the burger restaurant), and several other items that left me stumped. One looked like potato salad, another was filled with slices of something brown and floppy. There were no forks on the table, just a spoon and wooden chopsticks.

I weighed the odds of me actually getting food in my mouth if I used the chopsticks or spoon, finally deciding to give chopsticks a go as I squinted at Lee's hands and the way he held his own pair so easily in his long fingers. "What should I try first?"

"*Kimchi*," he said without hesitation.

Somehow that didn't surprise me.

"So, this is the amazing *kimchi*." I poked a small piece with my chopstick. "You really like this stuff, don't you?"

"We more than like it. We eat it with everything."

"Seriously?" I gaped at him. "Everything? Even breakfast?"

He nodded.

"But, uh, actually, what is it?"

"Pickled cabbage. Well, the most common type is cabbage."

"You have pickled cabbage with every meal? That's dedication." I just couldn't picture having this with waffles or toast.

He smirked. "Just try it."

I eyed the rather limp piece of cabbage warily, but couldn't refuse the challenge. Grabbing the spoon, because there was no way that I could do it with chopsticks, I scooped the piece up and plopped it in my mouth. Immediately my mouth puckered. "It's a little spicy."

He easily picked up a slippery piece with his chopsticks and stuffed it in his mouth. "This is actually really mild. And it tastes better when you eat it with chopsticks." He grinned around his mouthful.

"*Aigoo.*"

The sound he made at my pronouncement was a combination of a laugh and a snort. "What did you say?" he asked.

"I don't know what it means, but it works for you."

This time he definitely laughed, a warm and rich sound that rolled out of him and hit me like a tsunami. "Christmas, you...*aigoo*. Here—" He handed me a menu. "Pick what you want. I am buying."

I fumbled with the menu. "Oh, no, that's okay. We can go Dutch for this."

He lowered his head to pin me with that dark stare of his. "I do not know what that means, but I am buying."

I flushed and retreated behind the menu, studying it very carefully in a vain attempt to distract myself and cool my cheeks. I'd never be able to get through this meal if this kept up. *Deep breath in aaaaand exhale. Okay, pick a dish, Merri.*

But the menu was in Korean. Trying to decipher the pictures was no easier; it all looked like red meat to me. "So, what do you recommend?"

"Hmmm, I think this will be good," he said and pointed to a bowl of what looked like rice, meat, and vegetables. "It is *bibimbap*."

"Beebop what?"

He laughed, and my heart fluttered at his smile. "No, bee—bim—bap. It is a bowl of rice with meat, vegetables, and egg. It is delicious, you will love it."

"What are you having?"

"This." He pointed to what looked like huge slabs of bacon. "Spicy pork belly."

"Men and their bacon. Some things are universal, aren't they?"

A server came up to us and immediately locked eyes with Lee, staring at him in wonder. She began spitting out Korean, and he bowed and pointed at the menus. She bowed and backed away, still staring. *Man, they like to bow.*

I grinned at him. "Must be hard to be so popular with the ladies."

"What, that? She is just happy that I speak Korean. Now, show me some chopstick action." He waved his fingers like he was a conductor.

The server was more likely drooling over a good-looking guy, but whatever. I wasn't at all annoyed by it. Nope. Because this was not a date, and we weren't dating.

What *did* annoy me was my dropping food. Three times. "How do you eat with these all the time?" I asked, frustrated as once again I dropped the brown stuff that Lee informed me was fish cake.

"You have never used chopsticks?" he asked as he popped a chopstick full of the *kimchi* in his mouth before grabbing some salad. "You have them with Chinese food, right?"

"Yeah, I've never been good at it. And I definitely can't eat rice with them." Unless I ate grain by grain, which, at the rate I was going, would be faster than my futile attempts now.

"Here." He reached over and repositioned my fingers. "Hold them like this, and use this one as the base while moving the top one to pick up the food."

I nearly choked on my tongue as his hands, warm and huge and slightly rough, touched mine, making the skin feel like it was being brushed by delicate fire. Those hands were so big that they made mine look like a child's hands. But he didn't seem to notice my involuntary (and embarrassingly shaky) inhale as he guided me to the *kimchi* and helped me pick it up.

I nearly choked again, but this time from the taste. "That is really strong."

He grinned as if that was a compliment. "The best *kimchi* is. Here, try something else."

He insisted that I try everything on the table, always coming back to the *kimchi*. All the while the hostess girl hovered with an intensity that was starting to annoy me. But it gave me all the motivation I needed to actually get food into me; her fawning made me feel like spearing something, and it might as well be *kimchi*.

Lee guffawed after I stuck one chopstick in the dish to take a cleansing sip of water. "You are cheating. And you just insulted the cook."

I laughed. "No I didn't...wait, did I?"

"Doing that says you do not think the chef prepared the food properly and you are disrespecting them."

"*Kimchi*'s not my favorite, but it's not that bad." I furtively looked around, but no one else had seemed to notice. "Sorry, I had no idea."

"I will not tell if you do not." He leaned back, for the first time looking relaxed.

Always "I will," never "I'll." Was it deliberate, or had he never learned about contractions?

The girl came back to refill our water, even though we'd each only taken a couple of sips. I had a feeling that it was going to be like this all evening. She scooted out of the way as the waitress returned with plates of raw meat and put them on the grill set into the table. She handed Lee some scissors, which he used to cut up the meat, and he began turning it over with ease. The waitress went back to the kitchen to retrieve a sizzling bowl filled to the brim with food and put it down in front of me, along with a dish of some kind of red sauce.

I stared down into the heaped bowl—Korean portions were no

joke. "Maybe I'd better use a spoon for this." It would be a wonder if I didn't spill anything.

He grabbed a spoon and stuck it in, mixing up the egg and meat with the vegetables and rice before pouring the sauce over it. "Try to eat it with chopsticks. Just once."

"Is that a challenge?"

He grinned.

I carefully took the chopsticks and somehow scooped up some rice and meat. Not daring to breathe, I slowly brought the chopsticks to my mouth and, wonders of wonders, actually got the delicious food into my mouth. "I did it! Take that, Kimchi!" I jabbed the chopstick at him in victory.

Lee laughed on his own mouthful. "Is that what you are calling me now?"

"Well, if the chopstick fits."

He shook his head. "I have no idea what that means, but," he smirked. "Koreans do not use chopsticks to eat *bibimbap*. We use a spoon."

"You little weasel. You just wanted to see me spill food like a baby."

His nonchalant shrug wasn't fooling me. "If the chopstick fits."

"Fair play, Mr. Kimchi. Touché."

"Too-shay?"

"Touché. In this case, it's French for 'smart ass,'" I said, grinning.

To my surprise, conversation flowed easily between us for the rest of the meal. He wasn't sure how long he'd be staying in the States, but I got the impression it was for a while, although it was unclear as to how he felt about it.

When I asked him if he was having a hard time adjusting to living in America, he shrugged. "I have a better understanding of the language than a lot of my friends," he explained. "My parents hired a tutor to make sure that my English was excellent."

"Was your tutor Australian, by any chance?"

"Yeah, mate," he emphasized his accent. "You can hear it?" When I nodded, he shook his head ruefully. "I still am not used to the American accent. And everything is said so fast! All r's and vowels mashed together—sometimes I get tired listening."

I'd never thought about what English sounds like to a non-native speaker, and tried to imagine how exhausting it would be to listen to a foreign language all the time, no matter how fluent you were in it. "If it's any comfort, you're much better at English than I'd ever be at Korean."

"I should hope so, I practiced it a lot growing up."

He explained that, as with most Korean students, he had attended regular school, then gone to a special after-school that taught English, called a *hagwon*. When his parents decided to hire a tutor, he no longer had to go to the *hagwon*, but it still meant doing more work as soon as he got home.

Homework on top of homework before doing private lessons? That sounded hellish. "Did you ever do anything else besides homework?" I asked.

A shadow crossed over his face, and the easy friendliness that he'd shown for the past hour was snuffed out. "All I have known is work, in one way or another." He fingered his leather wristbands, not offering anything beyond that cryptic statement, before abruptly standing up. "Excuse me, I will be right back." He took off before I could apologize, although I wasn't sure what I should be apologizing for. But obviously my question had upset him.

I huddled in the dark booth, feeling out of place now that he wasn't there. Watching his broad shoulders retreat to the men's room, I ate more of the *bibimbap*. He was right; it was delicious. If Koreans ate like this all the time, then they won the best food contest, hands down. I could eat this stuff all day. Although maybe not the *kimchi*. That was something I doubted I'd get used to. As I ate, I wondered about these sudden mood swings. Was it his habit? Or was it me? It was so hard to figure him out.

The flashing colors of a music video caught my eye, drawing me in like a moth to a psychedelic flame. Looking around all the various screens, I could tell all-boy and all-girl pop groups were a big deal in Korea. Each group was comprised of brightly dressed singers who had impressive dancing skills. They wove among each other, every move seemingly effortless, against backdrops of flashing scenery. The men in particular caught my attention. With haircuts you'd rarely see on a boy here, they wore flowery pants and off the shoulder sweaters, and their eyes were heavily made up. They were certainly striking in a very different way. Lee was quite tame in comparison.

Take this group appearing on the screen, for instance. The men were surrounded by dancing girls in leather outfits while they stared soulfully off into the distance. They were belting their hearts out, matching expressions of anguish highlighting their handsome features, and wearing skin-tight suits of shiny material that emphasized their lean frames. The camera zoomed in on their heavily, and I do mean heavily, made up faces, swinging to the older one, who looked just like…

No way.

Noooo waaaaay.

The vegetable I'd just scooped up fell to the table with a splat just as an unsuspecting Lee returned, the aura of gloom gone. He stopped short when he saw me. "What? What is wrong?"

I raised my spoon to point at the TV, my mouth moving but no words coming. He looked, and I had my answer almost immediately. His face drained of color, almost matching his on-screen made up face.

"You're…you're…"

"Do not say it," he begged in a whisper as he frantically looked around.

"But you're on, you're…"

"'EE HYUNG-KIM!" The water girl's screech pierced through the room like a banshee's. The whole restaurant froze, everyone ogling a shell-shocked Lee, who stood like a deer in the headlights for what felt like forever before pure chaos erupted.

"Run!" Lee started to grab me, remembered my ankle at the last minute, and bundled me in his arms, somehow managing to dodge screaming women and maintain his balance.

"What's going on?" I yelped as we barreled through the door towards the car.

"Just keep your head down!" he shouted back, almost colliding with the car. Stuffing me into the passenger side, he flung himself across the hood and got himself locked in just before the wave of humanity hit us. We both just sat there, panting, as they screamed and hit the windows and screamed some more.

I turned to him with eyes as big as *kimchi* saucers. "Just what *are* you? Lee? Oh my gosh, are you okay?"

He was leaning his head against the steering wheel as a wheezing panting noise rasped from his throat. He was shaking so hard that I could see it even through the dim lighting, what little of his face that was visible waxen and sweaty.

I tentatively reached out and touched his shoulder. "Lee? Are you all right?"

He shook his head, muttering something in Korean. I jumped when one enthusiastic girl banged on the window; Lee flinched but didn't lift his head. His breathing was so fast now, I was scared he was going to pass out. "Lee? What can I do?"

Almost without thinking, I began to rub his shoulder, much like my mom had done to calm me down when I was little. He remained silent, but slowly, ever so slowly, his breathing slowed and his face regained color.

Finally, he raised his head and met my eyes, his own raw and glittering. "Christmas, we are in so much trouble."

Now I was the one who gulped loudly. "Just what kind of trouble?"

He didn't answer, just put his head back on the steering wheel.

I had a feeling that I would find out soon enough, and that I wouldn't like the answer.

Aiish.

Nine

"You're a K-POP STAR?"

Lee, all signs of his earlier worry gone, and his aunt paid my shout no attention as they volleyed shouts of their own back and forth in Korean. I had no idea what they were saying, but it involved a lot of *Aigoos*.

But I didn't care because I was still trying to wrap my head around this bizarre reality I'd been thrust into.

A K-pop star. Lee, my temporary next-door neighbor, was a K-pop star.

Visions of the guy who sang "Gangnam Style" danced through my head. That was Lee? Well, obviously not the same guy, but that's what he did? I examined him from head to toe: no sparkly suit, no makeup commercial-ready face, no hair brushed back like it had been caught in an artistic wind storm. It was just Lee, in jeans and t-shirt, and a worried expression pinching his face as he absently rubbed his arm.

While he and Ms. Park were going at it, I had my phone pulled out and was googling like crazy. And boy, oh boy, did I hit the mother lode.

Lee, annoying, drive-like-a-lunatic Lee, was Lee Hyung-kim, member of the group Thunder, and a heart throb of epic proportions in Asia. EPIC. Magazines, commercials, hit after music hit: Thunder had it all. And I got all of that after just a few seconds online. There was a YouTube channel titled Storm Warning, but I didn't dare open the link right now. Not with Ms. Park raging like a storm herself.

She smacked her hand against the table, jolting me from my tumble down the K-pop rabbit hole. Whatever she said next had Lee's eyes darting to me. *Uh oh.* If I was hoping to escape this unscathed, minus a swollen ankle, I was to be disappointed. Off she went again, her voice rising and falling in a rhythm that, once I gave up trying to guess what she was saying, was oddly soothing. Even if it was yelled at the top of her lungs.

Whose idea was it to come here again? He just had to insist that we go to his house first, not explain everything on the car ride home, then drop me off. Oh no. He had sat in silence, a muscle ticking in his clenched jaw, as we waited for the crowd to let up long enough to make a getaway. He hadn't even bothered to cover up his face as they took photos, while I had all but smothered myself with a jacket to keep hidden. And not a word was spoken the car ride back. I was too shocked to comment on his speeding, which just goes to show what kind of mental state I was in, and he had completely shut down, face impassive, whole body rigid. But being the perfect, if morosely silent, gentleman, he still helped me from the car and into his aunt's house.

He had taken off his shoes at the door, and so I did the same. There was a neat row of simple slippers lined up by the door; Lee had taken the biggest pair, and I slipped one on my foot, leaving my wrapped foot free, as Ms. Park had come out of the kitchen to greet us. All it had taken was one look at Lee before Ms. Park exploded with the first *aigoo* and launched into a tirade that was so long that I worried she'd pass out from lack of air. She kept it up while seating us at the kitchen table and getting ice for my ankle before hunkering down at the table and really going at it.

Now Lee suddenly deflated. Rubbing his face, he sat with his head bowed, resembling a scolded puppy. And that bothered me. Maybe now was the time to remind them that I still was clueless. "Um, excuse me?"

Nothing.

I tried a little louder. "Excuse me?"

Still nothing.

"HEY!"

Ms. Park froze and gave me an incredulous stare. I cleared my throat. "Sorry. Um, could someone please tell me *in English* just what happened back there. Just one of you!" I hastily added as they both opened their mouths.

Lee jumped right in to beat his aunt. "I am very sorry, Merri. I had no idea that people would have that reaction here, or I would never have gone in."

Ms. Park gave a very uncharacteristic snort. "Managers will not believe that."

My ears perked up. "Managers?"

Lee scowled at his aunt. "She meant parents."

Judging from the sheepish look on Ms. Park's face, it was definitely not parents, but I let it go. I had bigger fish to fry. "So, you're a celebrity?" I waved my phone around to flash a particularly stunning photo of him in a hot pink sweater holding a teddy bear. A teddy bear! "An actual celebrity?"

"Is that so hard to believe?" he asked, insulted. Well, that was too bad because I just didn't have it in me to soothe his ego.

"Never mind that. What the heck are you doing here?" They

exchanged glances, clearly not wanting to tell me anything. "Oh, come on guys. I just nearly got trampled. What's going on?"

Ms. Park spoke up. "Lee is on break. His studio said he needs one."

"And since *Imo* is already here, my family thought I could visit her," Lee finished. "I knew that there were American fans, but we thought it would be better."

Ms. Park rolled her eyes. "Without telling me before you come. Why they did not—"

"*Imo.*" The sharp tone in Lee's voice cracked through the small room, immediately silencing Ms. Park, who bit her lip and looked away.

I stared at Lee. "You came to a new continent for a vacation?"

He crossed his arms. "Is it any different from going to Europe for vacation?"

"I guess not…" But something still didn't sound right. "But why is it a big deal if people recognize you?"

"I just want peace and quiet," he said, shrugging.

I raised an eyebrow. Lamest excuse ever. "But I am sure it will be fine," he went on. "It is not like they know where I live."

The doorbell rang.

We all froze in various poses of horror before Ms. Park took a deep breath and left the room. Lee and I both relaxed as the high-pitched voice of one very determined Girl Scout reached our ears. She didn't pause for breath as she informed Ms. Park that now was the perfect time to order her favorites if she would please fill out these bajillion forms.

"*Aiiish!*" Lee abruptly stood up and began pacing, his breath coming fast and hard, getting more and more worked up. "This is all my fault."

I narrowed my eyes at him. Yep, something was up. "You know," I said bluntly, "you seem pretty upset by all this. Aren't you used to it? You *are* a famous singer."

"Can anyone ever get used to this?" was his cryptic response.

"Well, I certainly can't relate." He didn't react to my wry tone, too busy muttering to himself in Korean as he paced back and forth, back and forth, getting more and more worked up with each step as he unconsciously rubbed at his wrist cuffs.

I surreptitiously took out my phone, itching to look online again. Why was he really here? How had he become a singer? How long would he be living next door? Would I have to sign a non-disclosure or something now that I knew who he was? Hah! My dad would hit the roof. And here he'd thought it was such a good idea for me to go out in the first place.

Lee was still glowering to himself, checking his phone every few seconds as if expecting a phone call from his managers. No wait, his *parents*. No chance of getting any more info from him tonight. "Well, it's been fun." I got to my feet and hopped to the back door. "I'll just get home and put my ankle up." *Oh, nice one. Remind him of the ankle so that he won't try to stop you.*

Lee was suddenly crowding up behind me, going way into my personal space and making my breath catch in my throat. "You cannot go," he ordered.

I gave him my best oh-yes-I-can glare. "Lee, I'm tired, I'm sore, and it's a school night. I'm going home."

"You cannot tell anyone."

"Fine, I won't." Except for Ema and my dad. Wait, maybe not my dad. He'd definitely not take it well, and would probably insist that I stay inside when not at school. Fun side effect of being the only child of a military parent: extreme over protectiveness at times.

An arm came down in front of me, pinning me between the door and his rock-hard chest. Not that I'd noticed the rock-hard chest. "You cannot say anything to anyone."

"I already said I wouldn't." Yikes, could he read minds? Probably a result of eating all that miraculous *kimchi*. "Besides, who would I tell?"

He wasn't fooled by my innocent act. "Nothing. To. Anyone."

Boy needed a reality check fast. I pushed a hand between us and poked him in the chest. Hard. "Every person in that place knew exactly who you are. It's probably all over the internet now." Hey, maybe we'd go viral on YouTube, beat out whatever Storm Warning was. "Me saying anything is not going to make things worse." At least not worse than they already were.

He went from being angry and determined to wilted and defeated in 2.5 seconds. Unfortunately for me, he wilted in defeat against the back door. Just peachy. "Uh, Lee?"

He muttered something that sounded like *namoosgeya* and stayed put.

"Lee." I tried to push against that rock-hard chest. "Move!"

"Hyung-kim!" his aunt's voice rang out with impressive authority. "Let Merri go home. We have to talk." She brought my shoes over to me and bent over to help put them on, grumbling under her breath.

He tensed, and for a second I really thought he was not going to budge. But with a deep sigh he pushed himself away, opening the door for me. "Good night."

"Night. Good night, Ms. Park."

Her smile was both tired and sad. "Good night, Merri. I so sorry you caught up in this."

I casually shrugged. "It's fine." Having a mysterious celebrity with a dark secret move in next door? Bring on the google hunt...after explaining to my dad why I looked like I'd literally been dragged in front of a mob.

Instead of staying in the kitchen with his aunt, like I totally expected (and kind of hoped) he would, Lee followed me outside, offering a steadying hand when I wobbled with the crutches over the uneven ground. He didn't say a word, and I didn't try to break the silence—we both had a lot to think about.

He waited till I had unlocked the door, then gave a perfunctory nod and stalked back to his house. I watched him go, noting the tense shoulders and stiff posture. No doubt about it, he was upset. Upset to a level that my gut was telling me was not normal. Not that I'd ever met a celebrity before, unless you count Mickey Mouse.

Dad was in the kitchen, putting dishes in the dishwasher. He looked up as I walked in and raised his eyebrows expectantly. "How was it?"

Where to begin? *Dad, I left with Ms. Park's nephew and came home with a runaway Korean celebrity.* Or, *Don't freak out, but my face may be plastered all over the internet. How do you feel about moving to Hawaii?*

"Well, do you want the good news, the bad news, or the bizarre news first?"

Without a word, Dad grabbed his extra huge coffee mug, filled it to the brim, and sat down at the kitchen table. "Bring it on."

I'm not sure how coherent I was as the story spilled out of me ("Teddy bear, Dad, it was a teddy bear!") and his mug was empty by the time I finally stopped rambling. I eyed him warily, taking in the glazed look in his eyes. "Are you stunned or angry?"

"Let me get this straight. You're telling me that that boy is a famous celebrity, nearly got you mobbed, and your face might be all over the internet because he didn't tell you?" His eyes narrowed into slits. "I think I need to have a talk with him."

Oh boy. "Or, you know, I could do a little research and see just how bad it all is before you, uh, *talk* to him."

He rubbed his face, a classic Dad-thinking move he did, usually right before he said something that he didn't like saying. "Should I call your mom?"

The words hung between us as I struggled to think of what to say.

Did I want her to know? In all this time she hadn't reached out to us, hadn't shown any interest. She wasn't a part of our lives now…

"No. She doesn't need to know."

His shoulders relaxed slightly, and he nodded. "Okay. So, what are you going to do?"

"About Lee? Play it by ear, I guess." (In other words, internet stalk him until I had answers.)

"All right. Keep me posted, okay?" He got up and began reloading the dishes, muttering under his breath about how teenage boys are idiots as I hobbled up the stairs.

I quickly changed into my PJs, swapped out ankle wraps, and hunkered down into bed, sending Ema a message. *Text me when you're free. You won't believe what happened!* And then I opened the can of worms that was Thunder.

First up, there was Lee, obviously. Except I should be calling him Lee Hyung-kim or, if I *really* knew him, Hyung-kim. Lee was his last name. No wonder he had been so unimpressed when I'd first called him Lee; it's like if someone called me Hart. I'd have to ask him what he wanted to be called…if I saw him again, of course. Not that I was planning on doing it, because that would be weird and…okay, moving on. Blood type O, which apparently meant that he was confident, arrogant, and athletic, to name a few traits. Hah! He was the official spokesperson of the group, at least with English interviews, since he was the one who was the most fluent. Catchphrase: "It is not copy, it is coffee!" I have no idea why, but the fans ate it up; there were t-shirts with that phrase plastered all over it in bling.

Twins Choi Tae-min and Choi Tae-ho, both type AB, were the newest and, at fifteen, youngest members of the group, although no one could agree who actually was the youngest, since each insisted that he had been born first. There was a whole website devoted to fans weighing in on who they thought was oldest, complete with photos of when they were young and clips of different interviews. Tae-min and Tae-ho just laughed it off, more focused on creating challenging choreography for the group. And holy guacamole, their dancing. It was like every member's legs were made of rubber. No wonder Lee had run circles around me and then carried me home that fateful morning without breaking a sweat.

Rhee Jin-soo was the oldest member at twenty-three, also blood type O, and the quiet leader of Thunder as well as the genius behind many of their songs. Lee maybe the spokesperson, but there was something about Rhee and the way everyone else looked at him in interviews that gave the impression of leadership. They looked up to him, respected him.

Finally, there was Park Min-ho, blood type B. Orphaned when he was ten, he had the underdog story that fans, who called themselves Storm Chasers, loved. Tall, but not as tall as Lee. Handsome, but not quite as handsome as Lee. And popular, but not as popular as Lee. I was seeing a trend here, and he knew it, too, if the resentful glares and barbed comments in the videos were any indication.

And oh, the videos. Storm Warning. Nothing could have prepared me for the videos. Reality TV meets I don't even know; Thunder had a series of videos, where the cameras basically just followed them into different situations, like visiting Japan for the first time, a trip that involved a lot of random cafes, the group getting lost on the subway, and them marveling at an underwear vending machine. That's right, an underwear vending machine.

I was in the middle of video number twenty-five, right where Lee was yelling at Tai-min and Tai-ho to say "coffee" not "copy" (so that's where the catchphrase had come from), when I got notification that Ema wanted to video chat. "Ema! Oh my gosh, you won't believe it."

"Hey, what's going on? How was dinner?"

"Forget dinner! You are not going to believe what happened to me."

"I just got home from an early three-hour dance class. I have no imagination left."

"Lee is a K-pop star."

There was an expectant silence on the other end. "And?"

Not exactly the reaction I was expecting. "Didn't you hear me?"

"Lee's a K-pop star, I got it. What's the punch line?"

I rolled my eyes. "Ema, this isn't a joke. There is no punch line."

"Oh." She thought about it. "Oooh. Ooooooh. Oh wow." Another pause. "Which group?"

"You know about K-pop?"

"Merri, I'm Australian. Did you notice the number of Koreans over here? K-pop is everywhere. You've never heard of BTS? EXO? Girls' Generation?"

BTS sounded familiar. I'd probably heard about them from Bree, who loved listening to international music. "When did they start getting big?"

"They've always been big in Korea, but international fame?" She thought about it for a moment. "Probably a year or so ago."

Right when my mom had left, and my world narrowed down to supporting my dad and clinging to art.

"Merri?"

I gave myself a mental shake. "Sorry. Yeah, I might have heard of BTS. Anyways, have you heard of Thunder?"

"WHAT?" she shrieked, and the laptop fell over, giving me a close up view of her carpet. She lunged back into view. "HE'S LEE HYUNG-KIM?"

"I take it you know them."

"*Know* them? Hold on a sec." She disappeared, and came back wearing an over-sized hoodie that proudly proclaimed she was a Storm

Chaser, a cap perched on her head, and a red face mask with LHK embroidered on it.

"Oh my gosh, you're one of them."

"You're darn right I am. Thunder is *amazing*. Have you seen their dance moves? Oh my gosh, if I could dance like that I'd get a scholarship to anywhere." She let out a dreamy sigh. "And you're right next door to Lee Hyung-kim. THE Lee Hyung-kim. I can't believe it!"

"Yeah, well THE Lee Hyung-kim made it very clear that he doesn't want anyone to know where he is."

"I'll bet he did."

My ears perked up. "Wait, do you know something?"

Her eyes widened behind the mask. "Nooooo…"

"Ema!"

"Yeeeeah," she admitted with obvious reluctance.

"And?"

"And it's nothing. Don't even worry about it."

"He came to the U.S. to hide out and went all macho caveman, threatening me to keep his location a secret. It's not nothing." I crossed my arms as I tried to ignore the sudden pounding of my heart. What could he have possibly done?

"Leefoughtwithagroupmemberoveragirl."

"What?"

She sighed. "I think I better just show you." A link appeared in the message board, and I opened an article. My eyes skimmed all the exclamation marks, trying to find something to jump out at me. And then I saw it. A series of pictures at the bottom of the page that told more than all my past encounters with Lee combined.

Picture one was of Lee holding hands with a gorgeous Korean girl as they left a restaurant. A gorgeous Korean girl with long and lean legs, thick and shiny hair…and absolutely no freckles.

Picture two was a headshot of Park Min-ho, who was rocking the guyliner. He must have been at some concert, and was holding the mic as he stared off into the distance. There was something in his eyes, an almost tortured look, that caught my attention. I'd have chalked it up to his performance, except the next photo was a blurry shot of the beautiful Korean girl caught in a serious lip lock with Park Min-ho. They were in a park somewhere, and she had her arms thrown around his neck as he gripped her waist, oblivious to the world around them. Gee, where had I seen that before? Lee and I had something in common.

But it was the last one that made me catch my breath as a sick feeling churned my stomach. A furious Lee was glaring at the camera, one of his hands bruised and bleeding, while a couple of guys appeared to be holding him back from tackling the photographer. His face was white and pinched with anger and a raw pain that gripped at my chest. And that was before I read the blaring caption.

THUNDER MEMBER LEE HYUNG-KIM PUTS FEL-LOW MEMBER PARK MIN-HO IN HOSPITAL IN VIOLENT LOVE TRIANGLE!!!

Storm Chasers, I can't believe it: Lee Hyung-kim is in America!!! Check out this video of LHK taken last night at a restaurant just outside of D.C. What do you think of the girl with him?? KThunderfangirl. com

LHK!!!! <3 <3 <3

Who is she?? Is he dating again??

LHK IN THE U.S. ?!?!?

I just checked the group's website. No promotional dates were announced.

Is this because of Park Min-ho?

WHAT IF THUNDER IS BREAKING UP?

Worse, what if they replace LHK?

Chasers, don't worry. I will get to the bottom of this. We'll find out who this girl is. Keep watching Thunder videos and comment on LHK. Show him that we still love him! Remember, you can't have Thunder without the Storm [Chasers]! KThunderfangirl.com

Ten

A new video of Thunder member Lee Hyung-kim has surfaced. While many fans doubt that he is actually in the States, we have received neither confirmation nor denial from Thunder's company. Could Lee Hyung-kim actually be in America? And if so, why?

ARTICLE ON K-POP DREAMZ

The early morning light filtering through my curtains signaled that not only was it morning, but that I'd been up all night pursuing facts about Lee like I was a die-hard Storm Chaser.

Ema had been a font of knowledge. According to her, Lee and his girlfriend Park Su-sung had been the hottest new "it" couple. They'd met on set when she did a guest appearance in a Thunder music video and had been inseparable since. Or, at least, it appeared that way. It had been obvious to the fans that Park Min-ho was just as smitten with her as Lee, something that not only became increasingly apparent over the next few months but also helped with Park's popularity. Everyone roots for the handsome underdog in the love triangle. Including Park Su-sung, judging by that passionate kiss.

Lee had been blindsided, finding out along with everyone else, when the pic had been posted. He also happened to be preparing for an interview at the time, and supposedly lost it when Park sauntered in acting as though nothing had happened. The next thing everyone knew, Lee was gone and Thunder was taking a "creative break."

The Storm Chasers were frantic, Ema included, and worried that this meant an end to Thunder. "Did he say *anything*?" she'd asked several times. "Anything at all?"

"Ema, he didn't even tell me that I was technically calling him by the wrong name, let alone the fact that he's a celebrity."

She'd laughed at that. "I wish I could have seen his face when you did that. Wait! Can I?"

"If you're suggesting that I get him to video chat with you, you're insane."

"Yeah, I guess you're right." She looked so dejected that I immediately felt guilty, so before I could think twice I was offering to get her an autograph. Her squeal of joy had me covering my ears and shushing her so not to wake my dad. The last thing I needed was him overhearing anything about Thunder. Or Lee. Or how I was probably now on the Storm Chasers' watch list. Even Ema was concerned for my safety. "I think you need to talk to him, Merri. There are some pretty hardcore Chasers out there. Most of us are normal, but some of them…" She shook her head. "You'd better talk to him. And get me that autograph."

After promising three times that I wouldn't forget the autograph, I signed off and turned my attention to all things Thunder. Music videos and episodes of weird games shows that had them doing crazy things like climbing up a slimy stairway (a TV special filmed in Japan) or bungee jumping as they played Pictionary. True story. I thought Lee was going to break his neck as he attempted to draw a tree—never mind that he was upside down and being thrown off a bridge. After doing that, driving the way he did must seem like a walk in the park.

But nothing, not one dang thing, about him leaving Thunder. I tried my best to find out more, but all I could dig up was that Lee… Hyun-kim…Lee Hyung-kim…argh! The more I tried to call him something else, the more I stumbled, so *Lee* had thrown a very impressive punch, chaos ensued, and Min-ho ended up in the hospital. A week later, a Thunder spokesperson announced that Park Min-ho was fine and that Lee was taking a temporary leave of absence.

That was it. Nothing about if Park Min-ho would press charges, although the consensus was that he couldn't be after all this time, or when Lee was going to return. It was as if from that moment, Lee was off the grid, at least as far as the music company was concerned. It was a different story entirely on the fan sites. People were speculating on anything from Lee hiding from the police to plotting to kidnap his ex-girlfriend. There was even a forum devoted to letting Lee know that his fans were willing to hide him if he needed them.

What I couldn't get over was how big of a deal K-pop was. It was huge! And I'd never heard of it. Asia, America, it didn't matter, there were fans everywhere. And Thunder was at the top of each site's list. The only thing left was for a member to be cast in a K-drama, which was the name for their soap operas. And there were a LOT of K-dramas, every single one of them sounding crazy and awesome. I started watching one episode of *Boys Over Flowers*, which led to another episode and then another…I was in trouble. After six episodes, I rubbed my bleary eyes and finally closed my laptop.

After all the chasing, I was no closer to answers than I had been the previous night and had more questions than ever before, although I could tell you in great detail who I thought Jan-di should end up with, and it definitely wasn't the violin-playing redhead. But one thing was certain: I did have to talk to him, if for no other reason than to come up with a game plan to keep my face out of the spotlight. Waiting until

I could go next door was torturous. Out of habit, I began working on another sketch, but froze in horror when I remembered my panels. Oh my gosh, I'd posted panels with Lee on them! Had the Storm Chasers found them?

Fingers fumbling on the keyboard, I logged in and checked my account, sighing in relief when nothing seemed out of place. No unusual comments or anything, so I guessed it was okay. I immediately deleted all the posts I'd created sharing the link, and was ready to remove the panels featuring Lee...but did I need to? I knew I should take them down, just in case. But everyone loved and couldn't get enough of them. They were, without a doubt, my most popular panels. And it felt really, really good.

It wouldn't hurt to keep the panels up, right? I wasn't advertising them anymore. It would probably draw more attention if I did pull them. Besides, I was anonymous. At worst, they'd just think that it was fan art. Still, no more posting panels featuring Sparkle Boy. Not until we got this straightened out.

And speaking of getting things straightened out, I had a certain K-pop idol to ambush...I mean *talk* to.

At one minute past ten, I was making a beeline for next door, determination fueling each hop. Ms. Park's car wasn't in the driveway, but I knew that she went to the local farmers' market every Saturday morning because she and my mom had sometimes talked about finding the best produce. Mom had always intended on going to the market too, but never did. I wondered if she had the time now. Or was she too caught up in her new life? *No, do not go down that road. Focus on the here and now.* And right then I had to sit down with a certain wayward K-pop star.

It took a long time for the door to finally open. When it did, I couldn't help but do a double-take. "What's on your face?"

"*Bo*?" He could barely move his lips from behind the white mask that covered his entire face, his eyes squinting from underneath the eye flaps in confused annoyance. "It is my moisturizing mask. Why are you here?"

"We need to talk," I brushed past him, not bothering to wait to be invited inside. Remembering at the last second to remove my one shoe, I stood in the foyer, uncertain as to where to go. Lee motioned me down the hallway into what must be the living room. Unlike ours, which had slightly oversized furniture, the room was free of clutter, with simple furniture and a low coffee table. Everything was white, making the hardwood floors more dramatic. The only splash of color was to be found in the potted plants that were lined up on the bookshelves.

Lee fell onto the couch and tilted his head back, smoothing the mask across his face and, by all appearances getting ready to fall asleep. I settled in the chair beside the couch, and cleared my throat.

"Yes, Christmas?" he asked in a long-suffering voice.

"Well?"

"Well, what?"

"Lee! You know what."

He sighed. "It does not concern you."

"You were all worried last night—now you're not?"

"I do not want to talk about it."

"They were literally hitting the car, they were so excited. The restaurant isn't that far away. What if they track you down? What if they track *me* down?"

We were back to silent-and-angry Lee, who kept his mouth shut and stared straight ahead. But I wasn't about to give up. "What about if they figure out where you are? Do you have a plan?"

"*Deb.*"

I grit my teeth in frustration. "Lee, you have to—"

"Relax, Christmas. No one knows that you know me, so even if they do find me you will be safe. Is that what you wanted to hear? Here," he tossed me a package. "Try a face mask."

I almost threw it right back at him, but in a fit of inspiration—or insanity—I took him up on his offer and ripped open a package. I moved to sit down next to him, and he pried open one eye to watch me fumble with it. It took a little doing, but eventually I was leaning back in the couch, face mask properly smoothed, and ready to wait for however long it took for him to decide to speak again.

It didn't take long, but when he did speak his question hit me with the force of a two by four. "How long did you date the *baekchi*?"

All the fight left me in a *whoosh*. "What?"

"Your boyfriend. How long did you date him?"

"Ex-boyfriend," I corrected in a sharp voice. "And I don't want to talk about it."

"Why not?"

"Do you want to talk about why you're really here?"

"I do not know what you mean," he shifted in his seat.

"I know that there's more to the story than you told me last night. I did a little digging and know what happened with Park Min-ho. What I don't know is why you're here, but I think we both know there's something else besides punching someone in the face."

There was a long pause, then, "I do not want to talk about it."

"That's what I thought. But what are we going to do about what's happening now?"

He remained mutinously quiet, his jaw set in a stubborn line.

"Lee, talk to me. Come on, we have to at least figure out a plan. They were probably recording everything last night at the restaurant."

Thousands of Storm Chasers could be watching it as we speak. What had I done that night? Had I managed to cover all my face? I had covered it, right? I just remembered frantic screams of joy and Lee freaking out in the car.

I eyed him from under my mask, and he seemed his usual grumpy self. But there had definitely been something going on with him in the car. And the whole hiding out here was because he got in a fight? Not buying it.

Lee smoothed his mask yet again, quite determined to ignore me, and leaned his head back against the couch.

I sighed. Maybe I was coming at this all wrong. Sweeping in and demanding answers probably wasn't the best way to solve things. Taking one more deep breath, I quietly said, "Two years."

He opened one eye. "*Bo?*"

"I dated Luke for two years," I repeated, my gaze falling to my clenched hands, unable to meet his now alert eyes. "And I've known Bree since kindergarten. We were, uh, we were best friends. We shared everything. I just wasn't planning on sharing boyfriends." The lame joke stuck in my throat as memories of Bree crowded in. Amazing how years of laugher and fun had been overshadowed in one instant.

"My girlfriend, ex-girlfriend," he quickly amended. "We dated for a year, and in that time I never once thought that she would be interested in anyone else. So, when I found out she was seeing…someone behind my back, I…I did not handle it well. There were other problems, but what they did…he was like a brother to me." His was hoarse as he admitted, "I do not know what hurt more, that she cheated or that he did."

He surged to his feet and began pacing. "This was supposed to be a way for me to get away just for a while. I needed time to think!" he pushed fingers through his hair, making the strands stand up on end. He reverted to Korean, words coming out in an angry torrent, each one louder than the last.

The raw pain in his voice echoed mine. I knew all too well the bitterness of betrayal, and it was something that I wished with all my might we didn't have in common. I waited until he ran out of energy and words before standing to face him and saying, "I'm sorry." And I truly was. No one deserved what had happened to him, no matter how arrogant and eccentric he was at times. Without thinking, I reached out and clasped his hand, giving it an encouraging squeeze. "I really am sorry, Lee."

Startled, he glanced down at our hands. I began to pull away, embarrassed by my impulsiveness, but his grip tightened. I looked up at him in surprise.

"Thank you, Christmas," he murmured. And then he just stood there, watching me.

Desperate to change the subject, I eased my hand from his and gave him a grin. "Want to know what I did to him?"

"Bo?"

"I poured beans on his head. At school. In front of everyone."

For once I was the one surprising him. "You did *what*?" he asked in disbelief, laughter not far behind. "Really?"

"Really. Beans in his hair and all down his shirt."

He threw his head back and laughed—a rich, throaty sound of pure enjoyment that was contagious. I giggled, which turned into a full-on belly laugh as I relived the memory of Luke walking down the hallway, leaving a trail of beans after him. My mask began to peel away from my face, sending me into gales of laughter as it fell to the floor with a *plop*.

Lee and I looked at each other, and off we went again, collapsing against the couch as we guffawed and hooted and made idiots of ourselves.

"Christmas, you just wasted perfectly good moisturizing masks," he finally managed to say, peeling off his own to wipe away the tears on his cheeks. But his eyes were sparkling with humor, replacing the pain that had darkened them a moment ago.

"I gotta say," I said, "my face *does* feels super soft already. What's in these things?" I reached for the package, but everything was in Korean.

"Snail."

"*Snail?*" I shrieked, flinging the package away.

He shrugged, completely unconcerned. "It is harmless. Makes your skin healthier."

Obviously, given his poreless skin.

"Well, maybe it will get rid of my freckles," I joked, eyeing the soggy mask with distrust.

"I hope not."

I don't know who was more shocked by his words, him or me. His ears flamed red as I stared at him in stunned disbelief. But, almost like he couldn't help himself, he muttered, "I like your freckles." He was halfway across the room before I could blink.

I sat on the couch again, eyes huge in shock, as I took in the fact that Lee had complimented me. Lee Hyung-kim had *complimented* me. He liked my freckles.

The fact that he liked my freckles made my heart do things that my heart should not be doing. I liked that he liked my freckles.

Holy K-pop, what was I thinking?

Eleven

When asked what he thought about LHK being in America, Park Min-ho refused to comment. Could this all be over LHK's ex? Or is there more to the story?

Kthunderfangirl.com

Three days later I still couldn't believe that he'd paid me a compliment. I tried to tell myself that I was over reacting and being overly dramatic and ridiculous...but he liked my freckles.

Logging onto DeviantArt did not help. There was one common theme in all the comments, and they featured a snail mask-wearing runaway superstar.

No new panels?

Need more Sparkle Boy!

Working on anything new?

There was no escaping it. He was a hit, both in human and cartoon form, and by far my best subject. Of course he was. Thank goodness he didn't know it, or else who knows what levels his cockiness would reach. However, I couldn't help but smile at the thought of Lee seeing any of my panels; he'd probably tilt his head and say *"Bo?"* and then strut around like a king as we all basked in his glory.

Or he'll get angry that you've been making comics of him without telling him.

It was that scary second option that kept me from showing him. Stupid, because he wouldn't know unless I told him…but if I showed them then he'd know that I'd posted them. And what would I do if he didn't like them? Take them down? Would I still have as many comments? Or would people lose interest? That possibility was almost as scary as Lee's reaction. Because if I didn't have online support, what did I have? No, better to keep things as they were and just wait it out.

Reading through the comments one last time (really, when was the last time that I'd gotten such a response?) I closed the app with a sigh and began the arduous task of getting ready for school. Since spraining my ankle, I had to get up an hour earlier than usual so that I could get ready, eat breakfast, and get to the bus stop on time. It also took me forever to get off the bus, grab a snack, and get up to my room at the end of the day. By the time everything was done, I was exhausted, and I barely had the energy to get homework done, let alone draw new panels. But even if I did have the energy, I couldn't; it was just too risky to do any more, not with the Chasers determined to discover where their beloved LHK was hiding.

Oh, the Chasers. Ema was right, there were a lot of perfectly normal fans…and then there were the hardcore never-miss-a-song-release, stream-our-boys-to-YouTube fame fans who lived for Thunder. Ema called them the Chasers. For obvious reasons I'd lurked on message boards and scrolled through thousands of YouTube comments, and I realized two things. One: the fans were the reason why Thunder was getting so big. Their devotion and determination to promote the group in whatever way possible was a huge factor in Thunder's success. And two: I was in deep kaka if they figured out who I was because they absolutely, 100 percent, did NOT like me. Never mind that they hadn't actually seen me, just a picture of me hiding behind my sweater. They had decided that I obviously wasn't good enough for Lee, and that was that.

"Good morning, Merilee," the bus driver beamed at me as the bus doors opened.

"Hi Mr. Mathis." Interesting, he usually never smiled at me. Or talked, for that matter.

"Know what you're going to have for lunch today?" He leaned forward, grinning from ear to ear. "Maybe some beans?"

My face lit up like a firework, and I mumbled something before falling into the first available seat. Snickers broke out around me.

Great. Just great.

The rest of the day did not improve: I zoned out during trigonometry and got called out by the teacher; lunch was an agonizing trial of endurance as people eagerly watched me to see what food I'd choose, only to murmur in disappointment when they realized neither Luke or Bree were there; and the school nurse checked my ankle and informed me that I'd probably have to keep the wrap on for a few extra days because it was still swollen.

By the time the final bell rang, I could barely hop out to the parking lot. Just a bus ride left to go, then I could collapse into bed. If I could just make it to the bus…

I came to a screeching halt as I rounded the corner and saw a familiar tall frame leaning against a car. What was he doing here?

It was almost comical how Lee stood out from the crowd. It wasn't his clothes, since he was dressed rather conservatively in simple black jeans and a grey t-shirt with the sleeves rolled up. Rather, there was a raw magnetism to him, a vitality that demanded your attention. No wonder he was a fan favorite. If only they could see him now, leaning against the hood of his aunt's car as he scanned the tide of faces. An involuntary thrill shot through me as his eyes met mine. He straightened and came towards me, the few people ahead of me parting like magic for him.

For a moment all I could focus on was his striking face. Smooth skin darkened by a healthy olive tan, his cheekbones and eyes emphasized by the sweep of his bangs and the ever present guyliner.

I shifted on my crutches. "Hey, Lee."

"Is your ankle hurting?"

"Just a bit. Need to use the crutches for a few more days."

He winced. "I am sorry about that."

"No, no," I waved his apology aside, and very nearly lost my balance. Mental note: do not let go of the crutches while standing. "Not your fault. So, um, what are you doing here?"

His features tightened. "I, uh, came to give you a ride."

"A ride," I repeated in disbelief.

"*Deh.*" He glanced down at his feet in the most adorable display of shyness I'd ever witnessed. "I saw how hard it was for you to get off the bus yesterday, and I thought I could help."

The breath whooshed out of my body. He'd noticed that? "Thanks."

He bobbed his head and held out his hand. "I can take your bag."

He sounded confident, but his ears were flushed as he eased it off my shoulders and gripped it one hand. We both very carefully avoided eye contact as we slowly made our way across the parking lot, the silence becoming more and more awkward until I couldn't stand it anymore.

Words. Say words!

"Why didn't you tell me that I've been calling you by your last name all this time?"

He snorted with laughter, and the tension between us broke. "I wondered how long it would take you to figure it out."

"You are such a brat, you know that?"

"*Deh.*" He was grinning from ear to ear, looking ridiculously care-free and sexy.

"And that's another thing. What gives with all the Korean? You don't use it when you're talking to other people."

"But Christmas, where would the fun be in that?" He winked and smiled at me. But the smile quickly faded, and he leaned down to me. "I assume you know all about Thunder now."

No point in denying it. "Yeah. And I just want to say how sorry I am. I just made things worse. But Lee…I mean Hyung-kim, I promise I won't say anything. I'm just really sorry about the other night at the restaurant."

His brows lowered in confusion. "Why are you apologizing? It is not your fault. I could have refused to go in. I knew I was taking a chance. And just call me Lee."

"But—"

"Christmas." He lowered his head to look at me through his bangs. "*Lee.*"

It wasn't fair how he could make the smallest thing the sexiest. Not fair at all. Clearing my throat, I pointed out, "Your aunt seemed pretty mad."

"Ah." He glanced away, focusing all his attention on unlocking the car, fingers clenching the keys until I thought it would snap. "Not at you. Or me, really. Just at the situation."

"And just what's the situation?" I asked carefully.

He just shook his head and gave 110 percent of his focus into putting my bag in the back seat to avoid answering. I opened my mouth, ready to ask him again, but a flash of blue plaid shirt gripped my attention. "Oh no."

Luke was holding hands with a laughing Bree, the two beaming at each other as if they didn't have a care in the world. Perfectly happy with each other. How wonderful. NOT.

"What is it?" Lee straightened and was watching me closely.

"Don't turn around," I hissed.

But of course he did it anyways. Luckily, neither Luke nor Bree noticed since they were too caught up in their love bubble. I groaned and leaned against the car. "Why me?"

"I have no idea what you saw in that *baekchi.*"

"Not helping, Lee. Oh my gosh!" I ducked behind him, flushing in anticipated embarrassment and dread as the two drew closer to.

Lee eyed me with curiosity. "Are you okay?"

"Yes. No. I don't know! I just don't want them to see me."

As if he heard me, Luke's gaze met mine. He bent down to whisper in Bree's ear, causing her to whip her head around so fast she could have given herself whiplash.

"I *so* can't deal with this right now."

"Leave it to me," Lee said under his breath right before they came up to the car.

"Merri?" Luke said.

A world of questions in that one word. Luke and Bree's eyes were pinging back and forth as if they couldn't decide who to stare at first.

I had to force myself to answer, "Hey." That was all I could manage past my gritted teeth.

Lee cleared his throat and took over. "I do not think we have met. I am 'Ee Hyung-kim." He bobbed his head to each one.

Luke actually started to bow back until he clued in to what he was doing. "'EeHunim?" he asked instead.

"No. Lee Hyung-kim," Lee said slowly. For some reason, one that I was not willing to explore right now, it made me happy that he didn't offer for them to call him Lee.

Bree crossed her arms. "So, how do you know Merri?" she asked, getting straight to the point. "I've never heard her mention you." Dissatisfaction rippled over her face, pinching her features together like she'd sucked a lemon.

Lee smiled at her. "She never mentioned you either."

I would have laughed at the outraged look on her face if I wasn't too busy trying not to burn up from blushing. But Lee, cool as a cucumber, was not done. "Merri and I are next door neighbors. She has been showing me around the area." He reached for my hand and held it in a warm grip.

"She has?" Luke's eyebrows disappeared under his bangs as he shifted from one foot to another.

Bree widened her stance as if settling in for an interrogation, while I just stood there like an idiot, staring at my hand in Lee's. Lee was the only one who seemed to be relaxed.

"Yes, she has been very helpful. How do you know her?" he asked, all Mr. Innocent.

Luke frowned. "We've known Merri for a long time. Very long." Was that a possessive tone I detected? Unbelievable.

Lee gave him a polite smile. "Being away from my home has made me realize just how important friends are. It is good to have people that you can trust." Bree and Luke's faces both flamed red as they obviously tried to figure out whether Lee was insulting them or being sincere, while Lee smiled innocently at me. "Are you okay?"

"Yep! Never better. Let's go."

"Running away, Merri?" Bree asked in that new, sharp tone of hers. "Just like you always do. I can't believe you did what you did to Luke in the cafeteria. So unlike you."

"Well, at least I'm not running into the arms of my best friend's boyfriend." The words were out before I could stop them. But man, it felt good to say them! "You are the last person to lecture me about what I do. You don't have the moral high ground here, Bree, so just leave me alone. Come on, Lee."

Lee and Luke were currently in the middle of a staring contest, which ended as Lee took my hand in his again—to my shock—and murmured something in Korean, the words low and soothing. But his voice hardened as he switched back to English and looked at Luke and then Bree. "Normally, Americans say 'pleasure to meet you.' But I cannot say that since it has definitely not been a pleasure. And you," he said, looking again at Luke, "never deserved her."

Ooooh snap! I gaped at Lee, even as the imp in me laughed at their gobsmacked expressions as Lee opened the passenger door for me and calmly stalked to the other side. Rolling down my window, he leaned forward for one last parting shot. "You might want to stand back." He revved the engine for emphasis, chuckling when they both stumbled back. And with that, we were off, peeling away from the parking lot in a burst of speed that for once didn't bother me one bit. I was too busy analyzing every detail of what had happened.

Why would he…and then he said…it was almost like he felt…NO. Just no. Don't even go there.

Lee made a living from performing. This was just another performance. And I could never forget that fact, or else I'd be in a whole world of trouble. "That was…that…thank you."

"You're welcome. *Baekchi*," he spat out the last word. "I do not know why you dated him."

"That is the truest thing you've ever said."

He winked at me. "Koreans always tell the truth, Christmas."

"He liiiiiikes you," Ema sang out the words later that evening. "Mr. LHK himself likes you!"

I rolled my eyes. "First of all, don't call him LHK—it makes it sound like he's going to star in a lollipop commercial. And of course he doesn't like me."

"Oh really? How do you explain all the attention he's giving you?"

"He's just acting. It's all a performance."

She snorted. "Sure, and him deciding to pick you up from school before all this happened is a performance. Next thing you know, he'll pash you." Her puckered up lips gave a very vivid picture of what "pash" meant. "I'm still waiting on my autograph, by the way. Makes sure he spells my name right."

"Glad to see how concerned you are for me," I said wryly.

"Oh, please. You showed up your scummy ex, told off that witch of a so-called best friend, and managed to get the attention of one of Asia's hottest guys. You're fine."

"Yeah, well, enough about me. Catch me up on you."

Ema got me caught up on the latest drama from her dance class, describing in vivid detail how one girl broke a toe while practicing her *pirouettes* but kept going and now has to have surgery on her misshapen big toe. Seriously, there was no need to watch medical dramas when you're friends with a dancer.

All too soon she had to go, and I spent the rest of the evening idly doodling in my sketchbook (maybe one more Sparkle Boy comic wouldn't be so bad?) while my heart stubbornly warred with my mind, replaying everything he'd done that afternoon in vivid detail, zooming in on my response to it and highlighting an unsettling feeling in the pit of my stomach.

I couldn't possibly be falling for Sparkle Boy.

Could I?

To: Manager Sung Lee-hyuk
From: Seoul Music
Online activity about LHK has increased. Please monitor situation carefully. Contact LHK if needed.

To: Seoul Music
From: Manager Sung Lee-hyuk
Have tried to contact LHK about keeping a low profile, but have not reached him. Please advise on next step.

To: Manager Sung Lee-hyuk
From: Seoul Music
Wait and see if the situation dies down. If not, retrieval will be necessary.

Twelve

Park Su-sung, former girlfriend of Lee Hyung-kim, has released a public apology. "My actions were selfish and inexcusable. I can only hope that everyone can forgive me and know how I am ready to make amends in whatever way that I can." Thunder managers did not release a comment, and there is still no news of Lee Hyung-kim, although it is believed that he is in the United States. Will Thunder ever be reunited? Or will the group break up just as they've reached super stardom?
ARTICLE ON K-POP WORLD

Over the next few weeks a routine developed: Lee would be waiting for me outside each morning and offer to drive me to school, then be out in the school parking lot at the end of the day to drive me home. At first I didn't know what to think. Was he doing this because he felt sorry for me? If there was one thing I couldn't tolerate, it was pity; I'd gotten plenty of that when Mom had left. But he didn't treat me like I was about to break any minute, like people had in the past. If anything, he was the exact opposite: he'd tease me mercilessly as he drove at least fifteen miles an hour over the speed limit, weaving in and out of traffic with a casual ease that was both impressive and terrifying. Every now and then, I'd notice him glance at me before easing off the gas, although just when I was lulled into a false sense of security, an unsuspecting driver would pass him and we'd go back to warp speed.

As much as I hated hurtling from place to place, it did have its benefits. For one thing, Lee was fast but he was careful…if careful was defined by never actually hurting anyone and getting from point A to point B in one piece. And I never had to worry about being late to school, and I actually got to sleep for an additional twenty minutes each morning, spend ten more minutes in the shower, and take my time over breakfast instead of scarfing it down before rushing to get to the bus stop.

Another positive? He always came bearing—according to him—the best food on earth, courtesy of his aunt. *Bibimbap, japchae, bulgogi.* It all tasted fantastic, and it was ridiculously addictive, although I still couldn't stand *kimchi*, no matter how much Lee insisted my ankle would heal faster if I ate it every day. He wound up eating it himself when I refused the daily portion. The day I got the wrap off, he brought over a huge dish of home-made *bibimbap* to celebrate, complete with extra radishes and spicy sauce, just the way I liked it.

With all the eating I was suddenly doing, I needed desperately to start exercising again. The doctor had advised that I avoid running for a while, so I began going for a walk after school instead. After a couple of days of going solo, I came out one afternoon to find Lee waiting in the front yard, stretching and acting like it was the most normal thing in the world for him to join me. And, given the amount of time we were spending with each other, I guess it was. I liked spending time with Sparkle Boy. Who'd have thunk it?

The question was, why was he spending time with *me*?

He paused mid-stretch, looking over his shoulder at me, and winked. No one can say as much in a single wink as Lee Hyung-kim. Unfortunately for me, I still couldn't figure out just what he was saying…or what he wanted…or what he thought of me. Was I just a way to pass the time? Or something more? Why did it matter so much for me to figure out?

He became fascinated with my amateur photography skills, and loved to point out the things he thought would make good subjects.

"What, you don't want me to take your photo?" I teased one afternoon, focusing the camera on him.

He struck a pose, hand up to frame his chin. "If you did, you would break your camera."

A startled laugh escaped me. "Oh, really? How do you figure that?"

"If someone can break the internet, I can break a camera." He said it so matter-of-factly that I thought he was serious, but then he laughed. "You are so easy to tease, Christmas."

"I can never tell if it's teasing," I said. It was true. He had a wicked sense of humor and a naïve arrogance that was both hilarious and confusing, and I was never sure what he would come up with next. Just a week earlier, he'd refused to walk down a street because it only had four houses on it, and had stared at me in horror as I laughed. "Four is an unlucky number!" he'd insisted, eyes huge, and my laughter had sputtered to a halt when I realized that, in this case, Lee was absolutely serious. We'd avoided that street since.

He now settled back against a tree and watched me as I focused my camera on a tree, intent on capturing how the light filtered through the red leaves and lit up the veins. I hoped I could later recreate the effect with my alcohol pens.

"What are your secrets, Christmas?" he asked, out of the blue.

I fumbled with the camera, managing to stop it slipping from my hands at the last second. "Secrets? The runaway K-pop star wants to know about *my* secrets?" Had he found out about the panels? Was he upset? Did he know that I'd caved last night and posted another one, even though I'd promised that I wouldn't? But it was one panel, just one. Just to see what people thought. There was no way that he could know that I'd had to silence my phone because of all the notifications I was getting from the comments."

"So, you admit that you have some," he said, pouncing on my slip up with glee. "Tell me."

"Um, that would be a no." I swiveled to aim the camera at him and snapped away, relieved that he obviously had no clue about DeviantArt. And I absolutely positively would not post anymore panels of him from now on.

"Why not? You do not trust me?"

Trust him? I barely knew him! I wasn't about to bare my soul after a few car rides…and yet he sat there watching me, an almost eager expression on his face.

Clearing my throat, I put my camera away. "Let's go back, I want you to try some of my dad's pancakes. Time I feed you for a change."

You'd have thought I kicked a puppy, he looked so disappointed. Like it really mattered to him that I answered his question. But he took the hint and changed the subject, going off on a tangent about potato cakes and how they are most likely ten times better than regular pancakes, while I tried to process how once again he had slipped past my defenses.

The more time I spent with him, the more confused I got. Half of me was convinced he just wanted a friend for however long he stayed here, while the other half analyzed his every word, searching for hidden meanings.

Ema was thrilled. "I told you, he likes you!!" she crowed yet again later that week.

I groaned. "Ema, I wanted you to be the voice of reason, not the voice of insanity."

"Oh, please. The guy is obviously smitten."

"*Smitten*? Have you been reading your sister's romance novels again?"

"Maybe," she drawled out, "but that doesn't change the fact that he is. Come on, you'd say the same thing to me if the shoe was on the other foot. I wish it was!" She hugged her arms around her slim body, a dreamy smile lighting her face. "Of course, it would be you to meet the K-pop star and not me. And where's my autograph, by the way?"

"Don't hold your breath on that one."

"I can wait. Because if things go the way I think they will, he'll be more than happy to sign anything you give him," she waggled her eyebrows. "What does your dad think?"

"My dad? He thinks it's hilarious."

And he was loving all the food that Ms. Park was sending our way. Any reservations about Lee's celebrity status had vanished the minute he tried *bulgogi*.

"Anymore run ins with the witch and the idiot?" She gave an evil laugh. "I'd love to see Luke pitted against Lee."

"You know, I haven't really thought about them all that much."

And it was true. I was still hurt, of course, and would be for a long time, but as horrible as it was, what had happened had been very revealing. Luke was definitely not the kind of guy I could be with. I don't know if he was bad, per se, but one wrong choice had led to another wrong choice, and he clearly lacked the decency to fight it.

But it was Bree's betrayal that hurt most. No matter how much I tried to think of a reasonable explanation, nothing excused what she'd done. Bad enough that she'd made the mistake in the first place, but there had been so many times she could have fessed up and come clean. Yeah, it would have hurt, but at least she would have done the right thing in the end. But they both lied, only admitting it when they had already been caught. She and Luke deserved each other.

As I was climbing into bed later that night, I wondered what made people so selfish. My mom had also acted without caring that her actions left emotional devastation in her wake. And not once had she reached out again, not even on my birthday. She'd made it clear that she wanted a clean break, revealing a ruthlessness that still surprised me. Compared to that, Bree's betrayal was a cake walk.

It helped to put it in perspective, to acknowledge that it sucked and would suck for a long time and not waste my time trying to deny it. But I refused to wallow in self-pity. So, when I passed them in the hallway and happened to make eye-contact, I would smile (okay, it was more of a grimace, but it was a step up from bean dumping). When every inch of the school was decorated with posters advertising homecoming, I kept my chin up and refused to show how it upset me. I even agreed to help train the new person on the school newspaper team because, of course, I had to quit it. People stopped watching me expectantly, stopped whispering as I came in or left a room, and overall just stopped caring as they moved on to the next scandal.

Things were looking up.

Until they were not.

I knew the minute I saw the letters on the kitchen island what was coming, and sure enough, Dad announced over dinner, "You received several recruiting letters today. I thought we could take a look? You'll need to begin applying soon."

I stared at my plate, molding my mash potato into a mountain as I scrambled to come up with an answer that would spare me from the argument I could sense coming.

Finally, I plucked up the courage. "You know, I thought that I should look at some art programs. George Mason University has a Visual Arts program." I dared to peek at Dad and gulped at his hard, impassive expression, but on I blundered. "They also have a photography program, which I thought might be good to minor in. And I'd love to take some social media classes. I could go to NOVA, then transfer—"

"No. No art," he barked in a rough voice. "You know how I feel."

We'd been dancing around this issue for months, so it was almost a relief to finally get it out in the open. "Dad, I know how you feel, I do. But *you* know how I feel about art. It's important to me, why can't you see that?"

"Merilee, I'm not getting into an argument about this." He speared his meat and shoved it in his mouth, glaring as if to will me into obedience.

Unfortunately for him, I was just as stubborn. "Great, let's not argue. I'll go in and talk to the NOVA counselor next week and find out what I need to do."

"What you need to do is listen to me and respect the fact that I am looking out for your best interests. No art."

"Why?" I demanded. "Why can't I study art? Because *she* did? That doesn't make any sense!"

"No, what doesn't make any sense is becoming so consumed by something that you lose interest in anything else. What doesn't make sense is to be so set on one thing that nothing else matters, and you don't care at all about anything or anyone else."

"But that's her, not me! I'm not like that, Dad, trust me. Please."

I didn't care that I was pleading. I could go ahead and do this on my own, without his permission, and he knew that. But then I'd be just like her, wouldn't I? "This can't be just about art, Dad. Me taking art classes will not turn me into her, you have to know that. That was her choice, and I would never choose to turn my back on the people I love."

"Even if they don't want you to study art?" he shot back. "Because I'm not changing my mind. You do this, you do it without my blessing. End of discussion." He shoved his chair back with so much force it nearly fell over, dropped his dishes in the sink, then stormed out of the kitchen. The slamming of his bedroom door echoed through the house, and I was left alone, madly blinking away furious tears.

How could someone who was a retired military officer, who managed countless people and made decisions that most of us couldn't imagine, be so unspeakably illogical and pig-headed? Did he honestly believe that being an artist meant that I would become just like Mom? If we were in a soap opera, yes, but this was real life—*my* real life—and he seemed determined to keep me from doing what I knew was right for me.

I did some chair shoving and door slamming of my own, escaping outside to sit on the side porch in a vain attempt to cool off. He thought he could control me? That ordering me around like he was my commanding officer would do the trick? If he thought that would shut me up, then he was sorely mistaken.

"Christmas?"

I squeaked and jumped in my seat. Lee stepped into the lighted area on the lawn. "Lee! You scared me half to death!"

"Sorry. I thought you heard me. Are you okay?"

I scowled up at the house, imagining my dad sitting up in his room and ignoring the problem. "Not exactly."

"Oh." He fidgeted, then asked, "Did I do something?"

He sounded genuinely worried, and I forced myself to smile reassuringly. "No, Lee, I promise it has nothing to do with you. Just something my dad and I can't agree on." Or won't agree on, in Dad's case.

Lee did not relax at my words. If anything, he became even more tense, running his fingers through his hair as he shifted from one foot to the other. "Ah. Well, I came over because I...I wanted to ask you if you would come over for dinner. At my house…with me. You can have real Korean food, without the…"

"The mob," I supplied, being helpful even as my mind raced, hardly able to believe. He was actually asking me over for dinner.

"*Deh*. And we can watch a movie. If you like." Lee's ears were a flaming red. Not just the tip, the entire ear. They looked like they were sizzling.

What did he mean by dinner? Like, just dinner? Or date dinner? Or was I reading too much into it? I was probably projecting my own feelings onto him, and—wait. My own feelings? As in, I wanted him to want me?

No, no, no. Absolutely not. We'd become friends, sort of, but anything beyond that? No way.

"Christmas?"

Tell him no. You don't want to open that door. "Sure." *Oh my gosh. Have you no self-control?*

"*Deh*. Seven o'clock tomorrow night?"

"Okay," I said weakly.

His smile was equal parts relieved and hesitant, as if he were just as unsure as I was. He turned away, swiveled back, started to bow, froze, tried to smile, then strode away.

Was this a date? Was he asking me as a friend? Were we friends? Was this all too soon? Should I have said no?

I wilted back against the bench as I watched him go inside. No doubt about it, I was in big trouble.

Thirteen

Chasers, the numbers are rising! Keep streaming! Show LHK what he means to us! And if you need a break from watching videos, head over to SLAAC.com/SaveLeeAtAllCosts to find the latest updates on our favorite Storm.

KTHUNDERFANGIRL.COM

The next day, Dad acted like nothing had happened, and I was so distracted that I happily went along with the unspoken truce. Still, there was a cautious tension between us, one that I had a feeling would not go away. He was the immovable object, and I was the unstoppable force. Or maybe Mom had been the unstoppable force, and that was the problem. Question was, would I follow in her footsteps? Or could I convince Dad to change his mind? I'd have to solve that problem eventually, but I didn't have the energy to deal with it now.

It took me an hour to piece together my outfit. One hour. Just on the clothes. Clothes that I would be wearing to a dinner that wasn't a date. I mean, it couldn't be, could it? This was surely just another way of Lee offering his friendship. I told myself that repeatedly despite my inability to stop daydreaming about what it would be like if Lee and I began dating. Dating, of course, was ridiculous. K-pop stars didn't just fall for ordinary people, especially if that ordinary person was a clueless American who'd never even heard of their group. No, this was just me blowing things out of proportion. I'd go, have dinner, see for myself that he just wanted to be friends, and move on. And it was just a coincidence that I looked quite put together in my outfit. I chose jeans rolled up at the ankle, a white sweater and plaid scarf, and ankle boots, with my hair pulled up in a high bun and my face lightly made up. Yup, just a coincidence that this was one of my favorite fall outfits.

I was all ready to waltz out the door, cool and confident and detached from any anxiety, but then a thought hit me: should I bring anything? He hadn't said, but then again I hadn't asked. Would he notice if I didn't? Spying some orange and carrot muffins on the table, I grabbed them and hurried out the door before I could agonize over something else.

It took forever for him to answer the door. Eighty seconds, to be exact. I know because I counted them, my pulse rising the longer I stood there. Muffled shouting came from behind the door, then it was suddenly yanked open by a panting Lee, the shriek of the fire alarm ringing out from within the house. "Merri! Is it seven already?"

I couldn't help myself. "*Deh.*"

"*Aiish.*" He just stood there, clearly uncertain what to do.

"May I come in?" I asked hesitantly.

"Yes! Sorry, yes." He ushered me inside. The same pair of slippers that I had used the last time I was there was waiting for me by the door and I quickly slipped them on. I followed him into the kitchen; at least, I assumed I was. With all the smoke in the air it was hard to see.

"What happened?" I asked in between choking coughs. "What did you burn?"

He had grabbed a baking sheet and was attempting to fan the smoke out the open back door. "Everything. Here," he lunged sideways to hand me another baking sheet. "Using this helps."

"You mean it was worse than this?" I sputtered as I began to wave the sheet, holding my breath against the acrid stench of smoke and burnt food. It smelled like something had been sprayed by a skunk, then just gave up and died. He just grunted and waved harder, the movement riding up his shirt and showing glimpses of a toned stomach. I felt the need to waft my own face at the sight of it.

When the smoke cleared, I was able to see the culinary disaster that was Lee. A rice cooker was open, with the last of the smoke spiraling out defiantly. A pan of vegetables, somehow both soggy and burnt, rested on the stove, and another pan held the pathetic remnants of what I think had once been eggs.

The fire alarm cut off abruptly, and Lee groaned again as we got a good look at the disaster in front of us, muttering something under his breath that for once did not involve any *aishes* or *aigoos*. It didn't take Google Translate for me to get his meaning; I know how my dad would react if he walked into a mess like this, and Ms. Park was nothing if not particular.

I took it all in. "How did this happen?"

Lee appeared to be paralyzed by the extent of his disaster, eyes wide and a bit glassy. "I got, uh, distracted."

His cell was on the table, and I could only assume that he'd gotten another call from Korea. Whatever it was, he didn't want to say. Fair enough.

Rolling up my sleeves, I reached for the nearest item that needed washing, which turned out to be the blackened baking sheet. "It's not that bad," I said. "I think we can put the dishes in the dishwasher. They'll be clean by the time we're done with everything else."

Lee snorted. "That would be great, except my aunt does not have a dishwasher."

"Is it broken?" I asked, glancing at what was clearly a dishwasher.

He followed my gaze. "Oh. So that is what it is." He opened it up with the caution of someone dismantling a bomb, and crouched down to peer inside. "Why is there a fan in it?"

I swallowed the urge to laugh. "That's not a fan. It's where the water comes out. But it won't do us any good unless she has detergent." Rooting around in the cupboard only proved Lee's conviction; his aunt must not use it, because there was no dish detergent in sight. "I'll just do as your aunt does. Do you have a scrubber?"

He blinked at me.

"Wash cloth it is," I said, moving to the sink.

As I scrubbed the baking sheet, I could feel the tension in my body ease. Lee and I didn't talk, each of us focused on our tasks, but it was a comfortable silence, the only sounds being the gentle sluice of water and Lee muttering to himself as he worked on scraping the burned rice out of the rice cooker. At one point, he approached me, holding some of the rice pieces that he had pulled out. "They get crisped by the cooker," he explained. "Try it. It is like a chip."

Since my hands were submerged in the soapy water, I opened my mouth to have him drop it without thinking, only to have horror slam through me. Blushing, I fumbled with a hand towel, taking extra time to supposedly dry my hands while asking the universe to cool my heated cheeks. He just waited, holding the rice out to me, completely oblivious to my discomfort.

I gingerly took it from him and broke off a piece. Although maybe not as flavorful as a chip, the rice gave a satisfying crunch. "Not bad. Definitely better than *kimchi*."

His sudden smile, heart-meltingly warm, made my pulse speed up in ways that rivaled his driving speed. "At least I can make something."

Danger! Stop staring at those lips. You are not rebounding. And definitely not with a K-pop runaway. I cleared my tight throat. "I guess your aunt usually cooks."

Did he just move closer?

"I have never been good at it, although I pretend otherwise," he said.

"Well, we won't starve. I brought muffins." *Smooth, Merri, real smooth.* But dang it, it was hard to concentrate when those brown eyes were pinned on mine with an intensity that fried away all sensible thought. Maybe I should go back to staring at his lips.

But then his gaze dropped to *my* lips. And *his* lips turned up in a way that had my stomach plummeting to my toes before hurtling to my brain and then back again.

Quick, say something, anything, to distract yourself. I cleared my throat. "Do I have something on my face?"

"You have a piece of rice right," he reached out, fingers brushing against my lips. I froze, sucking in a breath as holding it as those fingers lingered on my skin. "Right here," he finished in a whisper.

My poor heart revved up again, pounding so hard it was a wonder he couldn't hear it as he shifted closer, those dark eyes still trained on my lips. Dark eyes that darkened even more when his hand drifted to my jaw, just in time for him to feel my huge (and involuntary) gulp.

The cursed motor-mouth kicked in (also involuntary). "So, don't take this the wrong way but I definitely don't think you should cook. Unless you want to set the house on fire. Maybe you should take a cooking class—"

"Christmas?"

"Huh?"

"You talk too much."

The words puffed gently against my mouth right before his lips brushed against mine once, twice, three times, before pulling back as if checking to see if I was okay with it. I stared up at him, eyes huge, not daring to move. And then he was kissing me, and I didn't care whether it was rebounding or insanity or insanely rebounding, because my world had narrowed down to the feel of his lips on mine, how his fingers gently brushed my cheek as if he couldn't help himself, how his other hand came around my neck in a warm and tender support as he pulled me closer.

I tentatively slid my hands up to his shoulders, and he made a sound at the back of his throat, a deep sound that made my knees go weak and my hands tighten their grip on shoulders that were now hunched around me, as if he was protecting me from the world.

Emboldened by a surge of bravery, I stood on tiptoe to reach better, and was rewarded by his low rumble of satisfaction and tightened grip. Our lips met eagerly, learning each other, lingering in the slightest of touches that slowly deepened into a kiss worthy of a ten out of ten score.

When we finally pulled apart, both gulping for air, I took in every detail: his dazed expression, flushed cheeks, slightly swollen lips, the nervousness in his eyes…an expression mirrored in my own face, I was sure. But neither one of us seemed ready (or capable, for that matter) to let go of the other.

"I…I…" My attention suddenly became very focused on the nearest thing to me, which turned out to be his (for once) simple t-shirt. I could feel my face reach solar levels of heat, and I was glowing with embarrassment.

"You cannot talk," he cocked an eyebrow. "That happens a lot."

A startled laugh escaped me. "So you've said. Have you ever wondered why, Mr. Kimchi?"

He shrugged, arms still around me. "I *am* charming."

"And so humble, obviously."

He puffed up. "*Deh.* You liked kissing me?"

I paused. "Before I answer that, *why* did you kiss me?"

139

His brow furrowed in confusion. "I think that is obvious."

I looked down to hide my frustration. Maybe it was obvious to him, but definitely not to me.

He put a hand under my chin and gently lifted it until I was forced to look at him. "Christmas, I am not like the *baekchi*. I kissed you because I wanted to kiss you, and I wanted to kiss you because I like you. I still want to kiss you," his voice deepened into a husky drawl, the accent sending shivers through me. "But I think it is better if I do not."

Cheeks still blazing red, I nodded, relief sweeping through me at his firm words. It wasn't just me who was feeling the attraction—miracle of miracles, he felt it too! He reluctantly let me go as I pulled away, which of course made me want to press myself closer. My mind raced with this new development.

He cleared his throat. "You never answered my question."

"About what?"

"About my kissing. You like kissing me." His voice roughened in a way that made my toes curl. "Right?"

I had to fight the urge to scuff the ground like a little kid. "Maybe."

His chest rose and fell in a big sigh, and he relaxed. "Maybe some *kimchi* will change your mind."

"Not even after that kiss, Mr. Kimchi." Hah! I'd regained some of my spunk back after all.

"Pizza?"

"Deal."

He turned away to pull out his cell phone, which was a good thing because the last thing I wanted him to see was me lean against the counter, my legs too weak for me to remain upright.

Holy K-pop, what was happening?

Chasers, the numbers are rising! Keep streaming! Show LHK what he means to us! And if you need a break from watching videos, head over to SLAAC.com to find the latest updates on our favorite Storm and the mystery girl.

KThunderfangirl.com

@KThunderfangirl.com do we know who she is?

OMO, is LHK actually dating? Can anyone blow up the picture?

Lucky girl, whoever she is.

Is she a Chaser?

Has anyone heard about PMH? Has he said anything?

No, but Thunder hasn't had a press release in a while.

Thunder is still scheduled for a concert in Seoul next June. Website is still selling tickets.

I can't find ANYTHING on this mystery girl, but SLAAC has message boards where you can share what you think. If we get enough hits, maybe people will notice! Come on, Chasers, let's SLAAC!!

KThunderfangirl.com

Fourteen

Guys, have you seen this awesome fan art of LHK? Love the comics! Stumbled across this account on DeviantArt—they are hilarious!

Post on Kthunderfangirl.com

The only thing worse than having to wake up to an alarm is waking up to an alarm only to realize that it's still the weekend. The blaring sound penetrated my consciousness, and I flailed to life, only to flop back on the bed with a groan when I realized it was Sunday. Burrowing back under the covers, I attempted to go back to sleep, but thoughts of Lee crowded in.

"You talk too much."

"I kissed you because I wanted to kiss you."

I shivered at the memory of his lips on mine, how his arms had wrapped around me to pull close, the sensation of feeling so protected as his shoulders had hunched around me as if I were precious. If I closed my eyes, I could catch a whiff of his scent, a combination of a smoky musk and ginger.

What was I doing? I was *not* the type to have a rebound guy. It had taken Luke forever to convince me to go out with him, and here

I was kissing a guy that I barely knew. It was like my life had become a K-drama episode.

Sleep was pointless, so I threw on some clothes, grabbed my camera, ready to capture the early morning light. But first, I needed to check the comments on DeviantArt. To my surprise, they had tripled overnight, each one raving about how awesome the panels were. But no one had said anything about Lee, so it must be fine. Breathing a big sigh of relief, I spent the next few hours looking through the lens of my camera, practicing various techniques and snapping away at anything that I thought would make a good subject.

That magical early morning light was just fading the Parks' front door opened. My pulse kicked into overdrive, but it was Ms. Park who stepped onto the front porch, squinting from the brightness. It didn't take her long to spot me, though. "Merri! You up early."

"Hi, Ms. Park. I couldn't sleep."

"Because of yesterday?" she asked in a knowing voice, and laughed. "I do not mind mess. Lee is happy again, that what I care about."

"He told me about his ex-girlfriend," I said in as casual a voice as I could manage. Maybe Ms. Park would give me more info.

A strange look flickered across her face, and she seemed to be thinking carefully as to what to say as she came closer to me. "She no good for him. Only like that he is in Thunder. He was, how you say, in bad places?" Her brown eyes bore into mine. "Lee need to heal. That why he is here."

Somehow, I don't think she was talking about a bad breakup. "Ms. Park, what happened?"

She bit her lip, clearly torn. "I cannot say. But doctors say Lee need to go away."

"Doctors? What doctors?"

She immediately drew back at my alarmed question. "I say too much. Please do not say to him that we talk." Taking my hand, she gave me a warm smile. "You good girl, Merri. Lee like you a lot. Happy with you. You like him?"

I nodded shyly. I did like him. I liked him a lot. And the fact that Ms. Park had observed that he liked *me* had butterflies doing cartwheels in my stomach.

"Good," she nodded. "Stay here."

I didn't have to wait long to know why she'd ordered me to stay put. About five seconds after she went back inside, Lee came bounding out, hair all disheveled and clothes wrinkled, like he'd literally just rolled out of bed. "Christmas!"

His face was tanned and flushed, eyes bright and eager as he looked down at me—the complete opposite of that night as we huddled in the car, when his face had been ghostly pale, his eyes glazed over as he struggled to breathe. I had known that he was hiding something, but I was starting to get a picture of just how big that something was. And it had not escaped me that he *always* wore those wrist cuffs, no matter what.

Doctors. His aunt has definitely said doctors. Was it for anxiety? Or something worse? Did I even want to know? Or was it better to remain oblivious?

He was waiting for me to answer, so I forced myself to push aside the worry...for now.

"Hey."

"Hey." His smile stretched from ear to ear, the warmth and happiness in his eyes impossible to resist, and I smiled back at him.

Lee took a tiny step forward. "You are awake early."

"So are you."

"I could not sleep." The way he said it, added to the intense way he was watching me, made it evident that *I* was the cause of his sleeplessness, and I felt my cheeks grow hot.

He leaned forward, hesitated, then swooped down and gave me a quick kiss on the lips, his mouth clinging ever so slightly to mine as he reluctantly pulled away. "I have been waiting to do that all night."

The heat of my cheeks spread to my entire face as I focused on those last two words. All night? He'd been thinking about me as much as I'd been thinking about him? Be still my K-pop loving heart. "You have?"

"*Deh.*" He bent down to kiss my cheek. "And that too."

My heart melted into goo. Lee Hyung-kim was kissing me. Lee Hyung-kim had dreamed about *me,* and I was officially in danger of becoming as starry-eyed as the girls in K-dramas.

Before the nerves got the better of me, I gently reached up to pull his lips back down to mine, giving him a kiss that, well, let's just say I'm glad my dad wasn't around to witness it. Lee enthusiastically returned it, wrapping his arms around me and pulling me up on my tiptoes so that he could deepen the kiss, mouth moving over mine until my brain turned to mush and I had to pull away to drag air into my lungs. Lee did the same, resting his forehead against mine as he took deep shaky breaths, arms still tight around me.

Finally, he drew back and cleared his throat. "So, uh, would you like to go out together? Today? With me?"

The display of nerves, coming from the normally cocky Mr. Kimchi, helped ease the remaining insecurity. I smiled up at him. "Have you been to an American movie theater?"

"Not yet."

"Perfect! There's a new action movie that just came out that I've been dying to see. I'll buy the tickets, you buy the popcorn?"

His smile lit up his whole face. "For you, Christmas, I won't even try to get dried squid."

"You know what? I'm not even going to ask."

I was definitely not about to ask about the dried squid. But the question about the doctors that Ms. Park had mentioned needed an answer. But not from Lee. My answer would need to come from a different source.

Talking to Ema about my suspicions turned out to be a dead end. "You think Lee hurt himself?" she asked for the third time, voice almost an entire octave higher from disbelief.

"It makes sense, doesn't it? I mean, the whole leaving the country because he had a fight with a group member seems a bit much, don't you think?"

She scrunched up her face as she thought about it. "Maybe. But I honestly don't know how he would have kept it all a secret. The guy basically lives in a fishbowl."

She had a point. Between the reality TV show that seemed to capture every waking minute of Thunder and their countless public appearances, it was a bit of a stretch to see how it could have been kept secret. But still, I knew there was more to everything than what people thought. "I've watched the videos from the past five years, and he wasn't wearing the wrist bands until a year ago. And then he's never without them."

Ema shrugged. "So? He probably got a new stylist. Some idols dye their hair all the time, Lee wears wrist cuffs."

"And then suddenly are hiding out while their fans are left wondering if the group will break up? Ema, he practically had a panic attack when the Chasers found him that night. And his aunt said something about doctors. There has to be something more to all this."

"Huh. Okay, so maybe you're right. It *is* weird that he be over here, although it could be a publicity stunt to make sure that Thunder doesn't lose fans. K-pop groups are expected to be perfect, not have two members fight over the same girl..." Her voice trailed off as she realized just what she was saying. "Sorry. Anyways, so what if there is?"

"What do you mean?"

She leaned forward, her face filling up the computer screen. "What if there is more to all this. What then?"

"I, I don't know," I slowly admitted, sinking back against the cushions of my bed. What *would* I do? Was it even my business to know in the first place? After all, Lee knew that my mom didn't live with us anymore, but he had not once tried to pry.

And then there was Ms. Park. Surely she would have said something if I needed to know what was going on. At this stage I didn't really have a right to demand answers. Maybe I just needed to accept that he had skeletons in his closest, and trust that he'd tell me if he needed to.

Ema gave me a superior smile. "You are having a moment of enlightenment because of my wisdom, aren't you?"

I snorted. "If that's what you want to call it, Aussie."

"Eh, I calls it as I sees it. Now, did he really say dried squid?" she asked in a bright voice, obviously ready to talk about lighter things, and I followed her cue.

"Apparently it's a common movie theater snack. I won him over to the side of popcorn with M&Ms, though."

"Good girl. Now, could you—" She frowned as her phone dinged with a notification. "Sorry, I gotta take care of this. Keep me updated, yeah?"

"Will do. Everything okay?" I asked as she continued to scowl at her phone.

She waved away my concern with a casual, "It's all good," although judging from her somewhat tense expression, it was definitely not all good. But before I could say anything else she quickly signed off.

Guess everyone had their secrets that day.

Fifteen

Once I made up my mind to stop trying to figure it all out and just enjoy the moment, life became a whole lot easier. Well, as easy as it can be when you are secretly dating a K-pop idol on the run from his alarmingly huge fan base. Both Lee and I were a little jumpy every time we went out in public, but as the weeks passed without incident, we began to relax. Sort of. I mean, I just couldn't turn off my concern like a switch and had to remind myself to respect his privacy and not hover, something that was a real struggle at first. But the more time I spent with him, the more he charmed me, easing my doubts and making me understand why LHK was the favored Thunder idol.

Charming? Check. Wacky sense of humor? Check. Good looks? CHECK.

Each day, he'd drive me to and from school, going a little under the speed limit as if he wanted to prolong it as much as possible as we talked about anything and everything.

"Christmas," he announced one particularly frosty morning, turning the heat up to full blast as if we were getting ready to drive through a blizzard. "What is your favorite color?"

"Blue, why?"

"It should be brown."

"What?" I laughed in disbelief, thinking he was joking.

"*Deh.* It should be brown."

"And why is that?"

"Because my favorite color is green," he stated as if this should be obvious.

"Okay."

"Your eyes are green."

"And your eyes are…oh, I see."

He nodded smugly. "*Deh.*"

"I still like blue the best," I said, biting at my cheeks to keep from smiling as he scowled and muttered something about finding hair dye. No way I would admit to him that there was a portrait of him in my sketchbook, and a great deal of attention had been paid to those brown eyes of his.

As if he'd read my mind, he said, "You are either a really good or really bad artist. You never show me." He was teasing, but there was a thread of curiosity, as if he'd been thinking about it for a while now.

Immediately, my thoughts flew to the cartoons, and I felt my face warm in a guilty flush. What would he say if he saw them? Would he laugh them off? Or would he be upset? They weren't mean…just, well, just cartoonish. And of him. That wasn't so bad, right?

If they're not so bad, why don't you want to show him? The voice of reason nudged at my conscious, and I squirmed. "They're not so great. Maybe one day I'll show you." Maybe.

"Okay." The way he just accepted my answer only made me feel worse, and I quickly changed the subject. He didn't say anything more about it, although I could feel him watch me with curiosity.

I really just needed to take the stupid comics down and be done with it. But somehow I never got around to doing it, possibly because when I wasn't at school, I was spending all my time with a certain Korean superstar. After a couple of weeks, the cautious awkwardness between us disappeared and we got into a routine, a.k.a. spending as much time together as possible. By mid-October we were basically inseparable. No matter what we did, Lee turned it into an adventure. Case in point:

Monday: walk with Lee. I had to take a picture because Ema had begged for photos, insisting that she needed visual proof that a guy could wear workout clothes like Lee's and still look good. When I told Lee, he threw back his head and laughed that throaty laugh of his before striking a pose, holding up one hand to form a "v" by his face. When I sent the pic to Ema, she gave me about twenty thumbs up and pronounced that his sweater had the perfect combination of swirls blue and purple and giant gold polka dots on his sweater, and that's when Lee decided that Ema was the best person to have as a friend.

Tuesday: bowling with Lee. He was very enthusiastic about flinging the ball down the lane, and shocked when an employee came over and insisted on putting up the gutter rail for him. "But I knocked them all over!" he exclaimed, gesturing to the pins.

"Yes, sir, but that's not your lane," the guy said in a very long-suffering tone.

Lee cocked an eyebrow. "I should get more points then."

"Gutter rail is fine," I interjected, stifling my laughter, and the employee sighed in relief while Lee huffed and grumbled under his breath. Best bowling adventure ever, hands down.

Wednesday: shopping with Lee, who managed to scoff at how small the mall was in comparison to one in Seoul while also marveling at the variety of random stuff the stores sold.

Thursday: K-drama marathon with Lee. We were camped out on the couch, with a huge bowl of popcorn between us, binging on *Boys Over Flowers*. I was enthralled: so much drama crammed into each episode! Lee? Not so much.

"Look at his hair! He is ridiculous!" he pointed at the male lead's hair which, I will admit, was curled to the point of absurdity. The guy currently had amnesia and refused to believe that the female lead was his true love, even though it was obvious to EVERYONE else that she was. Lee couldn't take it. "He is such a *baekchi*," he exclaimed for the fifth time, throwing popcorn at the TV. I was reminded of the fact that he had thought Luke was an idiot, and hid my smile by happily stuffing another handful of popcorn into my mouth.

The female lead threw herself into a pool, because apparently that was the only way to jog Mr. Amnesia's memory. Lee rolled his eyes. "This is ridiculous. K-dramas are ridiculous. So unrealistic."

I looked over at him. "Really? Everything in K-dramas is unrealistic?"

"*Deh.*"

"So what about when you carried me on your back?"

He gave me a heart-melting smile. "Maybe some things, then." A long arm came around me to tug me close, and he pressed a gentle kiss to my temple. I'd been getting a lot of those over the past few days; Lee never missed a chance to touch me, like he couldn't help himself. Holding my hand as we walked, giving me hugs, kissing me whenever he could. Lee was taking over my senses, and I was both scared and excited by it. What if it didn't work out? What if the whole thing blew up in my face?

I felt his lips on my temple once more, and my fears dissolved as I snuggled closer. One day at a time. I just needed to take things one day at a time.

Halfway through the second-to-last episode, my phone dinged with a text from Ema. Now, a friend would text back. But not me. No, because I was the amazing friend that I am, I invited her to video chat, thrust the phone at Lee, and told him, "This is my closest friend, and she's your biggest fan." And then I sat back to enjoy this new show.

Ema's face appeared on the screen and Lee flashed his most charming smile. "G'day Ema."

Ema blinked and her mouth fell open. Finally, she squealed, "LEE HYUNG-KIM!"

"Hi. Merri said that you are Australian. Have you ever been to Adelaide?"

"NO."

Oh, she was never going to live this one down. I wouldn't let her.

The Aussie side of his accent came out in full force. "Aw, that is too bad. If you can, you should go. The coffee is amazing."

"I LIKE COFFEE."

Okay, time to intervene. I took the phone back from Lee. "So? Am I the best friend or what?"

Ema was so excited, she was practically shaking. Actually, she was shaking; the screen was trembling like Jell-O in an earthquake. "That's Lee Hyung-kim," she said in a whisper that you could hear across the room.

"It is."

"Wait until I tell Lisa!"

Lee stiffened in alarm, and I hurriedly whispered, "Ema! You can't tell anyone, remember?"

"Oh. Right. Although have you been online recently?" she said, suddenly serious. A shiver of apprehension ran down my spine and turned into a chill. "No. Why?"

"You might want to check out SLAAC.com. Just don't kill the messenger. BYE LEE HYUNG-KIM!" And then she was gone.

It took me two seconds to pull up the website, and a millisecond to begin freaking out. "Uh, Lee?"

"What is it? Is it bad?"

I wordlessly handed over the phone, and he swore.

Some special, special soul had actually created a website called SaveLeeAtAllCosts, a site devoted in speculating who I was, who I wasn't, if I was furthering Lee's career, if his ex-girlfriend knew about me, whether I was the real reason they'd broken up. It was like looking at a psychopath's lair from the crime shows, complete with red string and oodles of photos.

There was a video of us, taken that night at the restaurant. Thankfully, my face was hidden behind a sweater, with just a few random curls sticking out. Lee, on the other hand, was in high definition, right down to the smudged guyliner and tussled hair. He was staring straight ahead, not making eye contact with anyone. I hadn't realized how angry he was; his face was drawn tight, his hands clenched on the wheel. He looked like he was ready to punch anyone who got too close. Kind of like right now.

"Lee?" I asked in a small voice.

He cursed again and jumped to his feet, gripping my cell in one hand as he pulled his out to make a call, back turned to me as he launched into a stream of angry Korean when someone answered. He didn't look once at me as he began to pace, seemingly shutting me out with an ease that cut right through the happiness I'd been feeling, leaving behind the all too familiar doubts. Only this time it was worse.

Never, not once, had I considered his fans. It just hadn't occurred to me that they'd find out. Why would they, when his being here was supposed to be a secret? And I'd been blissfully ignoring the fact that things were so uncertain between us; if I didn't think about the fans, then everything would work out.

Lee's tirade cut off abruptly, and he just stood there, staring at the phone in stunned disbelief. "He hung up on me."

"Who?" I asked even though I wasn't sure I actually wanted to know.

"My manager."

My stomach soured. "Is he mad?"

Lee barked out an angry laugh. *"Deh."*

I waited a beat, but he didn't add anything, so I asked, "Did he give any advice?"

Lee narrowed his eyes as he glared at the floor. "He did."

This must be what it's like to pull teeth. *"And?"*

"Never mind. It is not helpful." He offered me a weak smile and sat back down, visibly forcing himself to relax. "It will be okay, Christmas. I will think of something. I just need some time. And in the meantime, we still have some episodes that need to be watched."

I stared at him. "Are you serious? There's a website about us! And your manager doesn't know what to do?"

"I did not say that," Lee said, a muscle throbbing in his tight jaw. "He did have an idea, but it will not work."

"But—"

"Please, Christmas. Trust me. I will fix this." He turned back to the screen, conversation done.

We finished the series in silence, my mind racing the entire time, my interest gone. Why focus on the K-drama when my life was becoming just as convoluted?

The cursor hovered over the refresh button.

Should I? No, absolutely not.

I should go back to finishing my panel, one featuring a certain K-pop idol laughing at a K-drama. I couldn't seem to help myself, even though I couldn't post them anymore; all my inspiration came from exploring the adventures of seeing the world through Lee's eyes. My sketchbook was filled with episode after episode: him mocking the lack of realism in K-dramas, his continued mistrust of large glasses of water, and, my personal favorite, him giving me lessons in applying the perfectly smudged eyeliner—all equally hilarious.

Yes, that is what I should be doing. Not looking at SLAAC.com. Not torturing myself by hitting refresh.

I hit refresh.

And then blew a fuse.

SLAAC.com had been updated yet again. More photos of Lee, more postings of people determined to find out who I was, even a fan-made music video featuring various Thunder clips and ending with a screen shot of me cowering in the car, the video ending with a giant question mark on the screen before fading to dark.

Impressive, especially since it'd only been five minutes since I last refreshed it.

Lee had reassured me that this was normal. "Our fans are the reason we are so famous," was all he'd said. Fair enough, just as long as they weren't the reason that *I* became famous.

Restless, I went downstairs to forage for some food. Dad was out running errands, and the silence of the empty house prompted me to turn up some music to full volume—Thunder, of course, because that was all that I could listen to now. I wonder what Lee would say if he saw me dancing around the kitchen to one of his songs? *You cannot help yourself, Christmas, can you?* Then he'd strut around like he was king of the world, and I'd poke him, and he'd kiss me...

I had it so bad.

Oddly enough, though, the Chasers hadn't found my artwork yet. Or if they had, they hadn't commented on it. And why had I been worried? Not as though I posted my info on the site, so unless someone went all CSI on me and tracked me through my computer, I was fine. It was tempting to continue to add to the collection, especially since there were so many demands for new panels.

I jumped guiltily at knock at the door. Was it Lee? Had he come over to tell me that everything would be fixed soon?

I turned the music up full volume before flinging open the door, a wide smile on my face…except it wasn't Lee standing before me.

Bree.

"Hey, Merri."

The only sound was the music playing in the background as we eyed one another. She looked, in all honesty, awful. Her face was drawn and shadows under her eyes. Her hair, normally such a vivid red and shampoo-commercial worthy, was now dull and limp. And it could have just been my imagination, but I think her clothes were looser.

She was just staring at me, making no effort to speak, and since I wanted this interaction to be over asap, I took things into my own hands. "Why are you here, Bree?"

Her brow crinkled as if she was puzzled by something, but quickly smoothed as she focused on me. "May I come in?"

I leaned against the door in answer. "I don't think that's a good idea. What do you want?"

She rolled her eyes. "I want to talk to you, obviously. About, you know, everything."

"Why? I think *everything* is pretty clear. There's nothing left to talk about." Really, did she really want to talk it all out? Now?

"I just want…I just don't want you to be angry." Vulnerability flashed across her face. "I want things to go back to the way they were."

"Are you still with Luke?" I asked as hope rose in me. Had they actually broken up? Was she coming here because of a guilty conscience? But she was shaking her head, and just like that the hope shriveled up as it all became clear to me. She didn't want to apologize, or she would have done it by now. She knew what she'd done was wrong, but not only did she refuse to admit it, she didn't want to live with the consequences.

She wanted Luke *and* my friendship.

Um, no. "Bree, you made your choice. I think that says it all."

"So, you're not angry?"

"What do you think? You lied to me, *of course* I was angry."

"But you're not now?" she asked eagerly.

I shook my head. "I'm not angry, not the way you think. Just hurt. And, quite honestly, annoyed that you think that things can just 'go back to the way they were.' Because they can't. You were the one that decided to start seeing *my* boyfriend behind my back, and have not once apologized for it. That was *your* choice, and now *we* both have to live with it." My voice rose with each sentence until I was practically shouting. Forcing myself to take a deep breath, I added, "It hurts that you did what you did. And I'm angry that you still don't see how wrong it was. No matter what, we can't go back. I don't want to go back, I just want to move on. Now, I think you'd better leave."

She opened her mouth as if to argue, her face flushing red. Without saying another word, she whirled around and stalked off, angrily shoving at the trees at the back of our yard as she cut through to the next street. We'd worn a path through those trees, endless treks for sleepovers, bike rides, movie marathons...it hurt that those days were gone.

Tears of frustration burned my eyes, and I rubbed them impatiently. I couldn't look back. I wasn't the first person to be hurt by betrayal, and although I knew that I wouldn't forget all the memories that we'd created over the years, I knew that I had to put it behind me so that I could move on. Dad and I were still trying to do that with Mom, and I knew from experience that some days were better than others. But at least I'd made myself clear with her; I highly doubted that I'd have to speak to her again.

Still, I stomped around the kitchen, slamming dishes around as I fumed over her inability to see how her actions were wrong. No, not inability—refusal, which made it even worse. Had she seriously thought that if she waited long enough I'd be fine with everything?

Deep breaths, Merri, deep breaths.

At least I wasn't tempted to look at SLAAC.com anymore. And as furious as I was, I knew that the worst was behind me, at least with Bree and Luke.

Now, if I could only stop worrying about the future.

@KThunderfangirl I know where LHK is. PM me for details.
STORMCHASER007

Do you have proof?
KTHUNDERFANGIRL

I can get it. What do you need?
STORMCHASER007

Get pics of LHK. Do you know who the girl is?
KTHUNDERFANGIRL

I have pics of both of them.
STORMCHASER007

Sixteen

Over the next week or so I couldn't get rid of the feeling that something bad was going to happen. Worse, I felt like I was being watched. My neck would tingle as I walked down the hallway in between classes, my shoulders twitched as I ate lunch in the cafeteria. Even my now daily workouts with Lee felt invaded upon, although I never saw anyone. But eventually I wrote it off as me being paranoid—a result of stalking SLAAC.com—and I relaxed as the days of fall semester slipped by.

Lee was all for going to homecoming with me, mainly so he could out-dance a particular *baekchi*. But in light of Chasers, he admitted that it was probably best that we not go to a dance where there'd be a million cell phones taking videos that would be posted online. Instead, we had pancakes with my dad and started a new K-drama series, *Fated to Love You*. Lee was the one fascinated by it, while I kept wincing at the male lead's bizarre laugh. At some point, Dad joined us and soon enough the three of us were laughing, with Lee explaining random cultural references as the characters hurtled from one calamity to the next. The next day, I found Dad hunched over his laptop, watching the next episode instead of paying bills like he normally did. Score one for the Korean.

Halloween was the following weekend. Mom had loved Halloween and had stormed the local craft stores every year to get decorations that ensured that our house was the most decked out house in the neighborhood. It was the one day of the year that I knew that she would be in a good mood. She'd always dress in a costume, always a new one, and would sit on the front porch to hand out candy while Dad escorted Bree and me trick-or-treating, always making sure we hit the houses that gave out the biggest candy bars. This year, it would be me handing out the candy bars; I'd seen the lost look in Dad's eyes when I mentioned that we needed to get candy.

Lee was cutting the grass as I came outside; he immediately cut the motor and came over to me, a wide grin stretching across his face. "Are you going out somewhere?"

"I need to get candy before tonight. Halloween," I explained. He tilted his head in confusion.

"Candy?"

"You want to come?"

"*Deh,*" he said enthusiastically. "I can drive."

"Uh, no, I don't mind driving," I said. The cops would be out in droves that day, and the last thing we needed was Lee's crazed driving thrown into the mix. So, we climbed into my dad's little car and drove the exact speed limit to the nearest drug store, where we loaded up on so much candy that I'm surprised we didn't clean out all their stock. Lee was particularly enraptured by Reese's, although he was not impressed by the fact that there was no Pepero, chocolate-covered cracker sticks. We hauled everything back to my house, all ten bags, and set up on the front porch. Just like my mom had.

"Christmas?" Lee reached for my hand. "Are you okay? You are very quiet."

I ducked my head and shrugged. I'd never talked about my mom. Bad enough that he'd seen my love life explode in my face. If he knew that my mom had abandoned me on top of that? I'd be officially the most pathetic loser ever.

Lee was waiting for an answer, so I just mumbled that I was tired, but he didn't buy it. "Merilee." I looked up in surprise at him using my name. "You do not have to talk about it. But I am here to listen if you want to talk." He gave my hand a reassuring squeeze and a smile.

The first trick-or-treater was coming up the driveway, so I was saved from answering. Over the next few hours, we handed candy out to a steady stream of eager kids, all of whom were delighted with the handfuls of candy Lee gave to each of them. And every female, whether she was a tot, tween, or mom, melted when he smiled at them; no matter the age, no one could withstand the charm of LHK.

One mom supervising a gaggle of pint-sized superheroes caught my attention. Something about the way she smiled at the kids as they swarmed around Lee, laughing at their excitement, reminded me of Mom. Last year, we'd dressed up as the Queen of Hearts and Alice; she'd even convinced Dad to wear bunny ears and carry around a pocket watch. The present blurred with the past as I remembered how we'd giggled over his ears and his adamant refusal to wear the fake tail she'd bought. But he'd worn the ears, just to please her, so relieved that she had been in such a good mood. We'd been so happy that day, laughing and normal and unaware that just a few days later she'd be gone. Was there anything that I could have done to stop her? Or would it not have mattered?

The question lingered in my mind as we greeted kid after kid, until our bowl was empty and the street was dark. Lee helped me gather up the blankets and put everything inside. "This was fun. We should do this in Korea."

"Hey, maybe you'll start a new tradition." I tried to smile, but it wobbled at the edges.

He stepped closer, putting an arm around me to pull me close. Maybe it was the fact that he didn't say anything or press me for answers even though he was obviously curious, but the embarrassment that had gripped me faded as a rush of trust warmed me. Still, I snuggled close so that I wouldn't see his face as I admitted, "My...my mom loved Halloween."

His arms pulled me closer and he rested his cheek against mine, not saying a word.

"She left us a year ago. She'd never been happy, and decided that she wanted to travel the world and be an artist. Just packed up her things one day and left, without saying a word to my dad. She left me a text message, I guess I should be grateful for that. She didn't love us enough to stay." My voice broke into a sob, shattering the thin control I'd maintained all evening. I clung to him, and he held on tight, rubbing my back and murmuring Korean in my ear, the words melodic and soothing and just what I needed to hear, even if I had no idea what he was saying.

The tears eventually ran out, leaving me with a stuffy head, plugged up nose, and burning eyes. Lee tenderly wiped at my wet cheeks, dropping kisses all over my face as he did.

"Christmas, I am so sorry. I did not know."

"It's not your fault," I said automatically, the response that I'd said over and over in the days right after Mom had left.

But instead of nodding like everyone else had, he leaned down to look me in the eye. "I know. But I wish that you had not gone through that. Both you and your dad. You deserve better."

"Thank you," I sniffled, rubbing at my eyes. "Sorry, I didn't mean to bring all that up."

"Do not apologize. Here—" He thrust a candy bar at me. "Have some candy."

Mental note: candy is ranked almost as high as *kimchi*. I'd have to buy him his own supply for Christmas.

"Would you come over for dinner sometime this week? My aunt

would love to make you dinner." He gave me a smile, different from the one he'd given flashed all evening. Warmer, more intimate, one that chased away memories and filled me with a happiness I didn't think I could feel. "Please? No *kimchi*, I promise."

"Really?"

"Not for you, at least," he quickly capitulated, and I laughed. Well, more like honked, with my plugged-up nose, but a happy honk.

"It's a date, Kimchi Boy."

That night, I began a new piece; not a cartoon panel, but a portrait. Slowly the face came to life: eyes that crinkled in an almost constant smile, full lips, and faint lines that had been carved from years of laughing, curly hair that framed a heart-shaped face. My hand didn't waver as the pencil moved over the page, my hand capturing memories in a frozen image of a happy woman. No trace of the unhappiness that weighed her down more and more with each passing day, or the restlessness that would bring on almost manic energy that would result in anything from random adventures into D.C. to cleaning the house top to bottom. No hint of the unhappiness that would result in her deciding that her life with us was not good enough.

You deserve better.

Lee was right. I *did* deserve better. Better than the bitterness that I felt towards her, a weight that I carried every day. Maybe she deserved it, but I didn't. The only one that I was hurting was myself.

I'd never forget what she did, just as I'd never forget what Luke and Bree did. But how I handled their actions was up to me. And I wouldn't let my mom's decisions ruin my own dreams. But I also wouldn't be selfish in pursuing mine, like she had been. With her, it was all or nothing; she couldn't find a balance. Or didn't want to, more likely.

I'd be different. I'd *choose* to be different. I just needed to figure out how.

"And then she called Mr. Kimchi."

Ms. Park burst into laughter and nudged me with her elbow. "Mr. Kimchi. I like it. Here, eat more."

Eat more. The two words that Ms. Park loved the most. Over the past two hours, she'd pushed dish after dish on me. Tender *bulgogi* with lettuce leaf wraps, bowls of steaming rice, plates heaping with seasoned vegetables, steamed dumplings…and *kimchi*. Luckily, Ms. Park found my aversion to *kimchi* as funny as Lee did, and wasn't at all offended. She had even prepared a salad just for me, although it had some kind of sweet and spicy red paste on it instead of dressing. I'd obediently eaten everything she'd given me, and now I was in danger of slipping into a food coma. Both Lee and Ms. Park were fine, of course, using their chopsticks with an ease that I envied and eating to the point where I wondered how in the world they weren't two hundred pounds heavier.

But finally Ms. Park decided that we'd eaten enough and began gathering up plates. I offered to help, but she waved me away, insisting that Lee and I spend time together. "Go! I fine. Hyung-kim, take her outside to garden."

"*Deh.*" Taking me by the hand, he led me out to the backyard, a beautiful space where Ms. Park had set up an intricate garden, complete with a small pool and waterfall, bench, and trees that gave privacy. Privacy that Lee took full advantage of, tugging me behind one particularly shady tree so he could kiss me breathless. His lips sought mine out with an eagerness that made my knees weak, and I kissed him back, reveling in how his breathing hitched in his chest as I ran my hands through his hair. The feel of his slightly rough jaw against my cheek and his unique scent of sandalwood and citrus went straight to my head. Over and over our lips met, tasting each other, moving in tandem, our breathing mixing until I didn't know where his ended and mine began.

I abruptly pulled back, leaning my forehead against his chest as we both gulped for air. Lee muttered something under his breath and chuckled. I tilted my head back to look up at him, but his face was shrouded in shadows. "What? You find kissing me funny?"

"If I did, I would die happy."

"That has to be the cheesiest thing you have ever said."

His teeth flashed white in the dark. "You bring it out of me," he teased. But then he abruptly stiffened. "Did you hear that?"

"What?" All I could hear was a breeze rustling through the trees.

He remained tense, whipping his head around as if expecting someone to jump out at us. Gradually, though, he relaxed. "Sorry. I thought I heard someone."

"Let's go back inside," I suggested, even though I was sure he was imagining it. "I brought over some cookies, and I think it's time that I start pushing food on your aunt. Let's see how she handles my grandmother's molasses cookies."

He followed me inside, casting suspicious looks over his shoulder, and remained quiet the rest of the evening. But he managed to eat five giant cookies, so it was safe to say that he would recover. He happily munched on one as he walked me back to my house, swinging my hand between us as he asked how school was going. He was fascinated by the American public school system, commenting on how much more free time students have here. "In Korea, our studies are very important, especially learning English. If you want a good job, being fluent is essential."

"Is that what you did?" I asked. "You seem to be the most fluent in the group."

"My parents hired a private tutor for me and my sisters," he reminded me. "With my practicing and auditioning, there was not time for school and a *hagwon*."

There was a slight pause, like he had been about to say something else. Was it about his family? He didn't say it, but I got the impression that his parents were well off to be able to afford to do that. I knew a little bit about his family, courtesy of Ms. Park over dinner. His father was a surgeon, his mother stayed at home to look after their grandmother, and he had two sisters. Choon-hee was two years older than him and still in college, while Hyo-sonn was in ninth grade. But that's it. Lee was as mum about them as he was about Thunder.

"You must miss them," I said, fishing for more details.

"I do. My parents are proud of what I have done."

That wasn't exactly what I'd meant, but okay. "You are so young compared to how much you've done. When did you start?"

He gestured that we sit on the porch bench, and leaned back as he considered my question. "It is different in Korea than here," he explained. "You train for years to audition at one of the companies, and if you make it through the audition they place you in either a group or with a partner. You do not just start up a group of your own and get noticed. Well, you can," he admitted with a wry smile, "but you do not get anywhere. There are three big companies that launch careers, and it used to be that if you do not sign up with one of them then you rarely made it."

"Are you signed with one of them?"

"Thunder is with a smaller agency. We got lucky. We developed a strong fan base almost immediately, much like BTS. Other groups are not as fortunate."

I could only imagine. For every successful group there had to be hundreds that no one heard about. "How long did it take for you to get ready for the auditions?"

"I started when I was eight. My parents signed me up for voice lessons and had a private dance tutor come to the house. I also took guitar, piano, and drum lessons."

I gawked at him. "You did all that since you were eight?" He nodded, some of that light dying in his eyes. "No wonder you needed a private tutor. When did you audition?"

"At fifteen."

"You trained for seven years?"

He shrugged. "It is no different than athletes training for the Olympics, is it? Once I got through the audition, they decided that I would be best suited with the group they were forming, and we became Thunder." He stared off into the front yard, his jaw clenched.

"Do you miss it? Thunder, I mean."

"I do not know," he slowly admitted, as if reluctant to say the words aloud. "My life…it is very difficult, Christmas. We are given the best of everything, but it comes at a cost. Everything I do is judged, every decision criticized, and we must always be happy. There can never be anything negative associated to us, which is why what happened with Min-ho is so embarrassing, to the group and our managers. I think that they hoped my military service would save them from having to do anything."

I zeroed in on that last part like a hound dog on a scent. "Come again? What military service?"

Lee's face took on a deer in the headlight panic. "You did not know?"

"No, I definitely did not. *What* military service?" I asked in a completely calm, not at all panicked tone of voice. Or not. "Is there a war I don't know about?"

Instead of saying sweet reassuring things like I expected (and hoped for), he threw his head back and laughed. "War? There is no war, or at least not the kind that you are thinking of. Every male in Korea serves in the military, whether we are at war or not."

"*Every* male?"

"*Deh.*"

"And what, you are going to be drafted or conscripted or whatever into the army?"

He put an arm around my shoulder. "Yes. But probably not for a few years." He began nuzzling my neck, but I was not ready to be distracted.

"And then what, you go to a warzone?"

"*Aigoo*, you do not know anything about Korea, do you Christmas? No, I will not have to go to a warzone."

"Well, excuse me for being concerned," I huffed, shrugging him off, but he put his arm back around me and hugged me close, preventing me from running off to research what exactly military life in South Korea entailed. He leaned close and began toying with my hair, running the strands through his fingers and lightly massaging my scalp. "I like that you worry about me," his voice breathed close to my ear, indicating that he was more than happy to begin round two of our make-out session.

A bright flash, right on the edge of my periphery vision, had me bolting upright, nearly banging Lee's nose with my shoulder. "Did you see that?"

"*Aiish*, you nearly broke my nose," he grumbled, romance gone. "See what?"

I peered into the darkness, but couldn't make out anything out of the ordinary. "Nothing, I guess."

"*Aigoo*, next time warn me so I can goose out of the way."

"That would be *duck* out of the way, and yes, I'll warn you. Good night."

I gave him a quick kiss on the cheek and *goosed* inside before he could retaliate, chuckling at his surprise. I was still giggling as I climbed into bed, even as I blushed over his ardor. Had I ever thought that he was annoying? I was starting to understand the Chasers' enthusiasm. Ema would get a kick out of that.

OMG, it IS him!! StormChaser007, you are amazing!!! I will update SLAAC.com and let all the Chasers know. You are the best!!! Do you know the girl?

KTHUNDERFANGIRL

I do. They've been seeing each other for a couple of months. She didn't know who he was at first.

STORMCHASER007

SRSLY?? A non-Chaser?! Do you know where she lives?

KTHUNDERFANGIRL

Sending you her address. LMK if you need anything else.

STORMCHASER007

Chasers, I have incredible news. LHK is in Northern Virginia!!! And not only Mystery Girl here too, but she is living right next door to him. And SHE IS NOT A CHASER! Click on this link to find out how you can help show LHK our support so he'll return to Thunder. We are working on a plan, so be patient and keep checking for updates. Thunder must roll!!

KTHUNDERFANGIRL.COM UPDATE

Seventeen

The days were filled with homework, quizzes, a *Hamlet* project that would forever be ingrained in my nightmares, and glares from Bree. No one could hold a grudge like Bree, something that I'd always known. I just never thought that I'd be on the receiving end of it. But, honestly, it didn't bother me. I was too busy juggling school and time with Lee to worry about it.

Before I knew it, it was Thanksgiving. I'd suggested to my dad that we invite the Parks over, and he'd readily agreed. Halloween had been bad enough; we needed a big distraction to get through the Thanksgiving holiday. I didn't even want to think about what Christmas would be like…that was one ordeal neither of us was looking forward to.

We went all out, as much to prove to ourselves that we could carry on as to impress our guests. We spent three days—*three*—prepping for that one meal. You'd have thought it was a state dinner for fifty, not four, people. From stuffing groceries into the car to stuffing the turkey and then stuffing the turkey into the oven, we had enough food to feed an army. Given how the Parks could tuck away food, it might be just enough for the four of us.

We set everything out on the good china, lit candles, and had it all ready with just enough time for me to run upstairs and get changed into a burgundy tunic, skinny jeans, and a decorative scarf. I ran the brush through my hair, working out the tangles, spritzed it with some hairspray to get rid of the static electricity, and slipped on my ankle boots right as the doorbell rang.

"I'll get it!" I yelled, charging down the stairs to fling open the door. Lee grinned at me, looking so handsome in his black dress pants, white collared shirt, black jacket, and shiny silver shoes. Ms. Park, dressed in a beautiful flowing dress that showed off her trim figure, was holding a basket filled with what looked like twisted donuts. "From a Korean bakery," she explained as she stepped inside. "Hyung-kim say you like."

He knew me so well.

"And no worry, we brought our own *kimchi*." She held up two small cartons filled to the brim.

Lee winked at me as helped her out of her coat, lips twitching as I valiantly offered to put the *kimchi* on the table. "We have never had a Thanksgiving dinner before, but we are prepared."

"Being prepared is always a good thing," I replied. I couldn't wait for Dad to find the *kimchi* nestled between the green bean casserole and sweet potato pie, making sure to put it right next to the rolls right by his dish. Dad was just bringing in the ginormous turkey and valiantly hid his surprise, although his eyebrows did go up a bit. He greeted the Parks warmly and we sat down, starting the most hilarious Thanksgiving meal the Hart household had ever had.

Both Lee and his aunt laughed at the extra small glasses we'd put aside for them. Dad had looked at me like I was crazy when I put them out, and now I beamed at him in victory. He rolled his eyes, but his eyes were twinkling in a way that I hadn't seen in a long time. And he laughed out loud at Lee's awe of the turkey, offering him a piece so big I thought Lee's eyes might pop out of his head. But he gamely sawed away at it, and was sure to try each and every side dish: home-made stuffing, cranberry sauce, mashed potatoes, biscuits, green bean casserole, sweet potato casserole, gravy—and *kimchi*. At one point Ms. Park urged/ordered Dad to try some, and the three of us leaned forward as he took a bite. Lee hooted when Dad asked for more. "I told you, Christmas, *kimchi* is the best!" Ms. Park nodded and heaped more on Dad's plate.

I reached for another biscuit and slathered butter on it. "More carbs for me, Sparkle Boy."

Eventually, we all agreed that we needed a break before we were ready for round two with dessert, so the adults waddled off to the living room while Lee and I dragged ourselves outside to our bench.

"I ate way too much," I groaned as I tried to figure out if there was a way for me to loosen my jeans without him noticing.

"I like food." Lee stretched his legs out with a contented sigh. "And I really like turkey."

"I'll say. You had three helpings."

"Your dad had two helpings of *kimchi*," he pointed out smugly.

That's just what I needed, another *kimchi* addict. There'd probably be a container of it next to the milk in a day or so. I shuddered at the thought, and Lee chuckled. "It is not that bad, Christmas. If everyone else likes it but you, what does that tell you?"

I stuck out my tongue in response, and he laughed with that effortless boyish charm that I couldn't resist. But the laughter quickly faded into a worry that seemed out of place. "Are you okay?" he asked.

"With the *kimchi*? As long as I don't have to eat it—"

"I mean about today. Without your mom here."

"Oh." I braced myself for the usual wave of pain that accompanied any thought of Mom, but when it hit me it wasn't as bad as I thought it would be. "I'm really glad that you guys could be with us. I think it was good for my dad, too. And I had fun." I smiled up at him. "I was scared that it would be an awful, depressing day, but it wasn't. Thank you."

"Anytime, Christmas." He squeezed my hand, lacing his fingers through mine while his other hand lightly traced over the sensitive skin.

"What about the Chasers?"

He stilled. "What do you mean?"

"You know what I mean. Is everything okay?"

He looked away, jaw tensing, but when he faced me again his face was wiped clean of expression. "Everything is fine."

"Nothing from your managers?"

"No."

I almost didn't ask my next question, but curiosity won. "Have you been on SLAAC.com?"

His eyebrows lifted in surprise. "No. Have you?"

I couldn't quite meet his eyes as I nodded. "The Chasers are still not happy." Talk about understatement; the posts just kept coming, each one full of outrage over the thought of Lee dating. There were too many threads to count, and lately the website design had been changed; there were more tabs at the top, with reassuring names like Thunder Hotline and LHK Crusade. I was equal parts curious and determined to resist the temptation to look closely at it all, unless I wanted to sink into an endless pity party.

"Does it bother you that I'm not Korean?"

"*Bo?*" He snorted. "No. Would I do this," he gave me a peck on the lips, "if it did?"

"That could just be the happy hormones talking." *Great. Point that out to him. Smooth, very smooth.* "What I mean is that, I'm just an ordinary girl. An American one, with yellow hair and freckles. And you are a celebrity. Eventually you're going to go back, aren't you?"

"I do not know, Christmas. I really do not. But what I do know is that I like you, especially your yellow hair and freckles." He planted a kiss on said freckles, which just about made my heart explode. "Korean or American, you are you, Christmas."

"Good answer, Sparkle Boy. Very good answer."

I jolted awake, then groaned as the movement jostled my still-full stomach. Definitely shouldn't have eaten the pie *and* Korean donuts. A quick look at the clock told me that it was entirely too early to be awake on a holiday, and I buried my head in my blankets…only to jolt yet again as my phone buzzed insistently. I blinked bleary eyes at the screen was instantly awake. "*Ema*? Is everything okay?"

"Turn on your computer."

"What? You called me all the way from Australia to tell me—"

"TURN ON YOUR COMPUTER!!!"

"All right!" I shuffled over and swiped up my laptop, hurrying back into bed to cuddle under the warm covers. "Now what?"

"Go to KThunderfangirl.com."

The synapses in my befuddled brain began to warm up. I typed in the URL. "Okay, it's loading. But you're not telling me that this has to—OH. CRAP."

There, in high def, was a picture of Lee and me on a walk. And another of us in his backyard. And another of him kissing me, this one captioned "Thunder's Lee Hyung-kim's international romance?"

"That's…that's…" I sputtered.

"Scroll down, there's more."

"More? How the heck could there—WHAT?" There, right there, was Lee holding me on my front porch. "That's from last night. Literally last night, after dinner."

"They've been up since midnight, and look at how many hits they've gotten." In the corner of the screen was a section that proudly proclaimed that the posting had half a million views. And the number ticked up as I watched.

"Where did these come from?"

"She just says that she had a tip and got lucky."

"By stalking us?" I screeched. "A tip? Seriously? This is absolutely...hold on."

"What?"

"Shhh, I hear something." I padded over to the window. And was greeted by hell. "THEY'RE HERE!"

"Who's here, I mean there. You know what I mean! Who??"

I gaped at the scene before me. "Chasers. They are here. Outside. Here."

A swarm of girls was standing in front of the Park house, holding up signs with a scary amount of glitter and even scarier words painted on them.

I <3 LHK

Thunder rolls for LHK

I LOVE YOU LEE HYUNG-KIM!

Stay away from LHK!!!!

More were pulling up, the cars lining our quiet street until there wasn't a free place left. And they just kept coming and coming and coming. Oh my gosh, Ema, I gotta go."

"Wait! Tell me about—"

Too late. She'd just have to wait, because I had to call *LHK* and inform him that we were surrounded by Chasers. Not that he probably didn't already know that. But I needed to freak out at someone, and he was my target.

Except *someone* wasn't picking up his phone. Of course he wasn't, because why on earth would he pick up his phone at the one time I needed him to pick up the most? Fine. If you can't bring the person to the freak out, you have just got to bring the freak out to the person. He was a celebrity and must have handled this kind of stuff before. He'd know what to do. And it better not involve eating *kimchi* to make things better.

I marched downstairs, only to realize that I was still in my flannel PJs, so I had to march back upstairs, change into jeans and a hoodie, and march back down. Luckily, the backyard fence in between our houses was low, so I was able to haul myself over and sneak up to the back door. I had barely started to knock when Ms. Park wrenched it open. "Merri! Come in before they see you!"

"Where is Lee?"

"Upstairs. He is just getting...yah!"

She shouted something in Korean after me, but I was a gal on a mission. I flew up the stairs, charged through the closest door without stopping to think *why* it would be closed, and nearly ran smack dab into a startled Lee, who held his cell to his ear. A startled Lee without a shirt on. A startled Lee who had an impressively toned stomach.

Sweet mercy, were all those muscles his? What did he do, a million sit ups twice a day? Why was I here again? Oh right, hell. "We're on Kthunderfangirl.com," I blurted out, voice shrill in panic.

Giving himself a little shake, Lee shrugged and said coolly, "I know. They came a half hour ago." He carefully put the phone on his bedside table.

"Have you seen the website?"

"*Aniyo.*"

I pulled out my phone and all but shoved it in his face. "There. Right there. That's us. Taken yesterday!"

He looked down at the screen, face blank, all emotion gone.

"Lee, what are we going to do?" I prompted impatiently.

No answer.

I began pacing. "They found you. And me. Me with you! How? SLAAC.com was bad enough, but at least they didn't know where we were. But now they do! They are literally protesting me—who does that?"

Still no answer.

I shot him a glare. "Are you going to say anything?"

"Why? You are fine doing all the talking."

I gaped at his abrupt tone. "Excuse me? There is a literal horde of girls down there, chanting your name and protesting me, and there are photos of us online for everyone to see, and you're getting after me for wanting to talk?"

He rubbed his hand through his hair with enough force to make it stick straight up, which made his stomach muscles contract in a way that was, um, distracting. I mean, they actually *rippled*. "And would you put a shirt on!" I demanded in a fit of righteous indignation. As if I could concentrate while he was half-naked in front of me.

He abruptly turned away to stand by the window. "*Aiish*! This should never have happened." He cautiously parted two blinds to look through.

I was back to pacing, all three feet of clear floor space that there was. "How did they get the photos?"

"You mean you do not know?"

I froze. "And just what does that mean?"

It might have been a trick of the light, but I could have sworn that his shoulders tensed, as though he was bracing himself, before he turned to face me, face impassive. "I think you can guess."

"Why would you—"

Realization came in a cold, heart-stopping rush. "You think *I* had something to do with this? You must be joking."

He clenched his jaw but remained stubbornly silent.

Oh my gosh, he did. He actually thought that I'd ratted him out.

"How...how could you think that about me?" My voice sounded as bewildered as I felt. "Do you really think I'd betray you? Why would I?"

Pain flickered in his eyes, but almost immediately hardened with a cold anger that made my stomach churn. "What better way to become famous? I have seen your panels online, ones that you very conveniently did not show me."

The panels. Those stupid panels that I had so stubbornly held onto. "You saw those?"

"There is a link posted on SLAAC.com. I had wondered why you never showed me your art, and now I know. You have been using me, your *inspiration*," he sneered, "for what you want most."

"I'm sorry, I should have showed you the panels. But I stopped uploading them as soon as I knew who you were." I stuttered to a halt as I remembered that one final panel I'd put up, when I'd known exactly who he was. What had I been thinking? "You're absolutely right, I should have taken them down, but I thought it would look more suspicious."

"Really? Was that before or after you promoted them? I saw the links you shared. You wanted people to find them."

I fought off a wave of dizziness as each harsh word hit their mark. He was right. I had wanted people to find them, had wanted it so much that I all but invited the Chasers to come find us. I could have—should have—taken the panels down as soon as I'd found out who Lee was. Deleting the links wasn't enough protection, and I'd known that from the start. But I'd liked the attention they were getting. That I was getting. Liked how people looked forward to each posting, even asked for more. Liked how people had enjoyed my talent, how it made me feel knowing that people thought I was good. Nothing else had gotten that amount of attention; people loved them, and that appreciation had been easing that ache left by my father's disapproval.

Shame took a hold of me. *Had* I been using Lee? Just seeing him as a means to an end with my art? A way to distract myself from all the negative in my life? Yes, I'd eventually stopped uploading the work, but I hadn't stopped creating new panels. I'd filled up the rest of my sketchbook and started on another, thanks to him.

Lee pushed his fingers threw his hair like it was all he could do to control his anger. "See? You cannot deny, can you? You are just like her, using me for your own gain. She wanted to date the most popular member of Thunder, but that was not good enough."

"Lee!" I struggled to come up with a defense, but words eluded me.

He charged ahead, each accusation a blow to my heart. "It was not enough that I liked you, was it? Was that why you spent time with me? Because you got ideas for your cartoons? I saw the time stamp on each one. You began uploading them as soon as I arrived. You put those online without my permission!"

"But I stopped—"

"It never should have started!" he yelled, face almost purple with rage, veins standing out in his neck. "You used me! Just like she did!"

"And I guess I'm the mastermind behind SLAAC.com as well?" I fired back, a seething anger that he thought I was like his ex freeing me from my shock. "Because nothing makes a guy like you more than pretending to have an entire fan base blasting you online, right? I came up with the whole scheme to get more attention, and have been lying to you for weeks because that's the kind of person I am—I even arranged for Luke and Bree to cheat on me to get you to feel sorry for me."

He opened his mouth as if to argue, but I was so done with this conversation. "If that's what you think of me, Lee Hyung-kim, then SCREW YOU!" I said, spinning on my heels to make my escape before he could see the tears in my eyes. I saw a t-shirt on the floor and, snatching it up, I hurled it at his still bare abs. "AND PUT ON A SHIRT!"

Ms. Park was standing at the bottom of the stairs, obviously waiting for me as I hurtled downstairs. "What wrong?"

"What's wrong is that your nephew is a jerk! Sorry," I immediately apologized as her face blanched. "I mean, he's—"

"Did you?" she interrupted impatiently. "Did you use him?"

Maybe I should have taken down the panels. No, fine, I should have. I knew it, had known if for a long time, wouldn't have felt guilty about it for so long otherwise. I *had* taken advantage of an opportunity, but using Lee? Getting close to him just so that I could get ideas? "No," I said firmly. "No, I did not. I care about him. I'd never hurt him." Although I'd managed to do just that.

She shook her head, muttering under her breath. I braced myself for a scolding, but she patted me on the shoulder. "You right, he is jerk."

My lips may have lifted in the slightest of smiles at the show of support. "Thanks, Ms. Park."

A door slammed upstairs—Lee was not impressed with our gal talk.

"You go now," Ms. Park ordered. "I talk to him. And Merri?" She gave me a warm smile. "You are good girl. Not like Park Su-sung. She bad for him. Not you." She climbed the stairs without another word, thankfully not seeing me scrub at the tears now slipping down my face. At least one person believed in me. I automatically opened the front door, stepped out into a Thunder storm, and cursed my stupidity as cameras flashing like lightning, blinded me.

"THERE SHE IS!"

One girl, who was standing on the back of a pickup truck, pointed an accusing finger at me. "LEE'S MYSTERY GIRL!" She pulled out a bullhorn from her bag—*seriously?*—and started a new chant, urging those closest to her to join in. The chant quickly spread: "THUNDER NEEDS LHK! THUNDER NEEDS LHK!"

"That doesn't even rhyme!" I tossed over my shoulder before speed walking across the lawn, head held high, lips smashed together so no one would notice how they were shaking.

She stopped mid-chant. "Leave him alone! You're not even a Chaser!"

Horrified gasps spread through the crowd until all you could hear was one big never-ending inhale. The signs trembled, shedding glitter on protestors, turning them into a giant angry rainbow.

Forget pride. I sprinted up the remaining steps and closed the door with a loud *bang*, very grateful for the three inches of solid oak that was now between me and them.

"Merri?" Dad was coming down the stairs, hair sticking up on end as he rubbed at his face. "What's going on?"

I stared at him as the Chasers took on a new chant: WE'LL CHASE YOU AWAY. WE'LL CHASE YOU AWAY.

"You might want to sit down for this, Dad."

Eighteen

To: Manager Sung
From: Seoul Music Headquarters

Lee Hyung-kim has been discovered. Hiatus must come to an end. Please retrieve Lee Hyung-kim as soon as possible.

In the span of twenty-four hours, my normal life (if dating a K-pop star is ever normal) imploded. No wait, it was semi-normal now because Lee had dropped me...or I had dropped him. Whatever. We weren't talking to each other, and that was that.

Lee wasn't the only one. My father was, in a word, furious. I knew that because he also hadn't spoken to me, not since I'd dropped the bombshell of just why there was a swarm of people protesting in front of our house. "You mean you knew about this for weeks, and didn't think to tell me?" he'd asked in that deadly quiet voice of his when I made my confession.

Wincing, I'd nodded, and I almost kept the rest of it to myself but knew that it would only make things worse. "And, uh, I've been doing cartoons of him and putting them online."

"Why?"

I would have cheerfully thrown myself through a hole in the floor if I'd been lucky enough for one to appear as I admitted, "Because people liked them."

"I see." Those had been the final two words he spoke to me, and a condemning silence had reigned in our house since. I think I would have preferred shouting over the icy calm that usually descended whenever he was mad. When he realized that Mom had left, he was silent for three days. But that had been a wounded silence, not the deafening quiet he was giving me now.

My phone dinged with message after message from Ema, begging to hear updates. I ignored them, a growing suspicion gnawing at me until finally I couldn't take it anymore and arranged to video chat. That night I signed on, and she immediately launched into asking question after question, not noticing my silence at first.

"Are you okay? Oh my gosh, I can't believe it. What did Lee say? Are they gone? Or are they camping out? I told you, some Chasers are hardcore. They bring fandom to a whole new level. If I'd had known…" Her voice trailed off, and there was something about her tone, the way she didn't look at me, that made me feel queasy, and I finally spoke.

"If you had known what?"

Her eyes snapped back to mine. "What do you mean?"

"I didn't tell anyone where he was. No one. Except…"

Now it was my voice to fade away, unwilling to say what I'd been thinking since I finally had a chance to calm down and think about everything.

"Except me," Ema finished for me, her voice flat. "You think *I* told them?"

I remained silent.

"Wow. I mean, just wow. You really think I'd go behind your back like that?"

"I don't know. Did you?" It was the only explanation that made sense. She was the only one I'd told. And hadn't she been so insistent that I send a photo? "Ema, I just want the truth."

"The truth? Fine. Truth is that if I don't sign off right now I'm going to say something that I'll really regret. And when you're ready to stop projecting your insecurities on me, we'll talk." She reached out to snap her laptop shut, and the screen went blank.

Fantastic. I'd managed to tick three people off in one day. More if you count all the Chasers. Oh, and all our neighbors, because they were definitely NOT happy with the sudden traffic jam of humanity. Who knew so many people had our phone number? I ignored the incessant ringing (I bet Dad was regretting on his insistence to keep a landline) as I went on DeviantArt to delete my account, then watched the police disperse the crowd as I impatiently wiped at the tears that clouded my eyes.

Just what had I been thinking? How had I managed to fool myself into thinking that those stupid panels were okay?

The answer was simple: because I'd wanted to. Just like my mom.

No wonder Dad was against me and art. Maybe he was seeing something about me that I was blind to. That I was as selfish as Mom.

The thought hung over me like a guilty weight as I crawled into bed, but not before I peeked my head out my bedroom to see if Dad was still in his room (he was) and to check outside to see if the street was still clear of Chasers (it was).

Maybe things would be better in the morning...

Loud chanting, more effective than any alarm, woke me up early the next morning, killing any delusion that this was all just a nightmare. And Dad still wasn't speaking to me; he was too busy fielding calls from, well, everyone. Neighbors, news, random relatives that we hadn't spoken to in years—everyone. And, of course, there were the Chasers who, if anything, had grown in number. Police were called hourly; I think some of them were on first name terms with the Chasers by the end of that second day. Definitely by the third. And still more poured in, forcing me to hide in the house and watch it all from my window.

At one point, I could have sworn I saw Bree at the top of the street, taking it all in with wide eyes and an incredulous look on her face. Hah! Something that we had in common.

And still the Chasers came, armed with so many glittery signs that you needed sunglasses to go outside. Not that I could step foot outside. The minute I did, they got all riled up, shaking their signs at me and shouting for LHK. I bet the HOA meetings would get really exciting, thanks to us.

Checking SLAAC.com became a torturous way to pass time, with more and more messages being posted constantly. Boy, oh boy, were there messages. All praising Lee, most criticizing me. There were a few that stood up for me, a fact that I clung to. They didn't all hate me, just most of them...including Lee, apparently. Not that I blamed him; although part of me couldn't believe it, that he would cut me off so suddenly, believe that I'd betray him. The other part wasn't surprised at all. Because why wouldn't he? I had no excuse, other than my naiveté in believing that keeping the panels up was harmless. Heck, if I were in his shoes I'd probably do the same thing. My stupidity was impressive.

And then there was Ema. Was I wrong? She had sounded so hurt. Had I made yet another colossal mistake? But it was the only explanation that fit. For whatever reason—and maybe she really hadn't known how bad things would get—she'd told the Chasers about us. I can only assume that local Chasers were sent to take photos before everything got organized.

Sucked to be me, right now, not going to lie.

And it only got worse. Ema and Lee were avoiding me like the plague, but the Chasers were all too happy to stay and make their presence—and opinions—known.

I went outside to get the mail, they chanted.

I helped Dad bring in the garbage, they chanted.

I opened my window to air out the room, they chanted.

And, at one point, Lee must have poked his head outside, because the chant dissolved into a frenzied roar that echoed throughout the entire neighborhood. Of course, by the time I'd raced to the window to get a look, he'd vanished back inside.

Dad called the police and was told that as long as the Chasers weren't blocking traffic or destroying anything, they were allowed to gather. Something about conduct, not content. Since they weren't shouting obscenities or hurting anyone, there was technically nothing the police could do except disperse the crowd when it got too big.

"What about our piece of mind?" he'd shouted into the phone. "My daughter can't leave the house!"

"Are they following her?" the woman had asked in a bored voice.

"No."

"Threatening her?"

"Does slipping on glitter count?" I'd joked, and he'd shot me a glare before gritting out a "No."

"Then there's nothing we can do, besides come out if they are obstructing traffic. What are they protesting?"

He'd ignored my panicked head shaking. "My daughter's relationship with a K-pop star."

Her voice didn't change one iota—this was a woman who'd clearly heard everything. "Then tell her to date someone who is not a K-pop star. Have a good day, and don't forget to take our survey."

Dad had hung up before the automated survey began, then stalked out of the room, still intent on not speaking to me, although I swear

I overheard him muttering about contacts at the Pentagon and people owing favors. I held onto that for the rest of the day: he was furious at me, but he still cared!

And then, right when things couldn't get even crazier, more protesters showed up. But these protesters weren't joining forces with the Chasers; to my shock, they were protesting them. Their signs had new messages.

LOVE STRIKES!

LHK 4 LOVE!

CHASE LOVE!

That's not all. LTL.com (aka Love Thunder Love) began trolling SLAAC.com, complete with posts advocating that LHK date whomever he likes, a newsletter to keep on top of all K-pop dating news, and a GoFundMe to send me and Lee on a vacation to Hawaii. Seriously. There were people who actually wanted us to go to Hawaii. There was already five hundred dollars donated, with more coming in each second.

I, Merilee Hart, had a fan base. Me! And an international one, at that. There was an actual store on the LTL.com, complete with t-shirts, hoodies, blankets, and face masks with all proceeds going to the GoFundMe.

But that wasn't the worst of it. There was a link on the homepage, captioned with "See their love story from the start!" I expected more photos, but what I got was ten times worse—a compilation of all my panels of Lee. The Chasers had found each and every one. It didn't matter that I'd deleted my account; they'd saved them and reuploaded them. The Chasers had found my cartoon panels, even though I'd immediately taken them down after, well, you know. They must have saved them (total copyright violation, by the way) and uploaded them again. Worse than that, though; my dad, determined to find the source of all of this, did some internet research of his own, and found the panels almost immediately. Meaning Lee could too. Worst case scenario, he'd think I'd sent them to the Chasers.

All Dad said was, "I told you to do something other than art."

And for once, I couldn't argue.

"Dad? Do you want something to eat?"

"Nope."

"Are you sure? You've kinda been in there a while."

"Yep."

Ugh. Now I knew where I got my stubbornness from. He'd gotten a call that morning, and I hadn't seen him since; he refused to come out, and his silent disapproval was getting to me.

I leaned my head against the door. "I'm sorry. I am really sorry. I just didn't think anything would come of it."

The door was abruptly yanked open, and he just stood there in the doorway, arms folded in the universal stance of parental outrage.

I squirmed as he pinned me with a knowing glare.

"It was wrong, I know that. But you gotta admit, no one could have predicted all this," I said, waving an arm behind me as if the Chasers were standing in the hallway with us.

Dad's eyes softened for a split second but hardened again as he asked, "Why did you do it?"

He settled with no signs of moving until I spoke, so finally I admitted, "Because it felt good." Once the words started, the rest tumbled out of me in a rush. "People liked them, Dad. They liked them before they knew that they were about Lee. And it felt good to have people think that I was talented, to like what I was doing." *Unlike you.*

I didn't say that last part, but I didn't have to.

Dad stepped back as if I'd slapped him, his face tightening in pain. He opened his mouth, but I cut him off. "You were right. I got myself into this mess, and it was because I wasn't thinking about anything besides myself. About my art. I let it take over, and all I can say is that I'm sorry and I hope you can forgive me."

His sigh must have started in his toes, it was so deep and long. "Of course I forgive you, Merri. Yes, I was disappointed that you would do something so foolish. And yes, I was angry that you seemed to ignore all reason just to put some art online."

I winced but remained quiet. After all, he was 100 percent right.

He reached out and put an arm around my shoulders, a warm and heavy weight that almost immediately eased some of the tightness in my chest. His next words helped dissolve the rest. "But Merilee, no matter what, I will always love you. You made a mistake, but I'm starting to realize how I played a part in it."

I started to protest, but he cut me off. "No, I can see it now. In fact, I've been thinking of nothing else for the past few days." Taking a deep breath, he said, "I've been debating telling you about this, but you deserve to know."

"Know what?"

"Your mother." He squeezed me close, preventing me from raising my head to look at him. "She called me this morning. Now, before you say anything"—he cut me off as I open my mouth to hurtle questions at him—"just listen. She knows about Lee and all of this. She's offered to have you come and stay with her till it blows over."

"Mom wants me to live with her?" Never in a million years would I have predicted that.

"Yes." I could feel how tense Dad was, hear it in his voice how much this upset him. "And if you want to, I won't stop you."

Questions, all jumbled together, whirled in my mind like an out-of-control merry-go-round. But the first one I vocalized surprised me. "Why? Why now? Why not over the summer, or at Thanksgiving, or—" The sickening truth unfolded itself and cut through me with its harsh reality. "It's because of Lee, isn't it? Because he brings so much attention. She wants to be known as the mother of the Mystery Girl." A sadness, so profound that there was no room for anger, filled me. "She wanted to use me."

Dad's arm tightened. "Your mother does care about you, sweetheart. She just doesn't know how to have balance in her life, never has. She was obsessed with being the perfect wife and mother, and now she's obsessed with being an artist."

"Do you really think that I'm like that?" The idea that he thought I was *that* selfish, *that* flighty, hurt me more than Mom's attempt at manipulation.

"Of course not," he immediately replied, his voice strong and not wavering at all. "Talking to your mother today, hearing her try to justify her actions, made me realize just how unfair I've been to you. You know how bad it was after your mom left. I knew that she wasn't happy—she hadn't been for some time—but nothing prepared me for what happened."

He took a shaky breath. "Your mother is an all-or-nothing person. She's either all for something or against it. It's not about her art, per se, but I think she's decided that she has to reinvent herself to be happy. She's always enjoyed art, so that is what she has chosen to pursue." He paused to draw a deep breath through his nose. "But you? I've been so afraid that you will lose focus, will throw yourself into art—when really all I've done is projected my own fears on you. You are very much like your mother, in all the best ways: funny, spunky, and you have her looks, not mine, thankfully. But you are different, too—thoughtful, compassionate, and loyal. Yes, you made a mistake with Lee and the cartoons. But you acknowledged that you were wrong, and you will learn from it. And if Lee can't see that, then he doesn't deserve you."

My eyes welled up with tears. "I love you, Dad."

"I love you too. Even when you somehow get yourself in the middle of a fan war that is going on our once peaceful street." He grinned to show he was teasing. Sort of. "The media has caught on, you know. There were news trucks out earlier."

I groaned. "Great, just what I need. Are they still there?"

He gestured to the bedroom window. "See for yourself."

Sure enough, there was a local news truck wedged in the crowd, with a young reporter leaning into the camera as if to divulge the nation's next big story.

"At least the school understands," I offered in a lame attempt to make the situation sound better than we both knew it was. Technically, I could have gone, since no one was devoted enough to be up early enough to protest at the crack of dawn. But they were waiting for me by the end of the day. So, when Dad insisted that I stay home till we figure this out, I hadn't argued. Actually, the school administration found it hilarious. Dad had called to explain the situation and to ask that I submit my homework electronically, and the chuckling school secretary said that this was the first time she had to put "paparazzi" on a student file. Hilarious.

"Where are they coming from?" Dad marveled as the ring leader animatedly talked to the reporter, gesturing behind her to our house. We both ducked out of sight. "And just what is Lee doing about it?" he muttered. "That boy is the cause of this, he needs to take care of it."

I just gave a shrug. Lee had made it very clear that he wanted nothing to do with me.

Dad put an arm around me and pulled me close, "You know what we should do? Look at colleges. The ones that *you* are interested in. And I'll make pancakes. How does that sound?"

"I think that is the best idea that you've had in forever."

With one last squeeze, he headed downstairs and was soon making his usual loud clanging as he gathered ingredients. The sound, so normal, so much a part of my everyday life, brought a smile to my lips. We were still in the middle of kaka, but we were okay, in more ways than one. There was something in my dad's voice, when he'd been talking about Mom…no, that's not right…it was the *lack of something* that I'd noticed. Like bringing her up wasn't tearing up at his insides like it used to. And me? The fact that she'd actually wanted to use me was both painful and welcome, providing clarity and closure to something that had been hovering over me for so long that I'd gotten used to it. It hurt, but at the same time closed the door to those *what if* thoughts that haunted me, teasing me with alternate scenarios. If only I had been more attentive. If only I had cheered her up more. If only I had been a better daughter.

But nothing was good enough for her; I saw that now. Dad was right: I'd learned from my mistake. She, however, was trying to throw herself into another one, it seemed.

It hurt, and would hurt for a while. But just like Dad, I would be okay. And maybe, just maybe, I'd feel the same way about Lee, eventually.

Nineteen

So, I tried to focus on the silver lining, I really did. Dad and I had a great time stuffing ourselves with pancakes as we looked at universities; he was relieved that I still wanted to stay local and go to George Mason. We'd even worked out a plan on what courses I needed to take at the community college to knock my gen-eds out of the way, and marked registration dates on the calendar. It was the best dinner I'd ever had, hands down.

I automatically reached for my phone to message Ema, only to remember at the last minute that she was the last person I wanted to talk to. And just like that, my good mood plummeted, and if there was any hope of it improving, the Chaser's persistence stamped it out. That, plus the updates from SLAAC.com (reminder how Chasers didn't think I was good enough) and LTL.com (reminder how Lee and I were not together), had me wired up and jittery, twitching at practically everything.

By the end of the week, Dad was reaching the end of his rope. "If this keeps up, I say we go on a cruise for Christmas," he announced after one particularly loud chant. "We can just get away and relax…actually, we should do that anyways. Maybe the Caribbean? Or something longer, like a repositioning cruise."

"Hey, a cruise sounds good to me." My phone lit up, and "Ms. Park" appeared on my screen. She had insisted we exchange numbers after Lee had been discovered but had never called me before. I had a bad feeling about this. Sure enough, she was in a tizzy.

"They are here!" she yelled, making me wince and pull the phone away from my ear. I put her on speaker both so that Dad could hear and my ear drums would be spared.

"More fan girls?" As if any more could fit on our street.

"His managers! They are here!" The rest was shouted in Korean, but panic needed no translation.

"Okay. His managers are here. At your house?" I said in as calm a voice as possible as I tried to think of a polite way to ask why she was telling me this. Lee had made it painfully clear he wanted nothing more to do with me, and I had no desire to try to change his mind.

"*Deh*! They are coming!"

"When?"

"NOW!"

I looked out the window just in time to see a big black limo push through the crowd and pull into Lee's driveway.

"Yeah. I see them," I said.

"*Aigoo!*" She abruptly hung up.

The driver got out and hurried to open the door. Three men, all in very expensive looking suits, their faces expressionless behind sunglasses, got out and moved as one towards the house. It was creepy, like they had choreographed it.

Ms. Park opened the door and the fans came to life, chanting, "Lee Hyung-kim! Lee Hyung-kim!" The cry rose until it was an excited roar. I thought the girls would all spontaneously combust in a shower of sparkles. One of the Men in Black slowly turned and surveyed them, impassive face showing the height of disdain, before following the other two into the house.

Dad snorted.

"Good. About time someone did something. I have a feeling that this will all be over soon."

I should feel as he did: relieved that the end to all this was finally in sight. Instead, a knot of worry had taken residence in my stomach. "Ms. Park sounded really worried. Wouldn't she be relieved too?"

Before he could answer, my cell trilled again, Ms. Park again. "Hi. What's going on? Is everything okay?" All I got was a muffled moan in response. "Ms. Park? Can you hear me?" Rustling and a jumble of noises was my answer. "Lee? Dad, I think they're torturing him!"

"Merri, don't over-dramatize things."

"I'm being serious. Listen!" I put it on speaker phone, and the room filled with heavy breathing, followed by a groan and what sounded like a blender. And that was before the shouts erupted.

"I'm going over there," I said, grabbing my sweater.

"Merilee Grace Hart, don't you dare think about leaving—"

But I was already flying out the front door before he could finish his threat, only to realize my mistake when I was greeted by a sea of puzzled faces. The fans blinked in surprise at the first real look at me in days; I gave them a cheeky smile and the royal wave, making it to Ms. Park's door just as they came to life and began chanting. Miracle of miracles, the door was unlocked.

I immediately heard a chorus of masculine shouts. One of them was definitely Lee's deep voice, husky with anger and resentment...but not the tortured agony I'd envisioned.

"Merri." Ms. Park hurried down the hallway towards me, worry pinching her delicate features. "Why you here?"

"Is Lee okay?" I whispered back. Funny, she didn't look as upset as she'd sounded.

Her brow furrowed in confusion, but before she could respond Lee hollered in Korean. I had no idea what it meant, but it sounded like a desperate cry for help if there ever was one, and if nothing else, I could prove to him that I was on his side no matter what, so I charged into the living room. Four male heads swiveled, all owners wearing matching expressions of disbelief, Lee included.

"Merri!"

"*Oegugin?*" Man in Black number one pointed at me accusingly. With the sunglasses off, he looked like just another businessman, not a Secret Service agent intent on torturing Lee into doing who knows what. Still...

"Are you okay, Lee?" I asked, now blushing under the scrutiny even as I focused on Lee, taking in his messy hair, unkempt clothes, the bags under his eyes. The past two weeks had not been easy on him either. I braved a tentative smile.

Lee's face tensed into hard lines, his momentary shock gone. "This is Merilee. Merri, may I introduce you to Manager Kim, Manager Park, and Manager Sung." Each gave me a curt bow as his name was said. I tried to smile back, but it felt more like a grimace.

Manager Sung murmured something to Lee, who snapped back a reply that raised managers Park and Kim's eyebrows to their receding hairlines. Ms. Park caught her breath and held it as she eyed the group nervously. Okay, seriously, what was going on here?

Manager Sung turned to me and said in smooth English, "Miss Merilee. Perhaps you can talk to 'EeHyung-kim and ease his mind."

"Ease his mind," I repeated slowly.

"To leave," Manager Park supplied, his high voice thick with his accent. "'EeHyung-kim must go."

"Now," added Manager Kim, earning a scowl from Lee.

"Today?" I asked.

All three nodded. "*Deh.*"

I was really starting to hate that word.

"Flight is tomorrow," added Manager Park.

I let out a dry laugh, which sounded a little like a sob. "You're kidding, right?"

Manager Sung frowned. "He is booked on a flight tomorrow. First class, the very best."

"Best," agreed Manager Kim, who apparently only spoke in single-word statements.

I faced Lee, who was silent during this exchange. "Can they do that?"

"*Deh.*" One word, but so heavy with defeat. This *deh* meant yes. Yep, definitely hated that word.

He turned away and moved to the window, staring out at the signs being waved about with even more enthusiasm. They knew something was happening, the vultures. Just like I did. And I had a feeling I was going to hate it.

"We will give you a moment alone," Manager Sung said in that oily voice of his. Ushering everyone out, he shot me a victorious look before closing the door. And then there was just Lee and me.

"Was he serious? Are you leaving tomorrow?" I tried to keep the quiver out of my voice but failed. Not that he took any notice. He just shrugged and kept looking out the window.

"First lesson about managers, Merri: they never joke when it comes to making money. They have a contract, which says nothing about taking long vacations. My time is up."

The way he said it made it sound so final.

"So that's it. You are just expected to pack up and leave the next day?"

"If I can just suddenly be told that I need to have another surgery, I can certainly be told to just pack up and leave. *Aiiish!*"

"Surgery? What are you talking about? Are you sick?" I asked, failing miserably to keep the rising panic out of my voice.

He gave an angry laugh. "You think that I look like this naturally? As soon as I signed on to join Thunder I got a personal stylist, who insisted I needed plastic surgery to make myself more marketable. My eyes were the first—but no one counts that because everyone gets their eyes done. Then it was my nose—to fix the bump that I had not even noticed I had," he said, absently rubbing at his perfectly straight nose before clenching his hands into angry fists at his side. "You want to know the real reason why I was sent here? Why I was sent away to hide out from everyone, including my family?" He angrily ripped off the wrist cuffs and held up his hands, twisting them so that I could see his wrists.

Doctors say Lee need to go away.

A host of emotions—fear, heartbreak, condemnation for my blindness—choked me, the growing lump in my throat preventing any words from escaping as I faced the reality of Lee's secret. Lee Hyung-kim, who seemed to have everything he could possibly want, had tried to kill himself. But even worse than that, he'd been pushed aside, hidden like it was a horrible thing that needed to remain a secret from the world.

A burning anger swelled in me, pushing aside everything else. How could they treat him like this? Force him to have plastic surgeries, work at a grueling pace, and then drop him when he needed them the most? What about his family? Had they known? Had they tried to help? Or had they been just as clueless as I'd been?

The silence went on and on as I struggled with wanting to comfort Lee and barrel out to tell his managers exactly what I thought of them.

Moving even further away from me, Lee barked out a laugh, the sound abrasive and rough in its fury. "So now you know my horrible secret. I had just been told that the company wanted me to get another surgery, which I would have to pay for out my earnings, even though I send most of that back home so that my family can keep up the appearance of being rich. We were just about to go on tour, so more concerts, more cameras following us around, more fans meet-and-greets, all while making sure that we do not do anything to offend anyone. And then instead of having a break when I return, I have to go right into a painful surgery with several months recovery so that I can look the way someone else wants me to look, all while pretending that I did not have surgery because the fans would get upset. And then on top of it all, I find out that my girlfriend was cheating on me with my best friend."

All the anger drained out of him. "I just gave up. I wanted it to end."

The tears that had been burning my eyes, blurring out his features, spilled down my cheeks, and I covered my mouth with my hand to hold it all in. And here I'd been so focused on myself and my panels... how could he stand me?

"I failed, obviously, but it was enough to make the company worried. I had embarrassed them, and they wanted to see if Thunder could survive without me. I was in the hospital for several weeks, so they had time to come up with a plan. And what better way to make it all go away than to make me go away?" He impatiently snapped the wrist cuffs back into place. "My family suggested that I visit my aunt, and the managers loved the idea. Of course, they did not tell her just why I was suddenly coming to visit."

I remembered how angry Ms. Park had been that first day; somehow I had a feeling her fury had been directed at the managers, not Lee. No wonder she'd been livid.

"I thought," he shook his head. "No, it does not matter what I thought. Now that they know how much the fans like me, they are here to take me back." He turned away, shoulders drooping as if the weight of the world rested on them. And it sounded like he had been carrying that weight for a long time now. How could no one else see that? His managers? His family? Did they not care what their demands were doing to him?

I had to clear my throat, and still my voice was hoarse when I finally spoke. "What do *you* want?"

"What?" He obviously had not been expecting that question, which made me wonder if anyone else had ever bothered to ask it.

"What do you want to do? Stay here? Go back?" I laced my fingers together to keep from rubbing them and giving away my nervousness. "Your aunt mentioned doctors. Are you getting the help that you need?"

"You mean counseling? Yes. My father arranged for me to have weekly Skype sessions with a friend of his who is a psychiatrist. It has helped, but—" he shrugged. "My life is still my life."

The din outside surged into an excited roar, punctuating his words.

"What do you want, Lee?" I repeated softly. "What kind of life do you want?"

His eyes finally met mine, and the raw pain in them jerked at my heart. "That is the problem, Christmas. I do not know."

Those dark eyes searched mine, looking for…acceptance? Whatever he saw, it eased some of that pain glittering in their depths. His face softened, and hope flared in me as he opened his mouth. But just then, Manager Sung strode back in, speaking in rapid-fire Korean and ending whatever moment Lee and I had been about to share. Lee stiffened and glared at him, and Manager Sung pressed on, each word getting louder and louder until he was shouting in Lee's face. The only thing I understood was the one thing he kept saying over and over again: "*Oegugin.*"

The word that Lee had called me when we first met, which of course

I'd eventually looked up. Foreigner. Or in this case, outsider.

Lee's face hardened as he nodded. The smile on Manager Sung's was not reassuring, especially when he all but raced out of the room, shouting for the other managers.

"Lee, you're not going back, are you?" I asked in disbelief. He couldn't, not after what he'd just told me, surely.

But I was wrong. He drew himself up, every muscle in his body rigid. "I do not expect you to understand, Merilee. You are a—" His voice faltered.

"A what? *Oegugin?*" I demanded angrily.

"Yes. You are *oegugin*. You will never understand. Besides, part of this is your fault," he gestured to the window. "You used me, just like everyone else."

"No! I mean, I didn't mean to. Lee, I'm so sorry that this is happening. And I'm really sorry if I had anything to do with making it worse. You're right, I should have taken down the panels. But please don't think that I just saw you as a subject for them, because you're not. Drawing panels is my way of processing what happens in my life, and you are a part of my life. But I should not have put them online without your permission. I'm sorry."

For a second his face softened, and hope flared in me. We stared at each other, the only sound the faint chanting from outside; then his face hardened and the moment was gone. "It is too late for that, Christmas." Stomping over to the door, he yanked it open, and the three managers and Ms. Park almost fell into the room, having clearly been listening at the door.

"I will be ready to go by tonight," Lee said in very deliberate English. "The car can pick me up tomorrow morning. Ms. Hart is leaving now." And without a backwards glance he stomped up the stairs. The slamming of the bedroom door shook the house.

Ms. Park looked at me with uncertainty, while the Men in Black made no moves to leave. Manager Sung studied me with curiosity. "Ms. Hart, are you well? Your face is red."

Manager Kim nodded emphatically. "Red."

My red face became even redder, and my vision blurred until three uniformed blobs were all that I saw.

"Ms. Hart?" One of the suited blobs took a step towards me.

"I've got to go," I managed to say before stumbling out of the room, out of the house, across the lawn. Maybe the mini mob chanted something, maybe not; I didn't notice or care. I didn't even want to ask Ms. Park why she'd bothered to call me in the first place. Escape was all I cared about.

Dad met me at the door. He took one look at my face and went instantly into battle mode. "What did they do? Are you okay? Is Lee okay?"

I shook my head, unable to speak past the tears I was fighting to contain, and curled up on the couch, wrapping a blanket around me with no intention of ever moving again.

The cushions dipped as he joined me on the sofa. "Merri?"

One tear escaped, then another. "He hates me."

"Honey, I'm sure that's not true."

"No, he really does. And I don't blame him." He sat quietly as I sniffled my way through an explanation, silently handing me tissues to wipe away my tears. "He's leaving with them tonight," I finished, adding yet another tissue to the pile next to me.

"So soon?"

I nodded before burying my face in the blankets. "I've ruined everything."

Dad put a comforting hand on my knee. "Sweetheart, Lee had a whole bunch of problems that have nothing to do with you. You made a mistake, but that's it. You are not responsible for everything."

"But you didn't see his face." I'd never forget the scorn, the utter disdain as he called me an *oegugin*. He'd made it clear; I wasn't part of his world, or welcome to try.

Maybe this was for the best. My life would go back to normal. He'd go back home and…what? Just go back to his idol life?

As I sat there, Dad watching me anxiously, I let myself face the fact that it would be a long time, if ever, that my life would ever return to normal.

Not even an hour later, Lee was gone. I hid behind my bedroom curtains and watched him follow the managers to the car, smiling and waving to the screaming fans the whole time. I needn't have bothered to hide because he never once looked back; he just climbed into the car and waved and waved and waved until the car had disappeared around the curb, the Chasers rushing to get in their cars to follow him.

Still, I remained at the window, as if standing there would bring him back.

Twenty

The prodigal son has returned! Lee Hyung-kim reappears after several months' absence. He reassures fans that he is eager to resume his work and will begin touring with Thunder at the end of the month.

SEOUL MUSIC PRESS RELEASE

WE DID IT!!! Chasers, LHK is going home! Special thanks to everyone who joined me to show him our support over the past few weeks. This is the best Christmas gift he could give us!!!! Links to SLAAC.com will still be live, but all future updates will resume on Kthunderfangirl.com. Thunder Rolls!!

FINAL POST ON SLAAC.COM

"You okay, sweetheart?"

Dad entered my room with the apprehension of someone expecting to walk into an emotional hurricane. But I wasn't sitting at my window wrapped in my comforter this time. Oh no, I was pulling on my running shoes.

"I'm fine."

"Going for a run?"

"Yep."

"Want to talk about it?"

"Nope." I gave the shoelaces an extra hard yank, which threatened to cut off my circulation, but I didn't care. Lee was gone, still mad at me, Ema and I weren't talking, and my mom had magically lost interest in me as soon as she saw that Lee had returned to Korea. Talking was the last thing I wanted to do right now. I needed time away from everyone to think.

"Okay. I'm here when you do. And Merri?" He waited until I raised my head. "Lee is an idiot."

I just gave him a wan smile. "Thanks, Dad. I may be gone a while."

Skipping my usual stretches, I bent my head and started off in the opposite direction of the usual path that Lee and I used to take. I had been avoiding it for the past three weeks. "Out of sight, out of mind" was my new mantra. School had become my focus, and I threw myself into completing homework and doing all the extra credit assignments to boost up my college application. I met with a counselor at the local community college to make sure I signed up for the right fall credits, even began scouring online for deals on textbooks to get an idea of how much everything would cost. What I did *not* do was look for any updates about a certain somebody, go anywhere where we had gone together, or talk to Ms. Park. Avoidance was my middle name; if I didn't see it, it couldn't hurt me, right? Right.

Denial was a close second to avoidance.

The day was overcast and windy, the perfect reflection of my mood. With my headphones set to eardrum-shattering volume, I stomped past street after street as I did my best to forget Lee Hyung-kim. I had to. I'd been fooling myself into thinking that we could actually have a relationship. How could we? I'd always be the outsider, and he'd always be the idol. Not to mention that the guy had MAJOR problems that needed to be sorted out.

He'd said he was getting counseling, but was it enough? And what how could it help when he was returning to the situation that was causing the majority of his problems…or was there more? Would being back make it worse? What if he tried to… well, you know? What if this time he didn't fail?

The fears bombarded me, and I sped up, as if by running I could escape them. If only Ema hadn't told the other Chasers. Maybe I could reach out to her again, see if there was a way to fix things between us. She wouldn't have done it if she'd known, I was sure of it. Maybe there was one thing I could fix.

Just at that moment, I hit the ground awkwardly and my ankle turned as I tripped and stumbled onto the damp grass, burning with an all too familiar fire that left me gasping. When I dared to look, I could see it was already swelling.

"Seriously?" I shouted to the sky. No one's luck was this bad. A sprained ankle at the start and at the end of my relationship, or whatever it had been. It was like Fate wanted to remind me of he that will not be named.

A look at my cell gave me even better news: it was broken beyond repair. "You have got to be kidding me." The air filled with the sounds of my heaving, groaning, muttering as I forced myself to my feet. No guy in crazy workout gear to cart me home this time. It was up to me to drag myself back.

But when I put just the smallest amount of weight on my foot, my ankle buckled beneath me, causing me to yelp in a mix of pain and frustration. The doctor had told me that after a sprain the muscle can be weakened, but it hadn't given me problems since I began running again. Of course it happened when I had no way to call for help and no Lee to carry me…*no*, I wouldn't think about him. Couldn't think about him. Because if I did, I'd start bawling, and then wind up with a raging headache on top of a busted ankle. Instead, I focused on the more immediate problem and stared up the deserted street. Everyone was either sleeping or not home, and there were no passing cars to flag down, although my dad would have lectured me for hours if he knew I had considered it. I had no other option but to make the long trek home on my own. *Dang*, I thought. *And I had been making such good time.*

After some trial and error (and more yelping), I managed to move forward in what looked like a cross between a zombie shuffle and a Mexican jumping bean, with me going as slow as a snail. But it was motion, and I was moving forward, so technically it was progress. I could only hope that my dad would try to call me and somehow figure out that my phone was dead and come look for me. But the way my luck was going, that was way too much to hope for.

I had just made it to the end of the street when the first car of the day came up behind me, then pulled up to stop right next to me. The window went down, and out popped a familiar red head. "Merri?"

Great. Who else would be driving past me right when I needed help out of an embarrassing situation than Bree?

"What happened?" she asked, getting out of the car and approaching me with the caution of someone who had found a wounded wild animal. Well, this wounded animal still had her pride, thank you very much, even if she was hopping on one foot and waving her arms for balance. Before I could come up with reply that would save my dignity, she offered, "Do you want a ride home?"

I blinked in surprise. Just where was this coming from? After basically a semester of not talking, she suddenly wanted to play nice? Unfortunately, as much as I hated to admit it, I wasn't exactly in a position to refuse. "Uh, thanks."

She offered me an arm and gently ushered me to her car, hurried to the driver's side, then eased the car into a pace only slightly faster than what I'd been doing on my own. Huh. Bree was always super nice whenever she felt guilty about something, which was freaky because she hadn't been like that before I found out about her and Luke—she'd just been a nervous wreck. What else could she feel be feeling guilty about, or was that a question best left unanswered?

"Do you need anything?" she asked. "I have water if you're dehydrated."

Oh yeah, she felt bad about something. I waved away the bottle she held out. "No, I'm good. You can go faster, you know. I won't break."

"Oh." She practically deflated against the steering wheel in disappointment, but obligingly upped our speed to just fifteen miles under the speed limit. Her eyes kept darting to me, then away as if embarrassed I'd caught her. Yep, definitely guilty. And I was just too curious not follow up on it. "Bree, is there something you need to talk about?"

She stiffened but didn't say anything. "Talk about? What would I need to talk about?"

"I don't know. Just a thought. If not, then you can drive a little faster. I really need to get some ice on my ankle."

"Oh. Right." The car lurched forward, and just as suddenly slowed back down. "Actually," she began, "there is."

I knew it! I waited. And waited. And waited. And finally had to prod, "Yes?"

"The thing is…" another painfully slow pause stretched between us. Honestly, it was like she was thinking at the same pace that she was driving. If there was any hope of me getting home before noon, I'd have to take matters into my own hands.

"Is this about Luke?"

"We broke up," the words burst out of her like they had been bottled up for way too long. "Last week. He broke up with me last week."

Wow. They had lasted until last week. That's months longer than I'd have thought. "Oh. Did he say why?" Like, he was a jerk and selfish and a *baekchi...stop it! Stop thinking about Lee!* I refocused on what she was saying.

"No. Just sent me a text saying we're done."

Ouch. Words hovered on my tongue, uncertainty holding them back. But I finally said, "I'm sorry."

She gave me a sideways glance, skeptical. "Are you?"

"Yeah, I am." And I meant it. Despite everything, I felt genuine pity for her. She had made a choice, an awful choice, and wound up with nothing: no boyfriend, no friend. She had taken a gamble and lost, big time. Dang! I was so mature and enlightened I surprised even myself.

However mature and enlightened I was, though, the fact that Bree and I were technically in the same situation did not escape me. I don't know what prompted me to say anything, but before I could think twice about it I was telling her, "I'm in the same boat."

"I know."

I did a double-take. "What do you mean you know?"

Her face went bright red, and she didn't answer.

"You already knew about Lee?"

Her silence was louder than any confirmation. But how had she known? The only people that knew were Ms. Park and Dad. Well, I guess you had to include the Chasers, since they had watched Lee make his grand exit and put two and two together and had been going crazy online ever since.

The pain in my ankle was forgotten as my brain spun with the realization that Bree was following the site...which meant that Bree was a Chaser. I narrowed my eyes at her as the pieces of the puzzle came together to create a depressingly clear picture.

I had naïvely thought that after that initial sighting at the restaurant,

Lee had maintained his privacy because people just hadn't been able to find him. After all, the place was a couple of towns over, and it was a relatively small group of people that would recognize him. And to a certain extent, I'd been right. They'd marveled, wondered, and obsessed from a distance, an annoying online presence, but that was it. Until KThunderfangirl.com had received a tip. A very special, specific tip from a very special specific source.

Oh my gosh. "You're StormChaser007."

The accusation hung between us. Her sudden lack of color was all the confirmation I needed. Oh man oh man oh man, I'd messed things up with Ema big time. "You're the one that contacted Kthunderfangirl?" Shock was quickly overtaken by rage. "Bree, for real? Do you have any idea what they did? There was a horde of angry girls outside my house for days. Days! I couldn't go to school because they'd follow me. And Lee's managers found out and swooped in and...why?" The pained question was wrenched out of me. "Why did you do it? Did you take the photos too?"

Her hands tightened on the steering wheel. She opened her mouth, shut it, opened, shut it again, until she finally blurted out, "It wasn't fair!" That opened a floodgate of words that beat against my already wounded heart. "It just wasn't fair! You always land on your feet, you know? School is never hard for you. You actually like it! The first boy that you have a crush on asks you out, and then next thing everyone knows you are the perfect couple celebrating your second anniversary. And when that doesn't last, you find a hot Asian supermodel singer who's every girl's fantasy, and you start dating him!"

I sat back, stunned, but quickly rallied. "Bree, if you weren't driving I'd slap you to the middle of next week. You of all people should know that my life is far from perfect. You call what happened with my mom lucky? You think that my life is so perfect, when I haven't spoken to her in a year? And even if it was, does that magically excuse what you did? You were my best friend, and you didn't hesitate to go after Luke the minute he batted his eyelashes at you. I lost my boyfriend and my best friend in ten seconds. How is *that* perfect?"

"You bounced back fast enough with Lee."

Forget not hitting the driver—throttling her seemed more satisfying. I had to clench my fists from doing just that to her. "Yeah, and now he's gone because SOMEBODY was actually low enough to sell us out!"

"I didn't think they'd picket you! I just wanted to…" Her voice trailed off as if she realized that no excuse could justify what she'd done.

I thought I couldn't be hurt any more than when I had seen her in Luke's arms. Thought that there couldn't be any greater betrayal. But this? This kind of maliciousness? This was beyond what I could have imagined. And half of life's worth of memories, laughter, and dreams wasn't enough to mend the hurt.

Bree was eyeing me anxiously. "I know what I did was wrong. I knew it from the moment I saw the other Chasers in your yard. It just got worse and worse, and I didn't know how to fix it. I really messed up, Merri."

"Yeah, you did. Big time."

"Can you forgive me?" she asked hopefully.

That would have made me laugh if it wasn't so sad. But this was where we were now. A series of choices had been made, and this was the result. Instead of answering her, I said, "Bree, before I answer that, I have a question for you."

"Okay."

"Would you have stayed with him? Luke, I mean. Would you have stayed with him if he hadn't been the one to break up with you?"

I could tell from her expression that she had most certainly not been expecting that question. I almost expected her not to answer it, but to her credit she mulled it over before finally admitting, "I would like to say that no, I would have come to my senses. But I don't know. He had to be the one to break up, not me."

"What were you thinking?" The million-dollar question that had been burning in my mind all this time.

She gave a self-conscious laugh. "I've asked myself that a lot over the past few weeks. Remember that party we all went to? You left early because you had to finish that paper, but Luke stayed behind. A couple of drunk guys started bothering me, and he chased them off and offered to drive me home. And on the way back something, I don't know, clicked between us."

Clicked. Something just clicked between them. *How clichéd can you get?* But then again, I was the girl who fell for a celebrity and is surprised that she has a broken heart. We were quite a pair. "And then?" I snapped, now annoyed with both myself and Bree.

She took a fortifying deep breath. "Well, it just kind of progressed from there. He began hanging out at the ice cream stand. He offered to help me with my math homework. He drove me to school when my car was being detailed. Little things added up until you went away on vacation. He was helping me with SAT prep and, uhh..."

"Yeah, I get the picture." In vivid, obnoxious IMAX proportions. What got me was how in the world I had missed all of this. How had I not heard any rumors?

As if reading my mind, she said, "I think one of the things that bothered Luke was how independent you are."

I couldn't help but laugh. "And that's a bad thing how?"

She shrugged. "He said that after, you know, everything with your mom, you just kind of shut him out, did your own thing. You were too caught up with all your plans."

How had we gotten to talking about me? "That's the most ridiculous thing I've ever heard. It was a rough year, he knew that. I needed time, and if he was too immature to give it to me than that's on him. If it bothered him, he could have just…well, dumped me sooner." Man, what an insecure wimp.

"I kept telling myself that we were doing nothing wrong. No harm in getting a drive to work, right? How can SAT prep be bad?" She blushed. "And by then I wasn't really thinking beyond how wonderful it was to be wanted by a guy."

Oh, gag. "So you won Luke. Well done, Bree. Nice work. So, why bother destroying my thing with Lee? You hadn't had enough of screwing up my life?"

"I was angry and I stopped thinking clearly. After you refused to talk to me when I came over that one time, I just lost it. I overheard some girls at school talking about a K-pop group they love, and something just clicked. I had recognized him from somewhere, but he was always in full K-pop gear. But I found a photo of him without makeup and knew right away who he was. I saw KThunderfangirl's post on a forum, and you know the rest."

Did I ever. I'd had no clue about K-pop, yet there were fans of it at school. Yet another thing I had been clueless about. But I definitely wasn't clueless about what to do right now. In fact, for the first time in days I knew exactly what to do. "What you did was awful, Bree. It hurt more than I thought anything could hurt. It still hurts. I'm not minimizing what Luke did, but you were my best friend."

She flinched at my pointed use of the past tense and got quiet for a moment before asking in a voice just above a whisper, "No hope of, I don't know, fixing things?"

"To be jealous of me the way that you were, to do everything that you've done?" I shook my head. "There is no going back from that. I'm not going to constantly focus on the past, and maybe in time I will forgive you, because honestly, it's just not worth being angry at you all the time. But I don't trust you anymore, Bree. Not like before. And that's never going to change."

Her eyes welled up with tears, but she didn't look surprised. "I deserve that. I think that's why I got so mad last time. Deep down inside I knew you were right, and it made me furious. I got greedy and wanted both Luke and you." She pulled up in front of my house and put the car in park. "Mer?"

She had been the only one to ever call me that, the only one that I'd actually let call me that. The knowledge that I wouldn't hear it again, at least not in the same way as before, made my chest ache. "Yes?"

"I really am sorry. I don't blame you at all. And I'm kicking myself for having done what I did. I...it just started out so harmlessly, you know?" She gave herself a shake. "And then it was so easy to come up for a reason for the rest. But I am so very, very sorry."

Exactly what I had told myself about Lee's cartoons. Guess Bree and I were more alike than I'd ever want to admit to anyone else. And I believed that she was truly sorry, just like I was. But it didn't change anything. We both had to live with our choices, though her apology did help a bit. I gave her a nod and opened the car door. "Thanks for the ride."

"Is he really gone?"

I paused, then gave a nod. "Yeah. He left almost a month ago." I don't know what prompted me to say this, but I admitted, "I don't think it was all you. There were other things going on as well."

"Well, I'm sorry for what part I played in it,"

"Apology accepted," I said, now weary. The pain in my ankle returned full force.

"Do you need help to the door?" Bree asked.

Lee had used to walk me to the door. *Do not cry. Do NOT cry.* "I'll manage."

"I saw him," she blurted out. "Lee, I mean. I saw him the day after you saw, you know."

Oh yeah, I knew exactly what she was referring to, although the memory of seeing her and Luke on that first day did not hurt as much as it had in the past.

Bree continued. "He was out for a run, and I was in the front yard, raking leaves. He came to help me when I dropped the bag, and put the leaves in for me. When I thanked him, all he said was, 'She is a really good person.'"

I blinked in surprise. Lee had done that? Had said that? He'd barely known me then and...oh man, I could feel the waterworks coming.

Bree gave me a Bree smile, full of life and impishness. I'd missed that smile. "Mer, if the guy says that to a perfect stranger about another almost-perfect stranger, he's a good guy. I don't know what happened, but don't give up on him."

I gave Bree a sad smile of my own. "It's not up to me anymore."

I'd made my choice, Lee had made his, and now we both had to live with the consequences. I got out of the car and said "Thanks" before hobbling up the driveway. I felt her watching me the entire time. She waited until I was up the front steps before pulling away. I watched the car drive off, grateful for the sense of closure that I'd been given. If nothing else, her actions had shown me the truth, and I'd take that over living a fantasy any day, even if right now I was torn between wanting to cry for days and kicking a hole in a wall.

"Merri?" Dad was standing in the kitchen doorway. He caught sight of my gait, sighed and grabbed his keys. "Let's get you to urgent care."

I didn't even try to push aside the thought that Lee would have offered to take me to hospital. What was the point? The harder I tried to forget, the worse it got. I just needed to accept the fact that I was going to be miserable, both emotionally and now physically, and push through it. Taking it one day at a time had never seemed so overwhelming, though.

And I owed one spitting-mad Aussie a huge apology.

Sources tell us that Thunder has been working harder than ever. They have completed a series of photo shoots for the release of Handz new clothing line, and will begin rehearsing for a new music video. Fans can expect a welcome back concert held in Seoul, a New Year's Eve special to thank Thunder's U.S. Chasers. Sources say that things have been mended with Park Min-ho, who gave a statement that they would start fresh and Thunder will be better than ever. But will there be any interviews with Lee Hyung-kim????

KThunderfangirl.com

In his first interview since his extended leave in America, Korean heartthrob Lee Hyung-kim was all polite smiles until he was asked about the photo taken of him at a restaurant outside of Washington D.C., specifically about the girl with him. Lee Hyung-kim abruptly put an end to the interview; sources say that he was overheard ordering his managers to tell reporters to avoid asking about any of his time spent in America.

K-pop News

"I am eager to return to work, and am very grateful for everyone's understanding and forgiveness. I have learned from my mistakes, and hope to prove myself to Seoul Music."

Lee Hyung-kim in Thunder press release

Thunder members participated in a charity event, where hopeful fans bid on the chance to be taken out on a date with each member. Much to the disappointment of many, Lee Hyung-kim was the only one not included, saying he had an important prior engagement. More secrets?

KThunderfangirl.com

Thunder will release their latest music video next week. The video will be available on our website.

Seoul Music press release

Has anyone noticed that Lee Hyung-kim has become a recluse? Where are the new photos? Commercials? I've gotten tired of pausing the music video of *Dreamer* when he is leading. What happened when he was over here?

Kimchi4evr on a forum at KThunderfangirl.com

OMO! Thunderers, have you heard the latest? Lee Hyung-kim attacked a Christmas tree. That's right, attacked! From what's been reported, it seems that Lee Hyung-kim was doing a special appearance at a nightclub, and was given free drinks by the club's owner. A couple of fans got a little rowdy around him, and he was forced to leave early. On the way out, someone shoved a small Christmas tree at him as a gift. For whatever reason, Lee Hyung lost it! He grabbed the tree and threw it on the ground before storming out. The fan was rude, but did it really warrant such a dramatic reaction? Or is there more to Christmas when it comes to the increasingly mysterious Lee Hyung-kim?

KThunderfangirl.com

Twenty-one

As Ema very graciously put it, I'd "failed as a cobber" and had filled my head with "codswallop" and made a "beaut of a mistake." Or something like that. Bottom line, I sent her a request to chat, which miraculously she accepted, and spent a good ten minutes groveling. She remained impassive the entire time, until I finally ran out of words—and breath—and cut myself off before I made yet another mistake and said sometime stupid.

"So," she finally spoke. "Bree strikes again."

"Yeah."

She studied me, and I waited patiently. She was making me sweat, but it's not as though I didn't deserve it. Finally, she nodded. "All right. You were an idiot, you've admitted it, good enough for me."

I blinked. "Wait, that's it? You're letting me off that easy?"

"I'd say that nothing's been easy, starting from the day you learned that Lee was part of Thunder. And I can even understand how you'd think it was me. Stupid of you, of course, but if I'd been in your shoes?" she shrugged. "I might have thought the same thing. So yeah, that's it. Besides, you look like an angel compared to Bree." She gave me a wink but quickly sobered. "So, what are you going to do?"

It was my turn to shrug. "Just try to forget, I guess." If that was possible. "Maybe I should just pack up and move to Australia."

"Yes! We can live on the beach and be broke together. You can draw more cartoons about our fantastic beach-bum life and gain the right kind of fame."

She then kindly changed the subject and talked about the latest with her family, and I actually laughed for the first time in what felt like forever. When we signed off, I sighed with relief. At least there was something that I'd been able to fix.

With everything that was going on, I fully expected Christmas to be awful. There was no Christmas card from my mom and no fun dinner plans with Ms. Park and Lee. Had it really only been a month since Thanksgiving? The weather was dreary because in Northern Virginia, as everyone knows, it never snows until after Christmas.

Dad, however, had a plan. Two days before Christmas, he ordered me to pack my bags with my best winter clothes, and just like that we were on our way to the airport to go to New York City. He had somehow wrangled two hotel rooms (something about one of his naval buddies owing him) right in the heart of Times Square, so instead of moping around and trying to pretend that I wasn't in the depths of despair so that Dad wouldn't feel bad, I spent six amazing days exploring NYC with him.

The Christmas Eve service at the Basilica of St. Patrick's Old Cathedral brought tears to my eyes as we sang the familiar hymns with the rest of the congregation. And the giant Christmas tree at the Rockefeller Center was so much better in person, hands down. We acted like the tourists we were and walked around the silent Central Park on Christmas Day before exchanging gifts. He loved the TV streaming subscription I got him, and he surprised me with a sketch pad and set of alcohol pens, showing the acceptance that I'd craved for so long and which was hands down the best gift he could have ever given me. We even ordered room service for Christmas dinner, and camped out on the floor with pancakes as we watched our favorite Christmas movie, *Home Alone 2*. In the following days, we spent hours combing through the shelves of the three-story used bookstore, Strand, and saw not one but two Broadway shows (*Anastasia* for me, *Guys and Dolls* for Dad). We peered at the Statue of Liberty from the shore through those weird, freestanding binocular thingies, and had a contest to see who could find the tackiest souvenir (I won with the I <3 NYC beer can hat), and then rewarded ourselves with rainbow bagels with Nutella flavored cream cheese.

It was, without doubt, the best Christmas ever. It was so great that, when we got back home, I made a point to be friendly with Ms. Park instead of avoiding her. What had happened between Lee and me wasn't her fault, after all, and I didn't want her to think that I blamed her in any way. At first she was anxious around me, as if I would burst into tears at the sight of her. But one skill I had learned through the mess over the past few months was to have a good poker face. Besides, it wasn't her fault that he had resumed his life in Korea as if nothing had happened. Thunder was more successful than ever, and Lee and Park Min-ho had seemed to make up. It helped that Park Min-ho had broken up with his girlfriend shortly after Lee left and appeared to be genuinely sorry for the trouble he'd caused.

If my life were like the books and movies, I'd believe that this was only Lee putting up a good front because he desperately missed his "Merri Christmas." He'd be trying to distract himself but eventually cave and do something huge and romantic to win me back. Or I would do something bold and reach out to him first, only to discover that he had been waiting for a sign from me all along.

But this was not a fantasy. And as each day passed, the painful truth ached more and more until I cut myself off from K-pop news. No more pathetic searches, no more dreaming; I had to move on. So, when Ms. Park gave me a tentative smile when she came for dinner one night, I gave her a genuine one in return. Ms. Park was here, and he wasn't. Simple as that.

Ema offered unwavering support, even though her schedule was busier than ever. Not only was she filling out university applications, she was also rehearsing for auditions. One morning towards the end of winter break, we were video chatting, and she couldn't stop stressing over an upcoming audition. She had shared me a link to a master ballet class. "Look at her form! The arch of her feet." She sighed wistfully as I watched the video.

"You look like that when you dance."

"No I don't," she countered in a mournful tone. "I don't have that kind of extension, especially in my *arabesque*."

"I have no idea what that means, but you look like that when you dance. Actually, you look better." And it was true. I'd seen her dance over the summer, and had been struck by how graceful she was, how the music seemed to flow through each movement—each delicate motion a living embodiment of the notes. My eyes were just naturally drawn to her. "Don't ever let yourself believe that you aren't good enough," I said.

She beamed at me. "Really? Thank you! Can you tell that I'm nervous?"

"You'll be fine," I stated confidently. "You're fantastic, and that's that."

She quickly sobered. "And you? Will you be fine? Have you heard from him?"

"No."

"Have you been reading KThunderfangirl?"

"Noooo," I drew out the word as suspicion dawned. "Have you?"

"Well…"

"Ema!"

"What? The whole thing is ridiculous. No one acts like he did without a reason."

"Oh, I know the reason. I messed up, he is messed up, and Bree messed up. End of story."

"There's got to more to it than that. If you read the stuff that KThunderfangirl has been posting—"

"He *left*, Ema. He made it very clear what he thinks about me, and that's that. I have to get over it." The words would have been more impressive if my voice wasn't wobbling from tears.

Ema was immediately contrite. "I'm so sorry, I shouldn't have said anything. I was just trying to help."

"I know. It's just that I'm trying so hard to stay positive. I don't want to think about it because if I do, I'm afraid I won't be able to stop."

"It's way worse than the split with Luke, isn't it?"

I could only nod. It was so much worse. And I was scared that this time I wouldn't be able to bounce back. Between beating myself up for what I'd done and worrying that Lee would have a relapse, it was all I could do to keep my head up. Ms. Park and I had talked about it, and the fact that she shared my concerns made me worry even more. But she had assured me that she was talking to Lee regularly and he was getting counseling. Now that his managers knew that Thunder couldn't survive without him, they were making sure he got the help he needed, although they still insisted on keeping everything a secret. But, it was still progress, at least for him. And I had to stop obsessing over it.

After we signed out of the chat, I wandered around my room, too restless to go back to sleep even though it was 7 a.m. on a day off. I was randomly putting things away when my eyes fell on my sketchbook, and I was suddenly seized with the consuming desire to draw. And not just draw; draw Lee. Art had always been an outlet for me; this time was no different. Taking up my new sketchbook and pens (that still warmed my heart that Dad had bought them for me), I got to work on portraits, not my usual cartoon panels.

The sun had risen, and Dad was pottering around downstairs long before I'd finished the picture. I leaned back against my headboard, exhausted as I surveyed my work. I may not be able to talk about Lee, but what I lacked in words I certainly made up for in each line of my pen.

The first picture was of when he first arrived, drawn it from my point of view, hand holding a camera as he scowled at me. This time I had no problem getting the sparkles right; combined with the messy hair, perfect eyeliner, and brightly colored clothes—it was like reliving the moment all over again.

The next one was of him peeking over a menu, eyes a mixture of resentment and curiosity, long fingers gripping the menu to show his tension. I'd even included the glass of water that he had found to be so big that at the burger joint.

The next picture was how I'd imagined we'd looked when he'd carried me on his back. His head was down, walking towards the viewer, and my face was tight with pain. I'd almost not included that in the collection, but it somehow felt wrong not to. And that was the key, I think. Acknowledge that it had happened, not try to bury it. Acknowledge, but still move forward.

I went through the pad page by page, going over my interpretation of his time here, snapshots of what we'd been through together: my hand fumbling with chopsticks and *kimchi*, an image of his grinning face in profile as he drove (complete with blurred scenery drawn to show his crazy speed), and a picture of the fan girls standing outside his house.

It's amazing how you could know someone for such a short time but value them so much. Had I really only known him four months? It had been a fraction of the time I'd dated Luke, yet the hole that Lee had left seemed to only get bigger, not smaller like I'd hoped it would. Would I ever get over him?

I still didn't have an answer to that, so I did what I'd been doing ever since he left: I pushed the thought away and got ready to do something else. Lifting up the ledge to my window seat, I placed my sketchbook in it. Maybe someday I'd be able to look at it and only feel bittersweet nostalgia, but not right now.

The New Year's Eve concert sold out in five minutes! Since then Thunder has been busy shooting their next music video, although fans made sure that they were showered with Valentine's Day gifts when they returned. But the only present Lee Hyung-kim accepted was a flower from a little girl. Fans are worried that he will never be our beloved LHK again! What do you think? Comment below!

KThunderfangirl.com

I think he hasn't been the same since he left the U.S. Mystery Girl has his heart – LTL!

Park Min-ho broke up with you-know-who. Will LHK get back together with her?
New episode on Storm Warning channel. Promo hints of White Day fun!!

Here's a video of them going shopping for White Day. DO YOU GUYS SEE THAT LHK IS BUYING SOMETHING?!?!?!?

Twenty-two

Tune in @ 12:00 p.m. for a special LHK performance in celebration of White Day.

STORM WARNING APP AUTOMATED MESSAGE

January was its usual dreary self, complete with a halfhearted snow storm that managed to shut school down for a week. February, aka Singles' Awareness Month, was equally pleasant, and I spent the evening of the 14th not eating ice cream or chocolates, but cleaning my room with extra-strength attitude.

As the days soldiered on, the ache began to ease a bit. It was almost impossible to believe that the events of the fall had even happened; they now seemed so outlandish. And by March, I was actually feeling cheerful. Graduation was just a few months away, I was registered at the local community college, and Ema had invited me to spend the summer with her, joking that we could get a jumpstart on our beach-bum life by spending the summer there. I was overjoyed, relieved beyond words that I hadn't destroyed our friendship with my doubts. Bree and I were civil to each other when we ran into each other at class (Luke was doing an excellent job of staying as far away from both of us as possible), but I don't think the awkwardness that was now between us would ever go away, and I was doubly grateful for Ema's friendship. Dad had given his blessing, saying it would be my graduation gift—he didn't know about how I'd almost ruined things with Ema, but I know he was relieved that I was focused on moving on. Things were starting to look up!

One morning, I was sitting in my window ledge, working on a cartoon panel (me in Australia, this time), when I noticed a flower delivery van pull up in front of our house.

Weird. Did they deliver on Sunday mornings? And this early? It wasn't even nine yet. I tiptoed downstairs, not wanting to wake up Dad, and met the guy at the front door right before he was about to ring the doorbell. Seriously! Ring the doorbell on a Sunday morning! I kept the screen door closed between us as I told him, "I think you have the wrong address."

"Are you Merilee Hart?"

"Yeah, but—"

He peered at the slip of paper then held it out to me. "Is this your address?"

"Yeah, but—"

"Then these are for you," he said in a no-nonsense voice. "Says right here, 'Hand to Merilee Hart no later than nine-thirty.'" Opening the screen door, I dumbly accepted the bouquet of the most beautiful white roses I'd ever received. Make that the only roses that I'd ever received. I looked at the card included with the flowers, but it had a QR code printed on it and nothing else.

"Sign here please. And don't worry, tip has already been included." That hadn't even crossed my mind, but okay. And judging from the satisfied gleam in his eye, it was quite the tip for having to deliver at this time on a Sunday. After getting my signature, he trotted back to his van, leaving me to search through the rest of the bouquet to see if there was another clue. Nothing.

When Dad got up to make coffee, he was equally perplexed. "Maybe they are from Ema?"

"I highly doubt Ema is going to send me expensive flowers. Plus, what's up with the QR code?"

"Have you scanned it yet?"

"Not yet. Hold on," I pulled out my phone, quickly downloaded a QR scanner app, and held it over the card. I half expected it to be a dud, but the phone lit up right away, and I peered at the screen. "It's an app. But all it says is *Storm Warning: Expect Thunderstorms @ 12 p.m.*" My heart began to pound in my ears. Storm Warning? *Thunder*storms? It couldn't be…

It only got stranger. As we were cleaning the dishes, the doorbell rang again. Dad answered, spoke to someone a few minutes, and returned carrying another bouquet, this one of vivid orange roses with ribbons of pink trailing through them. My eyebrows arched up to my hairline. "Don't tell me those are for me as well."

"You guessed it. And here's the card." Same paper as before, with a time: 12 p.m.

"What's going on at twelve?" I said, not daring to give in to the spark of hope that was beginning to burn in me.

"Nothing," Dad said firmly. "I think it's best if you stay at home until we figure this out."

"Umm, sure."

Just to double-check, I texted Ema. But as I had suspected, she had nothing to do with it.

"Do you think they are from him?" she asked. "Because there's something that's gotten the Chasers excited; the posts have been nonstop."

I hated how quickly that spark of hope flamed into a full-on bonfire. After all my hard work of distracting myself, it was still so quick to rise to the surface. Ruthlessly squashing it, I replied, "I doubt it. Must be some kind of trick."

Ema and I left it at that. But the conversation had me all revved up for the next few hours, until I was as jumpy as a neurotic cat. Every car that drove by was another delivery truck, or maybe even Lee himself. And as each one proved insignificant, I got more and more frustrated until I finally locked myself in my bathroom to have a long hot shower, even though I'd already had one before all this started. Of course, it was during that time when a delivery truck did come with one more bouquet. When I came back downstairs it was waiting for me on the counter: lush red roses. This time the card had just two words on it.

Merri Christmas.

I suddenly felt light-headed. It *was* Lee. After all these days, weeks, months spent doing my best to forget him, he was...what? What was with the cryptic messages?

I checked the clock. "It's eleven fifty-five right now."

Dad crossed his arms. "Let's see what this boy has up his sleeve. It had better be good, after all the crap he's pulled."

Gripping my phone with shaking hands, I held it up to the QR code. This time, the app had a different message. *Storm Warning is live*, it read, and there was a live video being streamed, the camera pointing to an empty couch. In the bottom corner was a clock doing a countdown. The numbers flashed on the screen, each pulse matching the pounding of my heart.

The countdown hit ten.

This was it.

Five...four...three...two...one.

Lee came into view and sat on the couch, and I greedily took him in, noticing every detail. He looked tired: hair was shaggy, purple smudges under his eyes almost distracting you from how bloodshot his eyes were, and his clothes didn't quite fit him, as if he'd lost weight. The wrist cuffs were firmly in place—did any of the Chasers wonder about them? Had they figured out his secret?

He bowed at the screen. "Hello to all my fans," he said in that unique accent of his. "Thank you for joining me tonight for this special White Day webcast. For those of you who do not know, White Day is the day that men present gifts to women. As I promised, I am going to perform my new song, my gift to a special person. I hope that you enjoy." He grabbed a guitar, strummed a few practice chords, and then launched into a song.

My first thought was that I'd never actually heard him sing. With everything going on it seemed rude to ask him, like I expected him to perform for me. His voice was a beautiful bass, rich and warm like honey…and saying words I understood. He was singing in English, but not only that. He was singing about me.

I remember every drop of gold
As I wish you were here
The sun to light my soul
To banish all my fear.

I hear your laughter in the wind
Your voice in every song
A reminder of what I've lost
What I've needed all along

You just don't know
How you've changed my life
How you've made me strong
Through the pain and all the strife.

Your smile reaches my soul
Makes me tremble yet be strong
As you take me by the hands
And lead me to where I need to go.

You just don't know
How you've changed my life
How you've made me strong
Through the pain and all the strife.

I couldn't see the screen through the blur of tears flooding my eyes. Lee, private Lee, was making the most public declaration a guy could make, in front of 600,000 viewers who were most likely as glued to their screens as I was.

His ears glowed bright red, his voice shook a little, his hands fumbled on the guitar. But the mistakes made the performance all the more heartfelt. When he was done, he just sat there with his head bowed, as if struggling for composure. But when he lifted his head, his face was set with determination. "Thank you for listening. And here's a special message for Christmas. *Saranghae.*"

The screen went dark, leaving all of us viewers with our mouths ajar and minds buzzing...or maybe that was just my reaction.

He had written a song about me. Me. Merilee Grace Hart. Every line was about *me*. And he had sung it in front of everyone. In front of the Chasers. And his final words...thanks to my binging of K-dramas, I knew exactly what they meant.

Saranghae. I love you.

He *loved* me? He actually *loved* me? Why the heck had he left, then?

Dimly, I heard the phone ring, but I made no move to answer it. Couldn't move, actually. How could someone be numb and flooded with joy AND anger at the same time?

I love you. Lee had just told me that he loved me. No, had just told the K-pop world that he loved me.

Saranghae.

In a daze, I blindly accepted the phone that Dad pressed into my hand before making his exit, and that rich bass with its funny, sexy, *wonderful* mix of Korean and Australian accent was saying my name. "Merri? Are you there?"

My breath caught in my throat, and I made a choking whistling sound right into his ear, which quickly turned into a coughing fit. The perfect way to start a conversation with the guy that you've been pining over for what feels like forever.

"Merri! Are you eating *kimchi* right now?"

The ridiculousness of his question, so uniquely Lee, snapped me to reality. "Lee? Where are you?"

"In Seoul. Did you, did you see the video?"

Could he hear my heart pounding? Because I certainly could. "Yes."

He blew out a breath. "And?"

"You left me." The accusation was out before I thought twice about it. But I'm glad I said it, because I had to make sure that this wasn't just whim, that he'd change his mind yet again. "You just left. Not once did you try to reach me."

"I know." He almost whispered the words, each one filled with a pain that came right through the phone and gripped my heart in a vise hold. He took a deep breath. "Merri, I know that there is no excuse for what I did. Seeing those photos online, how the groups found us so quickly…I was never angry at you. I was *scared* for you."

"*What?*" I may or may not have shrieked that in his ear. "You left because you were worried about me?"

"Merri, I never once thought that you would do anything to hurt me. And yes, when I first saw your cartoons, I got annoyed, but then they made me laugh. Besides, fans do cartoons of us all the time. You have a real gift, and I am proud that I was included in it. You actually managed to make my life look bright and fun."

"But, but what about the Chasers?" I sputtered. "You said that it was all my fault."

"The only fault was that I had been avoiding my responsibilities for so long. I knew it was only a matter of time before they found me, but the more time I spent with you the more I became greedy for even more time. My managers had been warning me to leave you alone, and I'd been ignoring them, thinking they were just trying to scare me. But when the Chasers showed up on our street…" He expelled a breath in frustration. "I was suddenly faced with the reality of what would happen if I continued to be with you. Every movement under scrutiny, every second having to look your best, and I did not want that for you. And, I am ashamed to say, I got scared for myself. So much has changed so quickly, and I panicked, especially when I saw how the Chasers reacted to you. I still did not know if they were still mad about my fight with Min-ho, and I was terrified that they would blame you and take it out on you somehow."

His voice hardened. "But I will not let that happen. When I got here, everything slowly fell apart. No matter what I did, I could not forget you. Everything seemed so pointless and empty. And the more I tried to hide it, the more I realized how wrong I was." He stopped talking so abruptly I thought that he'd been cut off, but then he added, "I miss you, Christmas. *Aiish*, I miss you so much."

He had put his heart on the line, laid it bare—not once, but twice. First with the video, and now this. The question was, could I do the same? Did I want to? Could I trust him again?

"Christmas?" The uncertainty in his voice, the hesitant hope, was enough to help me make up my mind.

"What about your counseling?"

"I go twice a week," he said without hesitation. "I know that I have a long road ahead of me, but this time I am committed to it. And, when I am ready, I will share my story with others. Maybe it will help them." He paused. "Christmas? Do you miss me?"

I took a deep breath of my own. "I do miss you."

"You do?"

"Of course I do, you crazy Korean." I took an even deeper breath, but it had to be said. "Lee, I'll be honest with you. I don't know if I love you." I could actually feel his stillness over the phone, the stunned silence, but I had to say it. "It really hurt me that you not only accused me of what you did, but left me without looking back, or so I thought. But, it hurt me so much because I care about you so much. And I want to see where this goes."

A weighted pause, like he'd been holding his breath, that exploded into a joyful barrage of words, both Korean and English, finishing with "*Aigoo*, I wish I was with you right now. Are there flights? There must be flights. I can ask for a couple of days' absence and come next week and stay for the weekend and, and, I love you. I completely understand how you feel, and I promise that I will make it up to you."

"Thank you for the song, Lee. That's the most amazing thing you could have done, and it means everything to me that you did."

"Good, because I was scared stupid about doing it."

Scared stupid? Oh. "You mean scared silly?"

"*Aigoo*, those sayings. I will never get them right."

"It's okay. I'll tutor you, as long as you get me Korean donuts."

"It is a deal. And Christmas?"

"*Deh*?" I said, feeling downright cheeky.

"I *will* get you to say the words. You can bet your bottom dollar bill on it."

A hot Korean K-pop idol was determined to win back my trust AND get me to love him? Relief and pure joy bubbled up into a laugh, the first sincere one in weeks. "Can you really come back next weekend? Will your managers let you?" The MIB had seemed pretty hardcore and stubborn to keep their star away from a certain blonde-haired American.

Lee sighed. "Probably not. But, I think Thunder is due for a North American tour soon."

"I think it's safe to say that you have quite the fanbase in America."

He chuckled. "I am just interested in one particular fan."

I gulped even as my pulse thrummed in excitement. "Oh, I think this particular fan would like to see you in person. She may even have kimchi waiting for you."

"Christmas, as long as you are there I do not care about *kimchi*."

I gasped in mock horror. "Mr. Kimchi! You shock me!"

"I am going to do more than that when I get over there."

OMO.

Epilogue

Chasers, I have incredible news! Thunder has just announced that they will be doing a special North American tour this upcoming summer, pushing back their original Seoul date. Thunder is coming to America! Stay tuned, because I have a feeling we're going to be seeing way more of Thunder in the near future!

Author's Note

While Lee Hyung-kim is a fictional character, the struggles that he faces are very real. In December 2017, famed K-pop star Kim Jong-hyun of the group SHINee was found in his apartment after a successful suicide attempt, which was a shocking and bitterly painful reminder that all is not as it seems, even with those who seem to have it all.

I personally have been living with anxiety for most of my life—anxiety that has resulted in panic attacks that for years I had little control over. Thankfully, like my character, Lee, I was able to get help, and I spent several years in counseling to learn how to cope with my anxiety and its triggers. Anxiety can be overwhelming and frustrating, especially if you cannot fully express what you are actually feeling (as many people with depression struggle to do), but there is help available. Since I first started having panic attacks as a child in the 1990s, medical science has come a long way in learning how the brain works and understanding mental illness better, and we discover more and more each year. And the more information we have, the more we can help those who suffer from it.

If you or someone you know is depressed and/or anxious, there are resources that can help you on the next page.

- Depression and Bipolar Support Alliance (DBSA)
  www.dbsalliance.org
- National Alliance for the Mentally Ill (NAMI)
  www.nami.org

According to the American Foundation of Suicide Prevention, suicide is the tenth leading cause of death in the United States. In 2017, there were roughly 1,300,000 suicide attempts, of which 47,173 were successful. And that's just in the U.S. In South Korea in 2016, according to OECD.org, 25.8 out of 100,000 people died by suicide, which is actually an improvement considering that in 2009 it was 33.8 out of 100,000. There is no single cause of suicide; usually, it results from a combination of several factors, oftentimes when a person is battling a mental health condition, such as depression.

For more information on how you can help with suicide prevention, visit afsp.org/take-action/.

If you or someone you know needs help, the National Suicide Prevention Lifeline is available 24/7: 1-800-273-TALK (8255)

Acknowledgments

(aka Ode to All the Awesome People)

As I write this, I am still grappling with the fact that I am actually writing the acknowledgments page for my book. My book that is *published*!!!!!!!!!!!!!!!!!!!!!!! And if you've read this far, chances are you're one of the fabulous people who helped me in some way to get this book finished. So, let's get to it, shall we?

My family—who have had the dubious pleasure of living with a clueless author for the past three years—I thank you. I don't know how many times y'all have sat through an obscure plot summary, or held my hand as I bemoaned how I'd never finish, or read draft after draft (and always with an incredibly tight deadline). MC and Mom, you are officially the world's best and fastest proofreaders, and you made sure I ate by supplying me with Chick-fil-A and Korean food. Mom and Dad, your unflagging confidence and patience are inspiring, and you strengthened me more than you'll ever know.

To Samantha Olsen and Sara Spencer, who were my editors before I actually had an editor: Ladies, your insights and willingness to be thrust into the chaos that is my writing life are forever appreciated. Sara, do you think you can find an ornament to commemorate this book? And Sammy, your turn is next...

Swag Master. SWAG MASTER. WE DID IT!!!!! You were the first person to read *Hart & Seoul* in all its flawed glory. Bless you for your kindness, humor, and patience as you read drafts so numerous that you probably have the book memorized by now…really, it's a wonder we're still friends, given what I put you through. Thank you, thank you, thank you for all those nights of eating Korean barbecue as we brainstormed how to make Merri less annoying and Lee even more of a punk. Thank you for the ice-cream parlor runs whenever I hit writer's block yet again, and the car rides with K-pop blasting at full volume ("NOT TODAY!"), and the endless justification of impulse shopping, and of course the reassurance that you were not judging me…because you'd already made up your mind.

I am also forever grateful to the Mascot Books team, who were willing to take a chance on a debut author with a million questions and no clue about what she was doing. Jess, your enthusiasm for this project from day one still makes me smile; Nina, I'm keeping our email thread to see if we break the record for most replies. And Lorna, your editing skills ensured that this story is the best that it could be. The Chasers might be #LHK, but I'm definitely #JNL.

To everyone who has been involved in making my favorite K-dramas (and really, the list is still growing at this stage), thank you for providing the most hilariously dramatic form of escapism I could wish for. Thank goodness I didn't discover it until I was basically done with college, or I might never have graduated.

If you've gotten this far, then you must be a *really* dedicated reader. And if you're *really* dedicated, you must be a librarian. Librarians are the unsung heroes of the book world, and I salute each and every one of you, but a special shout out goes to the amazing people at Fairfax County Public Library System (HI, KINGSTOWNE CREW!!!) and Prince William Public Library System (CENTRAL AND BULL RUN,

I'M LOOKING AT YOU). Where else could I have learned all the amazing random things, like how to catch a lizard without its tail popping off? Or how to stay warm in a winter storm when all you have are some hole-ridden gloves? Library folk work so incredibly hard to help people, and it is a joy to learn from you all. Now, please, recommend my book to someone! I kid, of course, I kid (*cough*).

Heavenly Father, You amaze me. The door had been closed so many times, but then—POW!—You open an unexpected window with a view that takes my breath away. I don't know where this journey is taking me, but with You leading me, I know it's going to be amazing. As my friends have heard me say countless times, usually when I'm driving in rush hour: Jesus, I trust in You.

About the Author

KRISTEN BURNHAM knew that she was destined to be either a world-famous paleontologist or a writer. The dinosaur gig never took off, so it's a good thing she had a back-up plan. When she's not writing, she is hunting around for the best Korean BBQ food, reading, watching dramas (Korean, Chinese, British…if it's dramatic, she'll watch it), listening to music in foreign languages, and having arguments with her menagerie of imaginary friends (a.k.a. book characters). Find her at seoulofawriter.home.blog or on Instagram @seoulofawriter.